BOOK‹

MW00478858

Unequally Yoked: Staying Committed to Jesus and Your Unbelieving Spouse (2018)

—Miranda J. Chivers

Hope When it Hurts: The Scars That Shape Us. (2020)

(A Christian Writers' Devotional Collection)

Holy Resilience: Finding the Way Forward (2021)

(A Christian Devotional Collaboration)

Peace in the Presence of God: Devotionals for Women with Anxiety (2021)

(A Christian Devotional Journal Collaboration)

Stay updated with Miranda J. Chivers at

https://www.amazon.ca/Miranda-J-Chivers/e/B0791MGZP7

RUSSIAN MENNONITE CHRONICLES

Book One
Katarina's Dark Shadow

MJ Krause-Chivers

Sanctified Hearts Publishing

Sanctified Hearts Publishing P.O. Box 55 St. David's, Ontario LoS 1Po

For more information, email: the mennogal@gmail.com

Print: ISBN: 978-1-7751895-5-8
Hardover: ISBN 978-1-7751895-6-5

Scripture quotations marked KJV are from the King James Version of the Bible.

Scripture quotations marked NLT are taken from *Holy Bible*, New Living Translation, copyright © 1996, 2004, 2015 by Tyndale House Foundation. Used by permission of Tyndale House Publishers, Inc., Carol Stream, Illinois 60188. All rights reserved.

Editor: Nicole Lamont; Proofreader: Louisa Bauman;

Cover design: 100Covers; Formatting: Nola Li Barr

To my grandmothers: Anna and Katharine. Thank you for raising my father with a love for God and books, and for choosing Canada as your new home when you fled from the violence in Russia. May you rest in peace.

And to all the Mennonite survivors of the Russian Revolution — thank you for sharing your stories and encouraging us to fight for peace, freedom, and global justice; and for warning us to monitor world events.

You taught us that life is a gift. Open it wisely, take care of it. Cherish the memories.

All souls are created by a loving God. He desires for each to live, love, and be treated with respect and dignity.

INSPIRED BY ACTUAL EVENTS

AUTHOR'S NOTE

Russian Mennonite readers will argue this work of fiction doesn't hold a candle to real events — and they'd be right. The Russian Revolution caused catastrophic injury to individuals, families and societies. For the sake of the reader's sensitivities, the author chooses to minimize and fictionalize the gut-wrenching horror.

The best and the worst of humanity surfaces during wartime; but even in peacetime, the sins of racism, sexism, discrimination, and other forms of human degradation tear apart cultures and souls, infesting present and future generations with shame. Our spiritual task is to forgive the painful past and resolve to grow towards a future of unity and peace in a loving atmosphere. This cannot happen when we focus on our differences.

During WWI and the subsequent civil war in Russian Ukraine, deliberate political and personal agendas disrupted and destroyed our Mennonite culture. We can blame the era, the people, or the politics, but we must reflect on our own contributing bias and understand that none are immune to the consequences of their own sins.

To the non-Mennonite reading this story for enjoyment, please be forewarned that this is a work of fiction. This is NOT a de facto representation of the Russian Revolution or the Ukraine experience, nor is it an actual representation of the Mennonite experience in Russian Ukraine. Both the geography and the timeline of historical events were adapted to fit the storyline. None of the historical figures mentioned interacted with the fictional characters in this book.

The author has attempted to respect the historical process by referring to actual events that happened during the Russian Revolution in southern Ukraine, according to responsible sources. Historical records are often subject to the filters of analysts and may differ in content and interpretation based on the personal experience of survivors and historians.

The author is neither a historian nor an expert in the Russian Revolution and the Mennonite experience in Russia. The author urges the reader to consult historical documents to understand this era in greater depth.

This story is for entertainment purposes only and should not be used as a historical reference.

Please note: Although the land of the Mennonites no longer exists in southern Ukraine as it once did, some surviving buildings remain to remind us of this opulent era that once dominated the region. Most villages now carry Russian or Ukrainian names, although a few have retained their original tags. While those who lived during this time are no longer with us, their communal memories are stored in the souls of their descendants.

This author supports the registered charity: https://www.mennonitecentre.ca/Friends of the Mennonite Center in Ukraine Inc. and the Ukraine Headstone Project (through FOMCU). Please donate to this vital and ongoing work.

REFLECTION

"The wicked are stringing their bows and fitting their arrows on the bowstrings. They shoot from the shadows at those whose hearts are right. The foundations of law and order have collapsed. What can the righteous do?"

Psalms 11:2-3 NLT

JOIN MY READER'S GROUP

RUSSIAN MENNONITE CHRONICLES follows Katarina and Anna — two wealthy Mennonite sisters from southern Ukraine — during the Russian Revolution. While safe inside their patriarchal traditions, the World War seems a distant threat until Russia implodes, Ukraine pushes to separate, and anarchy reigns. Then the jaws of war strike.

When conventional structures fail and the religious prescriptions no longer fit, the Mennonites find themselves in a frightening and unfamiliar world. Raised under the banner of non-resistance, sisters Katarina and Anna come face to face with life and death decisions. How will they survive the horrors to come? Can their faith endure?

As Peter tells the story based on the diary of his deceased mother, he struggles to understand the impact of trauma on Katarina's life and its effect on his childhood. At the same time, he struggles with his own emotional wounds.

This series tackles the eternal questions: Why do bad things happen to good people? Where is God in times of trouble?

Find free stories, recipes, and other fun giveaways. Get advance notice of upcoming releases.

AFTER AND BEFORE

1951 MUNICH, POST-WAR GERMANY

KATARINA'S DIARY. ETCHED ON THE COVER:

"The voiceless dead lie buried in unmarked graves; their stories forgotten to the sands of time."

Peter swallowed hard. The lump landed in his stomach with a heavy thud. He reached for a glass of water and took a sip, then opened the book and stared at the familiar handwriting on the inside cover.

How did the diary end up in the rubble of their old apartment? He was positive he'd combed through every stone. But the box was found in plain sight — which meant someone put it there. But who? Was Katarina in Munich after the war? Had she wanted him to find it? If so, how could she know he would? He shook his head. That wasn't possible. She'd been gone for ten years.

KATARINA'S DIARY
(*Inscribed on the inside cover*)

> *Dear Reader,*
> *I'm rewriting this preface because the original pages*
> *are tattered. And I've had some time to reflect. First,*
> *I want you to understand how evil ripped apart our*
> *wonderful way of life and stole our souls. If not for*
> *the threads of faith and the bond with my sister,*
> *Anna, I would not be alive. The painful memories*
> *haunt me still — and for that you may think me*
> *insane. Nonetheless, I've persevered.*
>
> *I know I've made many mistakes. I ask for forgive-*
> *ness and understanding. But my decisions —*
> *whether good or bad — were based on the choices*
> *available to me at the time. The Revolution didn't*
> *leave me with many options. Eventually, survival*
> *was all that mattered. Even then, my best intentions*
> *were always for my sister Anna and our boys, Peter*
> *and Jacob.*

Peter closed the diary and stared at the cover while he toyed with the wrinkled corners. The story was too ugly to repeat, and yet it called to him like a filmy apparition. He opened it again and flipped through the pages.

What was he looking for? A secret message? A truth to heal his wounded soul? Would knowing the details of Katarina's tormented past silence his whispering demons?

"*I begin with the summer when the war became real to me.*"

She tried to tell him, but he refused to listen. He shouldn't blame himself. He was only a kid then. How could he have understood? What happened after their last meeting in 1941? Had she returned to Ukraine to search for Jacob? That would have been incredibly stupid — even suicidal. He should have gone with her. But it was too late. Katarina was gone and all that was left were her books.

One thing was certain. He needed help.

IN KATARINA'S HANDWRITING:
1915 RUSSIAN UKRAINE

I couldn't know the war would change everything.

At fifteen, I believed I was invincible, and the world was mine to own. Until that summer, I dismissed the global conflict and economic angst as irrelevant to my life. Father said that girls didn't need to know such things. Instead, I should study how to become a good wife and mother — since this was to be my subscribed role. But I craved a different future.

Unlike many of the local Russian children my age, I still attended school. Mennonites valued education highly and most of my peers had graduated from the primary levels. In addition to basic academics, the girls were also taught domestic skills such as cooking, baking, sewing and other similar crafts. This compulsory training — traditionally taught by our mothers and other female family members — guaranteed every young woman's future as a respectable member of our religious society. The more fortunate (like myself) received the added support of the watchful eyes and hands of our loyal servants.

I was born into a privileged class where land owner-ship defined wealth and demanded respect, and those who didn't have served those who did. We enjoyed more than most but less than some. Dad said our family was comfortable but not that impor-tant and emphasized humility as a facet of godli-ness. Money and land could disappear, but character shaped one's future. Mom said ambition led to greed and so we must watch our thoughts.

I didn't understand this until I was older.
Food was a serious subject in our family, and so I learned to cook before I could walk. By the time I reached eighth grade, my pies won the most ribbons at the church picnics, and Dad gobbled up my vareniki[1] even though half the filling disappeared in the boiling water. Extra portions of yeasty, molasses-rich bread and plates drenched with lumpy onion gravy covered my comestible sins. My older brother, Dietrich, was quick to point out my imperfections. I secretly wished for him to marry a grumpy chef. Thankfully, he was soon leaving for his mandatory four years of forestry service in the Russian military. There he would pine for my cooking.

Although I appreciated our community-based life, I yearned for travel and adventure as described in the books I'd read about exotic places like Germany and America. I balked at traditional goals and set my sights on becoming a missionary schoolteacher. To accomplish this, I strived to be the best student at school and a shining Christian example in the community to ensure my acceptance at teacher's college.

While Dad scoffed at my lofty ambitions and Mom rolled her eyes, my sister Anna cheered me on. "Why not you?" she said, "The world needs school-teachers, too."

Anna was the last of my sisters to marry. Even though Maria and Helena lived less than a two-hour carriage ride away, their busy farm lives and young families kept them close to home. Only our comedic sister-in-law Justina — married to our brother Heinrich — lived nearby. Our monthly family gatherings allowed little time to dig into each other's lives.

Weddings and funerals were extra opportunities to catch up. That summer, the sisters became almost inseparable as Anna's engagement and wedding — to the wealthiest bachelor in the land of the Mennonites — brought the women home to help plan the final details.

I thought seventeen was much too young, but what did I know? I was more concerned about losing my confidant and study partner. It wasn't the marriage that bothered me; it was the fact that Anna was moving across the mighty Dnieper River and far beyond the city to the other colony — a two-day carriage drive (in good weather) — and I hadn't yet learned to use the train. I despaired. Our future visits were bound to be sporadic.

Although I feigned joy for her marital bliss, Anna's departure meant this wedding was as much a funeral as it was a celebration. My fear of loneliness wasn't washed away by her promises of letter writing. I dreaded my bleak future without her.

The day of their wedding arrived in the middle of a blistering July heatwave, and my responsibility — as the single sister of the bride — was to manage the herd of younger cousins who accompanied their parents to the festive reception in our parents' backyard.

Instead of being one of the best days of our lives, it was the beginning of my nightmare.

1951 POST-WAR GERMANY

Reinhart Koehler leafed through the thick journal a second time before setting it down. Removing the spectacles perched on the tip of his broad nose, he placed them on the book, then lifted the gray cat with the yellow eyes — parked and purring in the middle of the oaken desk —and pulled it onto his lap. He cooed at the feline, scratching it under the chin and petting it for a long minute before acknowledging the thirty-three-year-old man in the brown tweed jacket seated across the room.

Peter tapped his fingers on the arm of the curved wooden chair, waiting anxiously for the editor's response.

"Well, it's a fascinating story, Peter." Reinhart set the

cat on the floor and dusted the hair from his tailored charcoal pants. "However, I have some concerns."

"Such as?"

"You said your mother wrote this?"

"Yes." Peter's gaze drifted over the cluttered bookshelves lining the walls of the dark, musty room. The late afternoon sunlight flickered through the murky tilt-turn window, casting the editor in an ashen tone.

"Did she give it to you for publication?"

Peter shifted and looked across the desk. "No. I found it in the rubble of our old apartment building before they demolished it."

"And your mother has passed on?"

"We believe so. She disappeared ... the government declared her deceased, missing in wartime. There's been no contact in ten years."

"I see." The editor twitched his mouth to the side and bit the corner of his lower lip. "And you're certain this information is factual?"

"I am."

"Her chronicle is unusually dramatic. It would be nice to have corroboration."

"Many Mennonites who lived through the horrors are still alive."

"I was hoping for a more unbiased source ... government documents or military records, maybe."

Peter rubbed the frayed threads on the hem of his jacket, pulled his feet under his seat, and crossed his ankles. "It's rather impossible to access Russian military information."

Reinhart leaned back, his balding head glimmering under the yellow light of the glass wall sconce. "Tell me, are you seeking to publish this as a memoir or a biography?"

"I'm not sure .... I was hoping you could enlighten me. I'm a bit out of my element here."

"Well ... one problem is the writer isn't present to clarify details. For all we know, this composition could be fiction."

Peter picked up the leaded glass goblet on the wooden side table and sipped the smoky golden liquid. "It fits with the stories I heard growing up. There are undisputed facts. For one, the mercenary, Nestor Makhno, led the Black Army. And the three armies — Red, White, and Black — converged at the site on June 20, 1920. This is documented."

"Yes, Peter, but I've read many fictionalized accounts of battles. Katarina makes serious accusations of war crimes. Unless we have corroboration, I worry about the families suing for libel." Reinhart scratched his square jaw.

"Makhno's daughter lives in Kazakhstan and his wife is still in prison, so I doubt they'll read the book. Besides, both Germany and Russia charged him with insurrection. He was exiled and died in Paris."

"Even so. Any legal interference in publishing will be costly. Regardless of whether they read it or not, the information is a political hot potato and a potential risk to us both."

Peter sucked on his lower lip, returned the glass to the side table, and flexed his fists. "Are you saying you won't publish?"

"I'm not saying no, exactly ... and that isn't the only problem. I'm just being cautious. Some may consider Makhno an honored freedom fighter."

"Perhaps, but not to my family. And not to those he tortured and murdered. Besides, Ukraine is a Russian republic now. They never gained independence." Peter squeezed his fists as he sniffed to control the sweat beading on his face. He glanced at the closed window. Should he ask the man to open it?

"True enough. But I worry about resurrecting more political wounds. The holocaust revelations are bleeding us. Katarina's story won't redeem Germany or fix my life. Tell me why I should care."

"Reinhart, speaking from my experience, many survivors are too afraid to speak out, or feel there's no point in obsessing about something that can't be fixed. They don't seek reparations. They want emotional healing. Sharing the past helps them to cope with the present.

"As children — myself included — we grew up hearing our parents' stories and we watched them suffer through night terrors, mood swings, depression, and alcoholism. In some respects, we are also victims. We need to make sense of what they went through." Peter felt his chest and jaw tighten as he glared at the man. Surely an expert like Reinhart Koehler understood the emotional consequences of war and the significance of history.

Reinhart stared back and paused for a long moment before responding in a cool, terse tone. "Yes, sad lives make for dramatic fodder. So why don't you write something like that? Why publish an unauthorized autobiography with historical details that may not hold up to public criticism?"

"Because the world must know what happened there. Thousands of bodies lie buried in those fields, forgotten to time. They need remembering." The interrogation was exasperating.

"Why? Why not let the dead bury the dead?"

Peter pressed his point. "If we don't record personal accounts, then how can we trust history? Future generations will speculate, and false theories will develop. Testimonials help to prove the existence of people, places, and events."

"Yes, I agree. But this isn't an English class where one can simply write a good story. A good researcher backs up a testimony with facts. We need to know if the existing data is myth, a subjective perspective, or objective opinion. Can it be qualified or quantified? Without confirmation, we've only got personal drama. Peter, you challenge intelligent minds at the university. Surely you understand the importance of asking these questions. Dig deeper. Convince me that this is an accurate record."

"Look, Reinhart, she was my mother. I heard many snippets over the years, and I watched her mentally relive the trauma day after day. I believe everything happened just as she said." Peter grimaced at hearing the lame plea leave his mouth. He wouldn't accept such a pathetic defense from any of his students. He half expected Reinhart to burst out laughing.

"Ok, Peter," Reinhart grinned and held up a hand in a stop signal. "Let's agree it's true. Let's say you find historical proof to her claims. We still have one other glaring problem."

"What's that?" Sweat dribbled down Peter's nose. He removed a handkerchief from his pocket and wiped his face.

"Her heroic presentation of Germany. Let's face it. It will be decades before we can erase the shame. You need to consider another angle." Reinhart walked over to the window, opened it and adjusted the tilt, then turned on the overhead fan.

Peter took a deep breath of the fresh breeze, leaned back, and crossed his legs. "Are you saying the entire world sees every German as evil?"

Reinhart sat down, folded his hands over his middle-aged paunch and rested his elbows on the chair's padded arms. "Well, honestly speaking ... most of us supported

Hitler in one way or another. Even if we didn't vote for him, we didn't fight his policies. We ignored the cries of the vulnerable. We placed ourselves on pedestals and pushed others off. Our plea for respect and validation seems rather pompous under those circumstances ... don't you think so?"

Peter squirmed. "Doesn't the rest of the world bear responsibility for their ignorance too?"

Reinhart's blue eyes crinkled, and his lips drew together in a tight smile. "I doubt they see it that way. The victor controls the retelling of the past. Therefore, Germany is always portrayed as the villain."

"But her life can't be for naught!" Peter didn't understand the man's point. What did any of this have to do with the manuscript? "If we can't depend on her diary as evidence, then how can we trust other texts discovered in similar ruins? I fear the discarding of the dead as if they never mattered."

"Peter, listen to me. Memoirs are slices of a person's life through their eyes. The way one views life reveals their inner self. Katarina survived a horrific ordeal, and her diary is dramatic. But her accounting is questionable. To publish this as factual would be irresponsible."

"Do you really expect academic accuracy ... from a diary?" Peter sensed the editor was stalling.

Reinhart pushed back his chair and put an ankle on his knee. "Peter, I have to sell the book. I can't spend hundreds or thousands on publishing and marketing a story that won't sell. It's my money. I'm sorry. From a historical perspective, it doesn't hold up. I appreciate your wish to tell your mother's story. But you have to give me something saleable."

So, it all came down to money. Why should that be a surprise? Even the media flaunted lies in their quest for fame and fortune. He had hoped Reinhart had more integrity. Peter crossed his arms over his chest. "Are you suggesting I rewrite my mother's story, twist the facts to match the audience's satisfaction? Falsify it or present it as fiction?"

"No, no," Reinhart chuckled. "Don't be jumping to conclusions, Peter. Hear me out. I suggest reworking it within the current parameters. Raw is good, but we need some context, err, corroboration to help make it believable."

Peter uncrossed his legs and arms and dropped his hands to the chair's sidearms. Perhaps he had reacted too defensively. He could see the man's point. "Hmm .... I want to be true to her. I don't want to take anything away from her experience."

"This document is a fragment of her introspective journey in the middle of a much bigger picture. If her writings are a true autobiography, they should be verifiable. Can you expand on that?"

"I feel as if you're asking me to break a priceless antique." Papers on the desk fluttered as a sudden gust blew through the window.

Reinhart placed a book on the moving stack. "The vase won't break, Peter. It's only another perspective. You can always put it on another platform later."

Peter sat up straight and brightened. "I suppose that's true."

"Don't let the past hold you captive, Peter. Society has a way of shifting long-held beliefs. Look at how slavery was embraced throughout most of human history but is now disgusting. Perceptions of religion change, too. Katarina saw the world through the Mennonite veil. The reader won't understand that life unless you show it." Compassion resonated in the man's tone.

"But her beliefs encouraged German loyalty — which

you say is unmarketable. I'm confused." Peter tapped his foot on the hardwood floor.

"Ok, let's explore this. If you were writing her biography, how would you address her attitude of German heroism?"

"First and foremost, the Mennonite communities considered themselves ethnic Germans, even though many were Dutch by ancestry. Their first language was German, and their culture was largely built on inherited German traditions from Prussia. As for their faith, their church preached the High German from the pulpit and considered it the language of salvation." Peter paused and rubbed his lips together. "To give you an idea as to how entrenched this concept was ... when I was a child, an old Mennonite woman told me that no Englishman could get into heaven unless they spoke German."

Reinhart threw his head back and roared.

Peter chuckled and nodded, "It's true. She really said that."

"That explains Katarina's unholy devotion to the German cause. And it's enough to throw her entire diary in the garbage, Peter. Who wants to read some teenager's romanticized view of a brutal regime?"

"No, no. It wasn't like that. It was because of their ethnic connections that Germany occupied and protected the villages and offered to rescue them from the Russian threat. Germany stood by the Mennonites when Russia didn't. Of course, she idealized Germany. She wasn't alone. However, I don't believe that her naivety diminishes her trauma. If anything, her acknowledgement of the betrayal makes it more believable." Peter paused as a shiver travelled down his spine. "Huh. I guess she embraced Germany much like I did twenty years later." Were their traumas comparable? He stretched his long legs, crossed his ankles, and tapped the sides of his shoes together. "Wow .... I'm not sure who was the bigger fool."

"You and me both. Tell me, you said her attitude changed during the second war?"

"It did. When she saw the truth up front and personal ... it sickened her."

Reinhart nodded. "I suspect reality slapped her in the face, the way it did most. Germany carries the weight of many victims. I fear survivor guilt may plague us indefinitely, but as to the Great War — like you, I was too young to fight, so my memories are vague. Can you draw a parallel to make it more relevant?"

"Yes. Mom was in a no-win scenario. She needed rescuing. Germany just happened to be the savior. She probably would've reacted the same to any rescuer."

"Peter, readers want heroes, not victims. What can we learn from her life?"

"Well," Peter rubbed his chin, "In order to survive, she manipulated the situation to the best of her ability."

"In other words, she was the hero in her own story. Now you've hit pay dirt. How she coped through the wars is a fascinating angle. People like reading survival stories — desperate situations that call for desperate measures — the raw grit that pulls on the heart. Keep going." Reinhart uncrossed his legs and leaned forward, then drew a pencil from the white ceramic cup on his desk and opened a notebook.

Peter took a deep breath and reflected on the dark memories. "Her perseverance kept her alive, but it came with a price. There were times when she acted robotic, emotionless — her body present, but her spirit elsewhere. It was hard to bring her back to the moment ... when she began translating for the SS, she said the labor camps reminded her of their last year in Russia — a time that she wanted to forget. I think coming to terms with the truth threw her overboard, mentally speaking ... and then she disappeared."

"The politics were very deceptive. We were all duped. Tell me, what was she like at home? Show me the real Katarina."

"She was ... troubled." Peter paused and sucked on his lower lip.

"Was she?"

"Disturbed? I suppose. Perhaps haunted by her memories is more accurate. She couldn't sleep. She'd wake up screaming, thinking her nightmares were real. During the day, she'd sit in her chair staring into space, daydreaming. Other times, her storytelling was unbearably emphatic and repetitive. I don't know who she was trying to convince — us or herself. Her unpredictable and violent mood swings kept both Dad and me on edge. We did a lot of fishing." Peter looked down at his scuffed brown leather shoes. *Was it really that bad? It was so long ago.*

"Keep going, Peter. Don't stop now." The pencil nib snapped. Reinhart flung it aside and grabbed another tool from the mug, then flipped the page.

"Do you want me to focus on the war or her troubled mind?"

"Neither."

"Huh? I don't understand."

"Her description of events and her suffering is clear. But who was Katarina, and why should we care?"

"She was a traumatized war survivor. She endured terror that I wouldn't wish on my worst enemy."

"How did she get through it, Peter?" Reinhart snapped

15

as the pencil flew across the sheet. "Who was this girl who became a woman during this awful time? Show me her strength, spirit, and resolve." He looked up from the notebook and stared at Peter with an astonished gaze. "Peter, use Katarina's story, even her words, but show us the woman who screamed at God, questioned her faith, and defied the odds while living through one of the worst horrors in history. Give us some hope that such atrocities will never happen again." Reinhart slapped the desk with the palm of his hand. *"Das ist gut fur alle,* man. Give us hope for Germany. Give us hope for humanity."

A seed planted itself in Peter's mind. He gaped and blinked as it took root. "That's it." He clapped, leaned forward, and knocked on the desk. "I've got it now, Reinhart. I can do this. When I'm done, the world will care about my mother and this history. I promise."

---

1. A large dough pocket filled with a variety of fillings such as cheese, onions, sauerkraut, or potatoes. Berry or fruit fillings were common during summer months. A Ukrainian version of the popular Polish food known as perogies.

2

THE WEDDING

1915 RUSSIAN UKRAINE—CHORTITZA COLONY

KATARINA TUCKED THE DAMP, BLONDE STRANDS BEHIND her ears and tightened her Dutch braids, then dipped the towel in the water bucket and rubbed her face and neck. Her head pounded, and her throat was parched from playing tag with her younger cousins in the dusty pasture. She squeezed the towel behind her neck until cool drops dribbled down her back. In a few hours, after the party ended, she'd strip off the fancy dress with its layered undergarments and take a refreshing dip in the pond.

She admitted that her mother had been right about the fabric. The expensive satin with its velvety raised pattern was much too heavy for the summer. With the war limiting the choices of such luxury items, it was only by divine providence that she spotted the champagne fabric at the very back of the seamstress's closet, lying right next to the bolt of Flemish lace for Anna's wedding dress.

"This is a sign from God," their mother, Lena Rempel, declared about the lace. "This marriage is meant to be."

When Katarina snapped up the adjacent fancy remnant and announced God's pleasure in her outfit too, her mother and sisters argued her choice. But Katarina stood her ground, insisting that at fifteen, she was old enough to make her own decisions on such matters.

She glowed in the exotic frock during the long tiring sermon in the unventilated church; but now, after an hour of romping in the fields, the sweat-soaked undergarments clung in twisted, sticky folds beneath the exquisite topcoat. She'd had enough of the dress.

Plunging the ladle down into the bucket, she scooped up the water, lifted it to her mouth, and slurped. The well water had lost its refreshing chill and turned lukewarm in the humid July heat. At least it was wet.

"Katarina, can you please help out here? The men need coffee. The servants can't keep up." Her mother jerked her chin towards the tiny summer kitchen behind her where the serving staff bustled, preparing the trays of food for the reception.

Katarina snorted. "*Nay.* I'm getting sweets for the children. I can't babysit and serve too. Besides, I'm exhausted."

"Don't talk back to me," Lena Rempel scolded in the Low German[1] language. "The *kjinja* need to learn patience. They can wait. We need more cups set and your sisters are busy serving at the tables. We need an extra hand here."

"Fine, but don't blame me if they get in the way." Katarina poured water into the washing basin and splashed her flushed face and neck a second time. She looked up to meet the glare of her mother's narrowed gray-blue eyes. Lena's pale lips tightened and disappeared into a thin pink line, and her bony knuckles glistened as her fists curled tighter around the handles of the two white coffee pitchers that she held in front of her chest.

When Katarina fluffed her skirt and waltzed into the flimsy wood and brick structure, Lena Rempel pivoted with a sharp quarter turn — her heels digging into the baked earth as she stomped away.

"Trouble much?" Katya, the head housekeeper winked. "The sisters of the bride must work hard on the wedding day."

"Three sisters and one brother married, but this is the first time I'm part of the sheep pen."

"Sheep pen?" Milica, the newly hired scullery maid, piped in with a giggle.

"*Tak.* You know, fenced in and kept in line with the shepherd stick," Katarina replied in the local Ukrainian dialect.[2]

"Oh, you poor girl. It's such a hard life to be the baby of the family, isn't it? Just imagine, only one brother to go, and then it will be your turn," Katya smiled.

Katarina picked up a tray full of cups. "My turn? Not on your life. I'm heading to teacher's college as soon as I turn seventeen. Then I will travel the world."

"Oh?" Milica raised her eyebrows while pouring coffee into a pitcher. "Which one are you applying to?"

"Rosenthal, of course."

"*Ty budesh.*" Milica grimaced, "I mean, where you live? In the residence there?"

Upon hearing the new maid's struggle with the local dialect, Katarina switched into Russian. "*Da*, of course."

"What does your daddy say about that?"

She set the tray down and — imitating her father — pulled back her shoulders, crossed her arms over her chest, and widened her stance; then, mimicking his deep voice, she said, "Oh, he just crosses his arms and says, God's will be done. He never says yes or no."

The servants giggled.

She relaxed her posture, picked up a cookie, and took a bite, "Yum, who brought these?"

"That would be your sister-in-law, Justina."

"I need the recipe."

"Katarina, are you hiding in here?" A beefy woman with mousy brown hair styled into a tight bun and covered in black lace poked her head through the doorway. Her billowy outfit filled the frame and shadowed the tiny room as she stepped inside. The long-sleeved white blouse with colorful floral stitching on its high neck and four-button cuffs gave a contemporary tone to the black cotton skirt with matching embroidery along the hem. Justina's reluctance in looking too modern showed with the added simple white bib apron — which took away from the costume's fanciness and made it seem puritanical.

"*Ja.* I'm bringing cups. I'm coming right now."

"The bride is looking for you."

"Well, I can't be three places at once. Where is she?"

"Katarina?" Frustration edged Anna's chirpy voice, "Is she in here?"

Justina backed away from the narrow entrance and onto the lawn to make room for a petite, slender woman in a high-necked, long-sleeved ivory lace gown and vinok headdress. The floral crown — composed of cornflowers, sunflowers, and periwinkle vines, woven together with a rainbow of ribbons — accented her brilliant blue eyes and hid her upswept honey-blonde hair.

Anna fanned herself with a colorful hand-painted oriental wooden folding fan — a personal gift from her new mother-in-law. "Oh, there you are. What are you doing? You're supposed to be looking after the little ones."

"Mom said I'm supposed to help bring out cups. She said they were fine by themselves."

"They are disturbing the men. They need some corralling."

"Good grief. Can't the men tolerate a few *kjinja* running around?"

"The conversation is not appropriate for the tiny ears. The men are almost past the coffee stage and ready for their medicine."

Katarina noticed Katya's smirk as she whispered to her young helper in Russian. "That's a discreet request for a stronger remedy like brandy and cigars. The women don't admit such things out loud. We'd best work a little faster."

"Politics again?" Katarina rolled her eyes.

"Yes, and it's getting volatile." Anna widened her eyes and jerked her head to the side twice to emphasize an urgent situation.

"Katarina!" Lena Rempel's voice bellowed through the thin walls.

"I'm here. I'm coming."

The towering peacock feathers on her wide-brimmed hat skimmed the frame as Lena ducked her head into the room. "Why is everyone gaggling here? The men need serving."

"And the children need order," Anna snapped back at her mother.

Lena's eyes widened and her mouth gaped. She glared at her daughters, then backed away from the door. Katarina bit her lip to keep from chuckling. Anna had a way of asserting herself that left others powerless. Katarina wished she had such a disarming skill.

She interrupted the awkward silence by pirouetting and throwing her hands in the air. "*Oba, nay. Oba, yea.* I'm being

21

torn in two here. What should I do, put cups on the table or babysit? Is there no one else who can help?"

"I'm sorry to put so much pressure on you," Anna's voice softened, "but as the youngest sister of the bride, you get to work the hardest. Besides, when it comes to the little ones, you're the best." Her face widened into a toothy smile, "You need practice if you want to be a schoolteacher."

In an act of sisterly defiance, Katarina flicked her index finger off her nose in Anna's direction.

The brim of Lena's fancy wedding hat came into view again as she poked her head around the door. "Get the cups, Katarina. Get serving. Justina, please get your boys to help out with *diesa kjinja*. They mustn't hear all the political gossip." Her voice was strained with exasperation.

"*Oba, nay*." Katarina stamped her foot and glared at her mother's silhouette in the doorway. "Again. Why is it so important for me to serve?"

"If you were doing your job, you wouldn't get switched out," Lena Rempel snapped. "Next time you'll stay where you belong."

Katarina turned her back to her mother, stuck out her tongue, and made a face that only the servants could see. They snickered and shifted their attention to filling the coffee pitchers and sweet trays.

"Behave yourself," Lena scolded as Katarina pushed past her. "This is your sister's wedding. You pitch in and help — where and when you're needed. No complaining. God doesn't —"

"— like complainers." Katarina stomped out of the tiny building carrying a tray of cups and headed towards the long rows of white tablecloth-covered tables stationed between the house and the barn.

The women had discussed the possibility of wind and

rain before deciding to hold an outdoor reception. The barn was the backup plan; it had been scoured and organized, and the animals moved to the far pasture in case of a last-minute change of venue. But the weather co-operated with blue skies and gentle winds, making for a perfect day for an alfresco affair.

Mason jars filled with wheat stems and field flowers heralding fertility and good fortune adorned each table and held the table covers in position. The yellow and blue ribbons tying the corners together kept the linens from flapping in the breeze while platters of meats, cheeses, breads, salads, and pitchers of water and watermelon juice provided the necessary weight to keep the decorated tables intact. Every practicality had been considered during the planning, and Katarina had been elected by the sisters as the primary party organizer.

She paused for a moment to admire her decorating before bustling over to her oldest sister, Helena Janzen, working at the far end of the men's section. Helena jerked her square chin towards the serving table. "Over there. Put the tray there. No. Never mind. See those two tables?"

Helena's pale blue eyes swept the crowd as she wiped her hands on the navy apron covering her full hips. She fluffed the multi-layered, crocheted collar of her new linen dress, straightened the buttoned cuffs, and tucked a stray ash blonde strand underneath her crown braid. "How do I look?" she panted in a breathy voice. Without waiting for an answer, she announced, "They need cups. And I need more coffee." She made an abrupt turn and dashed towards the summer kitchen.

"Right," Katarina whispered under her breath, "And they wonder why I get nothing done. How am I supposed to follow two directions at once?" She picked up the tray and sashayed over to the rowdy tables. Afraid of being hit by unpredictable gesticulations, she waited behind each man until the animated arms rested before planting the cups. *At this rate, I'll be here forever.*

She noticed the leering glances from the old men and cringed. Lately, her mother insisted on her presence as a server at every male dominated function, but the ogling made her skin crawl. She'd rather be babysitting. Children were curious creatures, but they didn't make her feel like a weed in a flower patch. If only her church friends or older female cousins had been allowed to attend and help with the function, as they had at last week's bridal shower, she wouldn't feel so conspicuous. But today was for important people, which they were not.

The booming voice of Katarina's father, Johann Rempel, roared from the head table. "And who hired that boy in the first place? You can't beat the tar out of a ten-year-old when he has no father to reinforce the punishment. He'll grow up to resent authority."

"J.P. was just trying to train the kid to be a man," Maria's husband, George Sawatzky hollered back. "Valenko came from evil seed. You can't blame him or anyone else. The boy would have turned out bad no matter what. His brothers were just as depraved."

Katarina rolled her eyes at her opinionated brother-in-law's negative comment and hoped someone would quickly shift the topic before the conversation got out of hand. She looked over to where George was sitting, immediately picking out his distinctive angular frame among the sea of black suits and white shirts. Today, the special effort taken to wax his facial growth only pinched his countenance more and made him look comedic. Katarina could never under-stand how such a short, wiry man managed to couple with her buxom sister, Maria. They were a strange looking pair in her mind.

A chorus of murmurs rising from the intimidating male crowd told her the conversation was heating up. Katarina groaned at the prospect of waiting another hour to eat.

Her stomach rumbled with an embarrassing loud moan and she grimaced, hoping no one noticed. She shouldn't have eaten that cookie. It only made her hungrier. In Katarina's opinion, it wasn't fair that the men ate before the women, but that was how things were done. It was tradition, and as such couldn't be changed.

Her mouth watered at the sight of the rapidly emptying plates and bowls, and she swallowed away the temptation to remove a platter from the table before it was empty. That would only get her hand slapped. The last item on the serving dish must be offered to the men first. She had to wait. She could sneak a few bites when she returned to the kitchen for another tray.

An unknown voice yelled from a neighboring table. "I agree, George. Without a fatherly example, boys run wild. When they mess up, they run to mommy and get coddled. Women know nothing about discipline. A good beating helps send the message home."

"Discipline, yes, but drawing blood goes too far," Johann barked.

"If the fire of rebellion takes root, the soul is destined for trouble. By the time they're twelve, it's too late. Get it under control early, I say." Helena's husband, Peter Janzen's comment was cheered with the sound of spoons clinking on glasses and accompanied by the rumble of yeas and nays.

Katarina took a deep breath and set a cup beside her father's plate. Anna was right. The conversation was testy.

"Confused youth can't be corrected easily. It's in their

blood. Do you remember Jake having trouble with some local smart mouth who blew up the police station back in '05? Makhno and friends, Jake said. They got the death sentence and for good reason."

"I heard it was life in prison ... the boy was too young to hang." Helena's husband Peter Janzen corrected Anna's new brother-in-law George Penner about the situation involving his father, the millionaire Jacob Janzen, who was known as Jake by his friends, but A.J. by everyone else.

"Either way, they're criminals and got what they deserve. And if today's youth latch onto those weird socialist ideas, mark my words there'll be trouble again. This latest round of political bickering makes the hair on my neck stand up. I don't trust it." The silverware rattled as Johann Rempel banged his thick fist on the table. The veins in his neck bulged purple.

Katarina grimaced. Her father hated to be wrong, and he seemed one step away from blowing his stack. But for what reason? Some miscreant farmhand who'd worked for the millionaire?

What did this have to do with politics? The questions begged to pop out of her mouth. She bit her lips to keep them at bay. As a child, she would have interrupted the conversation and asked. At fifteen, she was almost a woman — although not quite — and interrupting was improper. So, she wracked her memory and tried to piece together stories from the past that might fit this context.

She recalled hearing about a rash of burglaries and bombings in the villages when she was five or six. Her father and brothers had engaged in heated discussions about self-defence, and her mother fussed and cried when the men drove to town for supplies.

But that was old news. Why was this tale being

rehashed? Did it have something to do with A.J. Janzen, the absent, wealthy Mennonite? The pompous man had sent a letter of regret to the wedding party. Distance couldn't have been a factor since he owned two of those fancy new automobiles that drove faster than horses. He could have easily driven both directions in one day.

Although today's guest list read like a society register in a gossip column, the man was likely invited to the more extravagant reception to be held later at her new brother-in-law's family estate across the river. Either A.J. felt he didn't need to attend both functions, or their home wasn't fancy enough. Then again ... what if there was a clash between the men, and that's why he was avoiding the party? This would explain the crude talk. And it could invite delicious rumors. Katarina wiggled her eyebrows and grinned at the thought of starting a few. Then she cringed and scolded herself for thinking so.

She shrugged. In the end, it made no difference. The show-off wasn't present for the entourage to fawn over anyway. Besides, she didn't much care for those who acted like they deserved special treatment — like the owners of those two Opels parked beside the horse and carriages in the yard. Her father proclaimed such displays of wealth only encouraged greed and division and fueled the locals' resentments. However, the upper crust's insight into Russian politics *was* fascinating.

Today's event was bound to get tongues wagging at church. The more popular girls would pepper her for details — wanting to review the list of eligible future husbands. Katarina's inclusion in their exclusive circle would only last until they realized she had no intention of playing their game. The last thing she wanted was to become a society woman like her newly married sister. The trappings of wealth and a life of ease came with other challenges and responsibilities. Her father said it didn't guarantee happiness. And she believed him. Besides, she'd rather end up alone than pretend to be someone she wasn't.

Anna could have her fancy life. Katarina would enjoy the luxuries when she visited and that was enough for her. Although she respected her sister's choice, Katarina preferred a little dirt under her fingernails. But she had her limits there, too. Her older sister Maria — with her hands and feet in the muddy dairy barn — was a clear example of the other extreme. Too foul for her liking.

Teaching was a clean and honorable vocation. It kept her out of both the social spotlights and the farm fields. And *if* she ever married, her position as teacher would only attract intelligent suitors — men like her father. Her mind was made up. Her friends could strike her name off their matchmaking list. She would not compete with them.

Her daydreaming screeched to a halt as Abram Lentz's voice boomed, "It's those political radicals in Petrograd behind it all … encouraging the riots in the streets. They think the end justifies the means."

Katarina frowned. What did the protests half-way across the country have to do with the man's local farm machinery business? If he had enough to buy a luxury automobile, surely he could afford to pacify his employees with higher wages. Or … was she missing something?

"Violence is never justified," a voice hollered from across the multi-rowed square of tables.

Lentz sat back and toyed with the end of his waxed handle-bar mustache. He glanced at the cup as she set it down beside his elbow but neither thanked nor acknowledged her. "Then what do we say about war? What if it comes here?"

"We don't need to worry about that now. We'll find out more when A.J. returns from Petrograd." David — Anna's new husband — gave a calming and practical reply to the worried crowd.

Of course. Katarina smacked the back of her head with an invisible hand. The man had traveled to Petrograd with the regional committee to discuss political concerns with the Czar, over a fancy dinner.

"If those leftist social democrats gain any more power, they'll destroy the country," Lentz argued.

"Let's not get carried away by rumors. Let's trust the Czar to do the right thing." David lowered his tone in response to the raised voices.

"That weak, lily-livered autocrat? He keeps promising the world, but never delivers. Russia will lose the war if he keeps waffling." George Sawatzky jumped back into the controversy.

"Can you believe it? Russia and Germany at war," Katarina's brother, Dietrich, threw in his two kopecks, even though he was neither experienced nor rich enough to have an opinion. Katarina guessed that since he was soon leaving for his alternative military service in Berdyansk, Dietrich worried about the personal implications of the war.

"Ja, this is worrisome. The Russky differentiate little between us and the German colonists. They've already confiscated the guns. What's next? I feel like I'm sitting on my hands waiting to be slapped by the teacher while he's standing in the hall getting advice from the headmaster about how hard to hit," Johann D. Penner sputtered as he dipped his napkin in a glass of water before wiping the coffee dribble off his graying beard.

J.D. was David's elder brother. Katarina had heard that the man had a critical temperament — always preaching doom and gloom. She wondered if the rest of David's family were as negative, and shuddered, picturing Anna and her new husband sharing the estate's manor home with J.D. and his wife, Agatha, until their new five-bedroom house was built. Anna's perky personality would be challenged.

"We should have left for Canada when we had the chance." Bernhard (Ben) Heinrichs, Agatha's father, moaned. Many of their family had emigrated to the Americas following the wave of political changes in 1874.

"We? That was thirty years ago. A different generation. You can't compare that time to this. There was no war back then," Pastor Friesen interjected.

"I disagree. The signs were there. They warned us. We weren't paying attention," Ben shot back.

A raucous round of opinions fired around the tables. Katarina's head spun as she tried to keep track of the speakers.

"Gentlemen," Katarina's father bellowed, "We can't ignore the war or the problems in Petrograd. But it's our brotherly duty to serve Russia after all she's given us — as long as it doesn't conflict with our faith."

"Johann, it's more serious than that. Waving our conscientious objections in the country's face flags us as a problematic religious sect. Now add in our ancestry, our everyday use of the German language, and our celebration of the German culture. The Russky see us as a potential threat — possibly enemies. We could find ourselves in a jar of pickles," Maria's husband, George, whined.

"I'll add mustard to that, George. We're in a precarious position between Germany and Russia. Bear in mind, while Russia accuses us to be German sympathizers, the reverse may also be true. If Germany wins this thing, they may view us as Russian even though we're still technically German colonies — despite living here for a hundred years. They'll consider us Russified," J.D. added.

"Nonsense. I say this will all blow over. Besides, if it comes down to it, Germany will have our backs." Lentz reached into his pocket and pulled out a silver flask and poured a dark amber liquid into his cup.

Lentz was married to David's oldest sister, Mary, who had declined traveling for the weekend's events because of the wicked summer heat. Although Katarina suspected her absence had more to do with the fact that she couldn't bring her entourage of servants with her due to the parlor at their farm being too small. Instead, Lentz brought his business partner and brother-in-law Heinrich Pankratz. Pankratz was married to Lentz's younger sister, and also happened to be the first cousin to Katarina's father — which further legitimized the man's attendance.

When Katarina reflected on the attendees, she realized almost everyone was related to either the bride or groom by blood or through marriage. And this explained why some of her peers were not invited, as her mother normally insisted on for other social events. Not that this mattered to Katarina, as she preferred avoiding the twittering females and their teenaged parties when she could. The complex adult world was far more fascinating.

Ben Heinrich's arm sprang up, his hand almost hitting the cup Katarina was setting down. "If Russia doesn't send us to Siberia first ..."

"If I lose my farm because of this stupid war —"

Katarina's eyebrows knit together in a frown. *How does one lose a farm in a war?* She pictured armed soldiers fencing a farm after killing the owners. *That would require a lot of soldiers. But then, who would own it? The country? That made no sense.*

"— you'll do what, J.D.? You think you're in this alone? If we all stick together through this crisis, we'll survive and come out better for it." Johann slurped his coffee and signaled to Helena for a refill. She held up the carafe and waved at the scullery maid who raced over to exchange pots.

At the next table, Katarina's sister, Maria, nudged her husband George to shift while she placed a large platter of sweets on the table. Katarina held her breath and stared as Maria's ample bosom swept over the gravy bowl. George's arm shot up and moved the dish out of the way before damage could be done. Katarina exhaled a sigh of relief.

A man — whom Katarina recognized as her mother's second cousin, Cornelius Braun, and whose daughter Sarah was her rival at every spelling bee — cleared his throat and stood up to speak. "The war is shifting perspectives. We feed the country from our breadbasket and employ the locals, but they don't trust us because we speak German. Have we not proven our loyalty over three generations?"

"If we can prove our Dutch ancestry, then maybe we have a good chance for redemption," an elder with a tuft of shocking white hair in the middle of his balding head mumbled, as he reached for the last remaining slice of cheese on the platter and stuffed it in his mouth.

Johann Rempel belted out a hearty laugh. "Right. Let's see how well that line works on them. I'm more worried about things a little closer to home. If Petrograd looks at us with a slanted eye, then how do the Russky[3] see us?"

Lentz nodded. "It's the idealistic juveniles we need to worry about. They latch onto new political ideas to flex their independence. Every generation is the same — banding together to figure out novel ways to beat the system and get rich without trying."

Heinrich Pankratz banged the table. "We need to keep

them working hard and discipline them when they don't. Busy hands have no time to cause trouble."

Katarina rolled her eyes at the scrawny weasel-like character. It was known that Pankratz's position as Lentz's business partner was only to keep the family peace because he didn't have an original thought in his head. He would agree with anything and anyone if it saved his skin or made him feel likeable. And this undoubtably encouraged Lentz's drinking problem.

David's mellow voice flowed from the head table. "There's no time for idealism when there's a war to fight. With so many leaving for the front, I'm more concerned about labor shortages."

Lentz snorted. "The locals have no respect for orders from Russia. They form little gangs and disappear into the steppes, then have loud parties at night by the riverbanks."

"Ja. I heard they've got ideas for making easy money on the river by transporting drifters and defectors." Since George's dairy farm bordered the river, Katarina suspected he kept a close eye on the local water traffic.

"And bring them where? Not here. I won't have it. Those vagrant squatters make me nervous. We'll soon need more than just dogs to monitor our perimeters. If the war gets any closer or lasts much longer, I can foresee this problem mushrooming. They'll be invading our homes next," J.D. said.

"I disagree. Those vagrants need to eat. They'll want to work. It's cheap labor for us. This could be a good thing." Lentz nodded. "We could expand our businesses."

David interrupted the noisy chorus. "The danger of having no food or money is that one will do anything to get both. We must tighten the security around our estates and villages."

"I have my doubts we'll see that kind of trouble in these parts, David. You're too young to understand Russia's history. Our elders have seen political conflict before. They assure us the war will be over before long. Personally, I'm more concerned about the political youth. They inflame the peasants with their talk." Johann pulled on his long graying beard. "I've heard there's rebellion stirring at the university."

"Political activism is less worrisome than those criminal gangs back in '07. Poor Tante Trudchen never recovered from the robbery. The estate is barely recognizable anymore," Gerhard Penner croaked through a nasal voice. It always sounded like he had a perpetual cold.

"She was a fighter, for sure."

Katarina had heard about the deceased widow's courage during the attack, but she was unaware of the details. She made a mental note to ask her mother and sisters.

David shifted the topic back to his regional concern. "We need a plan to squash the protests before they silence us."

"David, you're being melodramatic. I realize you're supporting a lot of souls on your *grosse landwirtschaft*[4] but come on, now. It won't get to that."

"Look, the newspapers plant seeds in people's heads. If there's trouble in Russia, it's only a matter of time until things heat up here. The universities herald the Marxist dogma as the best solution to Russia's problems. If embraced by the masses, this ideology could push us off our farms."

Lentz dribbled more liquid from the flask into his cup. "That nonsense in Russia won't wash down here, David. These uneducated simpletons think different. They don't understand how the machinery of government works."

"Those are the worst kinds of activists. They want the wealth without the work."

"Da. But to prevent such, our workers need pacifying, and that takes money. High wages mean higher prices. We still need to make a profit. It's simple arithmetic."

Oberschulze Braun — the local mayor with a vested interest in the brick factory — who had been quiet throughout the discussion, now interjected. "Gentlemen, you're missing the point. Supply is diminishing while demand is increasing. Resources are going to the war effort and inflation is escalating. I agree we can't put more money into labor when we're pumping more into production material. We have to draw the line somewhere. At the same time, people need to feed their families."

"Things will go back to normal when the war ends. This is a temporary problem," David declared.

Katarina bobbed between the rapid fire of arms and elbows while keeping her lips clamped between her teeth so she wouldn't accidently blurt out one of the dozen questions popping in her head. She wished she could sit down and listen, or better yet — take part. But women weren't permitted to discuss such things with men. She was to be seen and not heard.

"I can tell you what my managers have told me," Katarina's older brother Heinrich Rempel added. "The workers are disgruntled, and unions are threatening to strike — again. They want shorter workdays and more money. Where there are no unions, they're being formed."

"They're always whining. It doesn't matter what we pay, it's never enough," Lentz snorted.

"The best way to deal with these union committees is to get rid of the organizers," Pankratz added.

"The Czar agrees. Make their lives difficult and drive them out," J.D. nodded as he clinked his glass.

"Now, now," Johann pounded the table with a tightened fist. "We need to be reasonable and talk sense into these khokhols. If we retaliate with force, we'll only light a fire for their cause. We need to keep the waters calm."

Katarina cringed. She hoped the servants hadn't heard her father use the pejorative term. She stole a furtive glance around the tables. A maid stood behind the back section with her hands clasped in front of her waist and her face expressionless except for the undeniable cold stare directed at Johann. She noticed Katarina looking at her and abruptly turned her back and walked to the serving table. Katarina determined to ask her father to be more polite in front of these house servants that she had grown up with. She respected them and saw them as wise and caring, not stupid.

Pastor Friesen stood up and cleared his throat before speaking. The crowd quietened and turned their attention to the middle-aged preacher from the eastern colony. "Let us remember — violence begets violence. We must be as swift as an eagle, as shrewd as a snake, and as gentle as a dove. We're not of this world, we're only passing through. God will have the last word." With that, he sat down.

There was a moment of silence before Johann responded, "Amen to that, brother. We can't allow the war or any political chaos to shift our faith. Our job is to grow food for the grand people of Russia and to keep our noses out of the country's business."

---

1. Low German, Low Saxon, or "flat" German is a west Germanic language used in common everyday speech by Russian Mennonites from southern Ukraine. High German (or proper German) was the

written language and used in church and school. Mennonites spoke both languages fluently. Russian was the language of business and spoken more by men than women. Many of the wealthy were also well versed in French—as this was used in legal documents in political circles. The servants largely spoke the local Ukrainian dialect informally, but it was not taught in educational circles until after the revolution.

2. Mennonites valued education and multi-lingual abilities. Raised in a wealthy family, Katarina could be fluent in Low German, High German, Russian and the local Ukrainian dialect. She may also understand some Yiddish, French, English and/or eastern European languages. She would easily slip between the various tongues depending to whom she was speaking.

3. Prior to the revolution, the present-day Slavic nations known as Belorussian, Ukraine, and Russia were one country, but Russians referred to the Ukraine region as Little Russia, and Russia as Great Russia or Velikorussy. Russian citizens were sometimes referred to as Russkye or Russky. Reference: https://www.ce.uw.edu.pl/pliki/pw/Stepniewski_YPES_2017.pf

4. Grosse landwirtschaft: A large farm or estate with much land.

3

REGIER

KATARINA FOUND POLITICAL CONVERSATIONS intriguing and far more interesting than the women's petty gossip about the latest social scandals. Today's rant led her to wonder about the war between Germany and Russia and to fantasize about the palaces and cathedrals of Petrograd. She envisioned the commanding and distinctive uniforms of the soldiers as they marched across the vast Russian plains and mountains, then puzzled over the sizes of battalions, the numbers of varying armies, and the scope of the war.

She pictured the opposing political parties in Russia as the Czar's spoiled children who — driven by jealousy of their fathers' wealth and power — inserted themselves into the middle of his business at the most critical time and demanded their own way. The storybook excitement faded as she realized the men seemed more afraid of union disagreements and local activism than the federal crisis. Perhaps she misunderstood. She made a mental note to do more research.

She reasoned the more she learned, the more she didn't know. This reminded her of a Bible verse which her parents often quoted to dissuade her from reading so much. *Of making many books, there is no end, and much study is a weariness of the flesh.*[1]

"There's no point in learning so much, Katarina," Lena said more than once. "It will only confuse you. Focus on what's necessary — the skills to be a proper wife and mother. Nothing else matters."

Except, to Katarina, the fascinating globe was more appealing than chocolate covered plums at Christmas. Teacher's college was her first step towards exploring these exotic details. From her standpoint, she was launching her own book after turning the last page of the final chapter of her great-grandparent's chronicles. Their story of searching for better opportunities began in Danzig and ended with a new life in southern Russia. Her adventure began *here*, and only God knew where it would end. The unknown future possibilities made her skin tingle.

Katarina knew there would be adversities along her solitary journey. Only a fool would assume otherwise, and she was no idiot. She had read enough tragedies to understand that fear accompanies change. But if her ancestors had overcome disasters and scary transitions, she could too. Their success lay in challenging old mindsets, finding alternative solutions, and embracing new realities. If she followed their adventurous example, she, too, would find prosperity and happiness. Then, when she was ready to leave the colony, her parents might discourage her, but she doubted they would stop her. Her resolute response was that she was only repeating a generational pattern infused in her bloodline. How could they argue with history?

There were only two further pieces of education needed until she could take that first step into her future: one more year of school and then teacher's college. As a top student, both goals were within easy reach. Nothing would deter her — not this war, and certainly not any local villains. In fact, if she applied herself, she might escape the predicted evil so feared by the men.

Just as Katarina envisioned the rising sun in her future, she set down the last cup and glanced over her shoulder to check on the whereabouts of Helena, with the coffeepot. A divot caught her toe, spilling her sideways into a young man in a black suit. His top hat flew forward, knocking a glass of milk onto his lap. He jerked backwards on the narrow board bench throwing Katarina off balance. As her feet and long skirts sailed to the sky, her shoulders and hips met the crusty turf with a thud. Her piercing screams shifted the men's heavy debate to a chorus of cheers and jeers as they watched the scene with great delight.

A hand shot out from the bench and she graciously accepted the support as she yanked down her skirts. She stumbled and winced as she stood, her palm flying to the burning pain spreading across her right hip and groin. Her focus shifted to the dirt and grass stains on the expensive satin. *No, not my new dress. Mom will kill me.*

She brushed the smudge with feverish swipes before noticing the gangly, chestnut-haired son of the veterinarian standing in front of her, flexing his fingers against his trousers. The redness of his face and his embarrassed smile told her he felt just as awkward as she did. When she looked up into his deep set, sapphire eyes that glistened like dew in an autumn sky, her heart fluttered, and a warm flush rose in her chest. She dropped her gaze and thanked him.

"My sincerest apologies, Miss Rempel." A proper upbringing reflected in his words and manners.

Anna's voice echoed in her head, "*Husband material.*"

She gulped and scanned the gloating crowd. "No, it was all my fault. I'm sorry. I wasn't paying attention."

Katarina felt her father's penetrating glare before she saw his flashing aqua eyes narrow to a slit and his lips tighten into a thin white line. She suddenly felt as obvious as a pink flamingo standing on one leg — not that she'd ever seen such a bird, but she'd read about them, and she imagined them to be quite arresting with their brilliant feathers and odd stance. She was, however, more familiar with mice; and right now, she wanted to shrink into being one.

"Katarina," the stern tone silenced the whistles and laughter. The men looked down at the table, straightened their posture and adjusted their top hats. "Don't you have duties to attend to?"

"Yes Papa. I'm very busy." Her hands flew to her hot cheeks, and she scurried away, pausing by the serving table to rinse her hands and pat water on her flushed face. Then, turning her back to the gawking audience, she squared her shoulders. Looking straight ahead, she strode quickly to the barn.

The fall was embarrassing, but it wasn't her fault, she reckoned. Even though she hadn't planned to trip behind the good-looking, eligible bachelor, her father's scrutinizing glare and gruff voice insinuated she had. Fifteen was too young to be attracting attention. The social rules of conduct expected a good girl to remain invisible around men until ready for marriage. If she had no intention of marrying in the foreseen future, then she needed to do a better job of being inconspicuous. She didn't want anyone to get the wrong impression, especially such gentlemen who were shopping for a wife.

Replaying the uncomfortable scene in her head, Katarina assessed she had been thinking too much rather than concentrating on the task at hand. She would apologize to her father later. Chastising herself, she shook her head to free her thoughts; then inhaled deeply and exhaled through her mouth in a long stream to calm the butterflies flitting through her stomach, and to erase the dazzling blue eyes from her mind.

Two blond-haired eight-year-old boys wearing white short-sleeved shirts and black pants streaked by, chasing each other around the barn with pointed sticks in a jousting contest.

Why are boys so obsessed with war games? I've never seen girls play at killing. "Men are weird," she declared to no one in particular.

The screams reminded her of why she had first gone to the summer kitchen. She pivoted and hustled back, choosing a detour around the reception area, hoping to avoid ogling eyes or getting pulled into another onerous chore. After gathering a plateful of cookies and a bowl of candies, she returned to the barn via the old creek trail, zigzagging around the craggy edges and gopher holes. As she passed under the weeping boughs of the ancient willow, a lean, nondescript figure in a tailored black suit stepped out from behind the tree and strolled in her direction, then stopped in the middle of the path in front of her and tipped his hat.

Katarina balked at the interloper and dug a heel into the grass. "Of all the nerve."

"Excuse me, Miss Rempel. I don't mean to startle you."

She stiffened her spine and furrowed her brows. "Well, you did." She glared at the man. What was he doing here, away from the others? Probably using the tree as his personal outhouse, she surmised. Or was he following her? Her stomach tightened. "Do I know you?"

"I'm sorry to be so forward. I'm Jacob Regier, your mom's cousin, from Regier Press in Halbstadt. I was hoping to speak to you." He extended a hand, then immediately withdrew it and put both hands in his pockets, took a polite step back, and cast his gaze to the ground.

"Oh?" She studied his face. Thick wire-rimmed eyeglasses floated awkwardly at the bottom of the man's narrow nose. He snuffled and pushed them further up the bridge with a manicured finger, then removed a handkerchief from the pocket of his suit jacket and wiped his *schnauze*. Katarina sensed nervousness in the man's quiet demeanor and analyzed him further. Despite his unwelcome approach, the graying temples relayed trustworthiness.

If anyone noticed her talking to a man, there'd be questions later. She'd had enough trouble for one day. She turned her head and scanned the crowd, searching for her father's overprotective eye. He was nodding at the man on his right, his face turned away from her. She looked back at the interrupter. He was at least ... forty? Perhaps she wasn't violating any social proprieties.

She relaxed her stance but kept her guard up. "What about? I have my hands rather full right now." *Ooh. That didn't come out right. Now, he'll think I'm impudent.* She sniffed and bit the corner of her mouth to keep from blowing the strands out of her eyes. Her chest prickled under the damp underwear. *I need to ditch this dress.*

The cousin looked over at the crowded tables and then back to her. The corners of his mouth turned down when he smiled and the creases around his gray-blue eyes crinkled upwards. "I hear you have aspirations of becoming a school-teacher."

"Yes." Katarina scowled. *Who's been talking about me? To you?*

"I was wondering — with your sister moving to Halb-stadt ... have you considered attending teacher's college there?"

"No, I'm planning to study over here. Why do you want to know?" *You're awfully nosey.*

"Yes ... well." Regier toyed with his lapel. "Rosenthal has an excellent reputation, but Halbstadt is equally fine. I assume an intelligent woman like yourself is evaluating both options."

Flattery will get you nowhere. "I see. Thank you for the information, but I don't understand why where I go to school is important to you," Katarina said with deliberate insolence.

"Well, yes. I'm getting to that. Your teachers informed me you're an astute student with excellent writing skills. I'd like to get your opinion on a new concept for the newspaper."

"Oh? I see." Katarina beamed. *He wants my opinion? Who thinks so highly of me to suggest this to him? And what does this have to do with college?* She shifted the dishes, placing the bowl on top of the plate, lacing her fingers between the layers to prevent squishing the cookies.

"Yes ... well." Regier watched as she juggled the dishes. When she looked up, he looked down and chipped at the rocky soil with the toe of his boot. Katarina guessed he was just as uncomfortable with this conversation as she was — maybe more so. She frowned. *Why do I get the distinct impression this conversation was not your idea, Mr. Regier? Who put you up to this?*

He wiggled his chin as if he was thinking about his words, then focused back on her. "You see, Katarina, we want to expand our readership at *The Post*. We're searching to hire a novice reporter to feature a new social column — something to attract our female readers. Perhaps news from the villages, church functions, recipes ... that sort of thing. What do you think of our idea?" The shifting of Regier's rate of speech reminded Katarina of a steam locomotive, starting with a slow German drawl and chugging along until it increased into a staccato beat. He spit out the last sentence like an engineer blowing the final boarding whistle.

Katarina pasted a grin on her face and nodded stiffly, while biting her lower lip to keep from laughing out loud at the man's funny way of talking. His demeanor bore a clear family resemblance to her mother, except he was funny. And polite. And respectful. But what man wanted a fifteen-year-old girl's opinion? Goosebumps formed on her damp neck as she realized his importance. This *educated* man wasn't a simple farmer like others. He was cut from a different cloth. She wasn't familiar with such fabric, but she liked it.

Katarina pulled herself up straight. "*Ja*, I suppose more women would read your paper if there were articles pertaining to day-to-day life. We all want to know what's happening in the other colonies. Most women don't enjoy reading about politics or war. But it needs to be factual, not gossipy. One mustn't spread hearsay." She emphasized *hearsay*, thinking it sounded adult and biblically correct.

"I heartily agree with you. Your insight's very thoughtful." His gray-blue eyes flickered and connected with hers, then drifted to the boisterous crowd and back to her face. He smiled another thin, tight upside-down grin. "Katarina, I understand your first loyalty is to the ladies' school in Rosenthal, but your stellar academic achievements will be well received in Halbstadt. I'm on the board, and I'll be happy to vouch for you."

She furrowed her brows. "I'm confused. What does my schooling have to do with your paper?"

"Yes, well ... if you attended there, we could offer you a part-time position as a writer. This would be a great asset in your teaching career."

Is he offering me a job? "Huh?" Katarina mulled over the offer. "That's an interesting proposal. To be honest, I haven't considered Halbstadt as an option."

"I understand. Travel in the winter can be a bit tricky. The Kitchkas Bridge ices up fast. But it's still better than the old cable ferry." He glanced up and scanned her face, then looked away as he continued talking. "Those were scary days. Do you remember that big platform trying to scrape through the ice jams at Wolf Throat Narrows?"

Katarina scrunched her eyebrows trying to recollect crossing the rapids before the bridge was built. "I think so."

"I believe it's still there, though it's not used much anymore. Back in the old days, it was too treacherous to cross the river in the winter. Every year, we lost a man or his horse to those icy waters. Having teacher colleges on both sides was a practical imperative then. Now, the bridge unites the colonies in more ways than one," he chuckled, "and makes travel easier. Although, no one wants to drive two days in miserable weather to do so."

"*Ja,*" Katarina nodded. "But it's not an everyday trip. Anyway, Rosenthal has a students' residence onsite. I'm planning to live there and go home on weekends and holidays. It's not that far from home. And there's no river crossings. So, travel isn't a concern."

"Oh, they have a residence in Halbstadt, too. Although, I don't know why you'd want to stay there if you could live nearby at your sister's. Katarina, imagine the fun you'll have competing against your old schoolmates during inter-collegiate academic games. They'll shake in their boots when they're forced to compete against you. You know their weaknesses. You'll win the championship for sure. I know you're no stranger to a good old-fashioned spelling bee. I've been to a few of your performances." Regier's eyes crinkled upwards. "You know, I'm almost jealous of the opportunities in front of you. We didn't have many choices in my day."

That he was familiar with her academics confirmed his trustworthiness to her. He wasn't a widower looking for a wife, or just a relative making conversation. He knew her and liked her. She relaxed her shoulders, hugged the dishes and laughed, "*Ja*. I appreciate a little rivalry now and again."

"The Halbstadt college will help you exercise those skills a bit more. And you and Anna can visit your parents when the weather is good," Regier added.

I could leave home AND live with Anna. What a great idea! Why didn't I think of that? Her eyes widened and she bit the corner of her bottom lip to keep the smile from forming.

Regier held up his hand in a cautionary sign. "If you wish to pursue this excellent opportunity during your studies, I must warn you; apprentice wages are minimal ... I should say almost nothing. But the teaching profession doesn't fare much better for young women. However, you'll soon discover creativity has its own rewards. In time, you'll earn a living wage. I'm sure staying at your sister's *wirtschaft*[2] could aid a bit in the cost of your keep until then."

Although his emphasis on the word *opportunity* captivated Katarina's attention, she was taken aback and confused by the comment about finances, and she wasn't sure how to answer. She'd never given much thought to expenses. Money was obviously a necessity. But how much was enough? And how did one acquire it?

What does he mean, the cost of my keep? Dad will pay for my schooling. And Anna will never charge me to live with her in that castle. Or does he think Anna won't have access to David's money? She chewed on this thought. *I'm not sure either. I never thought to ask her. Good grief, this moving away is complicated.*

"I need to discuss this with all concerned." The memorized response was always the correct one. It would buy her time to think.

"Of course. Your father and brother-in-law would expect no less."

She nodded. "Thank you for the invitation. I'll consider it."

"I believe you'll be perfect for the job." He gave a slight bow, then turned on his heels and returned to the party.

Katarina waited until he had cleared the path before proceeding. *According to him, I'm both special and intelligent. Just imagine — me leaving home and becoming a journalist on lady issues? What will the women say? The gossip ... They'll accuse me of being full of pride. It'll be a scandal.* She sucked in her waist and pulled back her shoulders, envisioning herself as the center of attention parading through the town square with a red parasol and a large shopping bag and catching the green-eyed attention of chinwaggers. She smirked, then shook her head. *This sounds too good to be true. I doubt Mom and Dad will let me go that easily. I'll talk to Anna. She has answers for everything.*

Feeling ten feet tall, she strutted to the rear of the barn where a group of children were climbing fences and playing tag. "Thank you for helping out, George," Katarina nodded to her thirteen-year-old nephew.

"No problem." George brushed the dirt off his black suit jacket and yelled out, "Who wants sugar?" He stared at the heaping plate of sweet treats in Katarina's hands. "Is that all you brought? That's just enough for me."

"Get lost. Don't you know we are learning to share?" A bevy of laughing and screaming faces with outstretched hands encircled them.

"Eww," George made a sour face and laughed, "sharing at a wedding? That's so unfair." He grabbed two squares and popped them both in his mouth, then pivoted and sauntered towards the barn.

A foggy, acrid wisp floated across the pasture. Katarina frowned and sniffed the air, "George, what's that stench?"

George turned and scratched his ash-blond brush-cut. "What?"

"It smells like smoke."

---

1. Ecclesiastes 12:12
2. Wirtschaft: a word typically used to describe a large farmstead

4

WHERE THERE IS SMOKE

"SOMETHING'S BURNING." KATARINA WRINKLED HER nose, sniffed, and examined the haze.

"The harvesters are probably burning garbage again." George peered at the sky and shrugged.

She shook her head. "They shouldn't be. Everyone knows we're having a wedding here."

She scrutinized the thick gray plume billowing on the horizon. "The smoke is too heavy for a field fire. George, can you please alert the men?"

As her nephew raced off and disappeared around the far side of the barn, Katarina watched the acrid smog drift towards the farm. *Where is it coming from? The mill? No, it can't be. They're shut down today. Everyone's here.*

She scratched her head and acknowledged the dusty young charges circling around her. "Come, let's feed the chickens. We can take turns."

"What's that smoke?" eight-year-old George T. wrinkled his nose.

"I'm sure it's nothing we need to worry about. Come on. Let's do our chores. Everyone needs to eat." She picked up the feed bucket and started towards the chicken coop.

"I hear yelling," his brother Helmut said. "Is there a fight?"

Katarina listened to the discordant noise. Male voices shouted over the clanging dinner bell. "Here," she shoved the pail at ten-year-old Gerhard. "Can you take the others to feed the chickens? I'll find out what's going on. I'll be right back."

Without waiting for an answer, she lifted her skirts above the ankle and dashed around the side of the long barn and up the trail. When she rounded the corner to the reception area, a chaotic scene greeted her as a wave of black suits and white shirts surged towards the carriages, knocking over the neat rows of tables in their wake. The planked tabletops toppled into piles of lumber and dishes and food flew into the air.

Dimitri, the stableman, stood on the back porch and shouted, "Fire! Fire!" He walloped the dinner bell with repeated and violent strikes.

Katarina collapsed on a straw bale and stared in horror at the strewn chaos. "My decorations ... all that work ... now what?"

As the yard emptied of men, she saw the crowd of women congregating outside the summer kitchen and ran over to them. "What's going on?"

"Fire at the mill."

"How can that be? Nobody's working today."

"We don't know. But the men will handle it."

"All right, ladies — let's stop the jibber-jabber. We better clean up before the sun goes down," Justina shouted.

Like a well-oiled machine, the women snapped into a memorized clean-up routine. Wooden apple boxes appeared from their hiding places behind the summer kitchen to serve as carrying trays for the food and dishes, and teams began dismantling the makeshift furniture. Katarina ran over to help.

"Are those *rotznasen*[1] staying out of trouble?" Lena asked.

"Yes, they're fine. I'll check on them in a minute."

"Never mind helping here. They need to get washed up before they go home."

Again? I'm never doing the right thing at the right time. Katarina threw up her hands and stomped off, almost bumping into Maria with her beefy arms wrapped around two large amber bottles. "The smoke is getting awfully heavy," she chortled as she bounced past. "We best tuck this medicine away. Someone might need it later."

Ja. Give some to mom so she can calm down. Katarina admired her older sister for her positive can-do attitude and forthrightness, but often wondered if Maria's cheeriness was more of a cover-up for her inferior physical attributes.

She had learned that a large dairy farm was heavy work and assumed from that information that a strong back was a necessary asset; so perhaps the heavy bosom and large frame weren't such big deficits as she imagined. Since — according to her parents — the challenging life had molded Maria into the best organizational manager in the family. Therefore, controlling this unruly crowd of anxious women couldn't differ much from keeping the cows in line.

On second thought, she reasoned that nursing eight children in twelve years required substantial breasts. Did childbearing create such monstrosities or were some unlucky women destined that way? She gawked at her sister swooping across the yard with her arms laden with plates and some balanced on her chest. Katarina shuddered. She hoped she wouldn't end up looking like Maria.

Her hand swept over the edge of the table and stopped by a plate of pickles and cheese. Her stomach growled reminding her she'd missed lunch — the biggest meal of the day — and now *faspa*², too. She scouted for a roll. Finding one in a shallow serving bowl, she created a make-shift sandwich and gobbled it down. The juicy dill mingled with the squeaky cheese, dripped down her chin, and she wiped it away with the back of her hand. Her eyes wandered over the tables searching for sausage or something more substantial to satisfy her ravenous appetite, and a glass of watermelon juice to wash it down and quench her thirst.

The old widow, Aganetha Peters, nudged her out of the way with her elbow and seized the plate before Katarina could grab another pickle. *Of all the nerve.* She threw up her hands. *I guess I'll eat later.* She wiped her mouth with a dirty napkin and tossed it back on the table, then ambled towards the barn.

As she passed the back serving table, Lena yelled a second time, "Katarina, bring those tots to wash up and get ready for bed."

"Right." She threw a back-handed wave to let her mother know she'd heard and meandered towards the pasture, ignoring the open barn doors and gates as her stomach growled. Her thoughts and gaze drifted with the thickening haze on the horizon. A knee-high tug on her skirt redirected her attention.

"Aunt Trina, Hans and Gerhard are riding sheep in the sheep pen."

"Oh, for crying out loud. I told you to feed the chickens, not harass the animals." *I can't leave these rascals alone for a second.*

"I'm not 'rassing aminals,'" five-year-old Wilhelm pouted.

"Sorry, Wil. I meant your cousins, not you." Katarina paused and reflected on the crisis. *Did I leave the gate open? Where are the goats?* "Good grief, Wil. I hope the goats aren't in with the sheep. If they are, your silly cousins could get hurt. They bite." *And if they're not there, we'll never find them in the dark. How will I explain this?* Her stomach tightened at the fear of consequences from her oversight.

"I don't know." Wilhelm shrugged.

I messed up by leaving the tots unsupervised. I'm going to be in big trouble. Katarina faked a tight smile and put an arm around his tiny shoulders. *Don't get upset with him. It's not his fault.* "Thanks for telling me, Wilhelm. Let's go see what those foolish boys are up to."

They dashed to the pasture behind the barn where a cheering group congregated around the sheep pen while some perched precariously on the upper rung of the wooden fence.

"Everybody off!" Katarina hiked up her skirt to side-step the manure piles in her path. "Hello? I'm talking here," she raised her voice above the din. The laughter dissipated into giggles and whispers. One by one, the children jumped down from the fence, emerging with sheepish grins.

"Enough already. I leave you for five minutes and this is how you behave?" She walked into the pen and closed the gate behind her. "You're all in big trouble. And you *spitzbubs*[3]," she pointed at Hans and Gerhard still seated on the ewes, "You'll be tarred and feathered when your parents hear about this. Now get out."

The boys dismounted and proceeded to the gate, snickering, and elbowing each other as they maneuvered around her.

"This isn't funny, boys," Katarina twirled and put a hand on Gerhard's shoulder. "I left you in charge. That means you're accountable for the safety of the others. Do you think you were being responsible?"

Gerhard shrugged. "I guess not."

"You both could've been hurt. Now go to the house and wash up."

The brothers scampered away, leading the animated trail of cousins to the farmyard.

Katarina shook her head. *How does Maria manage with two sets of twins around her busy farm? These boys have way too much energy.* She turned her attention to the animals, scanning the flock and the nearby pasture for wanderers. After counting the goats in the pen and satisfying herself that none had escaped, she breathed a sigh of relief and double-checked the bolt.

She acknowledged her two nieces watching her from the dirt pile beside the chicken coop. "All right now, everyone back to the yard. It's time to wash up and go to bed."

"Oh, do we have to?" Five-year-old Margaret pouted as she twirled, watching her skirt fan out.

"Yes, we do. Let's go."

As Katarina escorted the girls from the pasture, she noticed the rear door of the barn was still open. "Was anyone playing in the barn?"

"*Yo.* Weren't we allowed?" Six-year-old Mary fingered her pigtail.

"*Yo,* of course. I'm just wondering if anyone's still in there."

"I don't know," Mary shrugged, "Maybe Hank."

"No, he's up ahead," Margaret lisped.

"All right, then. Let's get washed up. I'll check the barn

later." She marched the pair to the rest of the group and then led the charge to the well. When the eager flag of arms demanded rights to the pump, she gave in to the noisy chorus and jumped aside as the muddy puddle grew under her feet.

"Is everyone rounded up?" A husky feminine voice boomed behind her.

Katarina's hand flew to her chest. She spun around and laughed, "Justina, you scared me half to death. I didn't see you there." She took a deep breath to settle her jitters. "I believe so. But the barn doors are still open. I'll take another look."

"Good. I'll send the strays to catch up to their mamas. Go finish your jobs."

"Right." As Katarina sauntered back to the barn, a soft breeze blew a cloud of thick white ash into the yard, irritating her sinuses. She sneezed, then coughed, inhaling the funky taste of charred wood and grain through her mouth. She looked up at the darkening sky. Fiery bursts of orange and red punctuated the rolling charcoal billows. The scene reminded her of the fireworks at the harvest festival, except she knew it wasn't.

A piercing crack split the air behind her. "Is that a gunshot?" She pivoted and searched the horizon. A column of dust moved towards the farm, and a faint thundering sound rolled across the fields. *Horses? They must be heading to the mill to help.* Another volley of shots caused her to stop and listen. "Oh, Katarina, you're imagining things. It's just fieldhands alerting the others," she scolded herself to settle her nerves.

She shrugged off the noise and marched to the pasture to complete her errands. After double-checking the locks of the sheep and goat pens and chicken coops, she returned to the barn, entering through the rear and bolting the back door. She wandered through the belly of the building, carefully scanning the stalls, tack, and storage rooms, then climbed the narrow wooden ladder to the hay loft. "Anyone up here?"

Finding no one and hearing no voices, she opened the loft door and searched for the dust cloud. A moving formation emerged, the sound rumbling across the field. Now, the rat-a-tat-tat of gunfire was clearly audible. She squeezed her eyes, blinked, and scanned the roadway a second time, and frowned. *Are they coming here?*

Her gaze darted across the clearing at the flurry of activity in the yard as the women raced to the house, dragging their tots behind them. The thundering of the galloping horses almost drowned out Justina's booming voice as she yelled at the women to hurry.

An icy shiver passed down Katarina's back as the gravity of the situation grew in her mind. *Who are these riders? What do they want?* She tried to remember details from the men's discussions. *River gangs? Local troublemakers? Did they torch the mill?* She frowned, trying to make sense of the seemingly disconnected details.

She sucked in her breath as the realization slowly dawned. *Oh, dear God. It's a set up. They're going to attack us.* An ash-filled gust of wind lifted the loose straw near the open door and sent it swirling around her. She scanned the murky sky. *The wind's picked up.*

Her stomach tightened, and her heart raced. *Should I stay up here? Surely, I can hide in the straw. They won't find me here.* As she turned to scan the soft golden mounds, she noticed the layers of smoke drifting through the loft. *Smoke from the fire. It's spreading. Are the fields aflame? What if the barn catches on fire? Straw burns fast ... I could burn to death.*

She inhaled sharply of the smoky air. It scorched her lungs, and she dropped to her knees in a coughing fit. *I've got to get out of here. But can I make it back to the house before they get here?*

She regained control of her breath and re-surveyed the scene from the loft door. The group was now visible. She counted — four, five horses, or was it seven? Her mind fought to make sense of the sight. *I'm not wrong. They are coming here.* She sat back on her haunches. *But why? What do they want from us?*

She looked around the loft again. *I should stay. I'll be safer here. They won't find me here ... No, too much smoke. It's not safe. I can barely breathe.*

"Make a decision, Katarina," she cried out. She looked back at the riders. "If they torched the mill, they could set this farm ablaze, too." *But surely, they won't kill the women and children.* Her mind grappled with the possibility of violence. *They have guns. If they started the fire, they're likely prepared for murder. And they won't think twice about lighting this barn on fire. And with me in it.*

"No one knows I'm up here. They'll never find me until it's too late," she said out loud as her eyes widened and her imagination raced with the mental picture of her scorched body.

She stood up and turned to run, but the barn's open doors had created a funnel effect for the wind, and the air had become a thick, gray haze — blurring the path to the ladder. Instinctively, she dropped to her knees and found a clearer layer. She sank to her belly, held her breath, and crawled. The blood pounded in her head. Her chest heaved. Inhaling in rattled gasps made her dizzy and light-headed.

Large gulps choked her lungs. She heaved and scraped her way to the small opening. Upon reaching it, she stared down to the floor below. *I must get out; they'll burn the barn with me in it.*

The ladder seemed too long, the ground too far away. As she shifted her weight onto the narrow rungs, one foot slipped. She hugged the rails and stood motionless, waiting for her jelly-filled legs to steady. The ladder vibrated beneath her.

"Don't you dare fall." She squeezed her eyes to push away the queasiness. "I'm not scared of heights. I'm not. I'm not." When had she become so fearful? She had climbed trees with the boys when she was a young girl. Of course, she could manage the slatted wood. She goaded herself to carry on.

Every movement felt like it was happening in slow motion, the seconds ticking by as if they were hours. On the next step, her skirt caught on a nail and threatened her balance. She gasped and white-knuckled the rails, trying to force the move, but the heavy fabric wouldn't give. With the side of her face embracing the wood, and one arm wrapped around the rail, she clawed at the expensive satin with her free hand. A final yank caused a loud ripping sound and the material yielded.

She groaned as she examined the tear. "Shoot. Mom will kill me. This will not be an easy fix."

Letting go of the skirt, she jumped the final four rungs to the cement floor. Her ankle twisted upon landing, and she dropped to the ground. "Ouch."

Gunfire popped and horses neighed.

They're here.

An unintelligible cacophony of shouting men and screaming women rose from the yard.

Katarina paled. *I won't make it to the house.* She looked around for a safe place to hide. *I don't want to die in a fire.* Her mind argued with options. *Think, Katarina.* She rationalized that if the front door was shut, it might keep the raiders from the barn. She could then run through the back door and hide among the sheep. *But what if they go back there and shoot the sheep? Oh, dear God, then they'll kill me, too. Where do I hide, where ... show me where?*

She darted left, then right, then stopped, trying to gather her thoughts. With her heart racing and her head throbbing, she scanned the organized and clean barn. Her thoughts felt jumbled. The barn was a fuzzy maze of uncommon order, but she had no idea where anything was anymore. The stalls were empty; the cattle, horses, and the new foal moved to the pasture beyond the sheep pen, and the feed supplies were neatly stacked along the walls and tucked away for the reception. Where could she hide so she wouldn't be found?

She raced towards the tack room at the front of the barn, her chest heaving as she struggled for breath in the dank air. *You won't make it. Think, Katarina, think.*

The din grew louder. Horses neighed. Men shouted. A whip cracked. Once. Twice. Gunfire split the air.

Katarina shuddered. *If they don't shoot me, they'll burn me alive. God, please save me.* She stood paralyzed in the middle of the smoke-filled room while her legs acted like two concrete pillars holding her upright and refusing to budge. She cried out, urging herself to move, "The front door, Katarina — just get to the front door. Close the door. Go."

Her clumsy legs obeyed the verbal command and she wobbled to the sliding panel. As her shaking hands grasped the handle and inched aside the heavy wood, the setting sun flashed a brilliant yellow ray through the ashen clouds, obscuring her view. As she squinted, trying to see beyond the light, the silhouette of a tall, dark horse with a rider on its back suddenly appeared in the doorway.

She froze and held her breath. Her eyes widened, and her mouth dropped open. Her heartbeat pounded in her head. *No. No, please. God help me. I don't want to die like this.* The horse and rider galloped through the entry. A flash of red clothing caught her eye. *Cossacks.* Her eyes widened and she turned to run — fighting with the air to propel her back to the tack room.

More cracking sounds. Gunfire. Men's voices. Laughter. Horses neighed. In that moment, she knew she was destined to die at the mercy of the bandits. There was no hope left.

Whoop. Whoop. Something whistled past her head. There was a pinging sound, then a sharp crack, and a loud pop. A heavy object struck the back of her head, then her arm and her knees buckled. She dropped to the ground with a dull thud. The slippery satin dress caught the rough concrete floor, and she sailed into the path of the unwelcome visitors. A loud crunch in her left shoulder produced an explosion of searing pain that shot through her body. Terror and torment mixed with the stink of the horse's belly before darkness enveloped her.

---

1. A German slang expression generally interpreted as snotty nosed brats.
2. A late afternoon meal usually consisting of bread, cold meats, cheeses, pickles, accompanied by coffee and tea and followed by plates of tea cakes and cookies, or pie.
3. rascals

5

TERROR AND TRAUMA

KATARINA WOKE TO THE HUM OF WOMEN'S FRANTIC voices and the stink of torched grain and smoldering wood. A scorching flame blazed down her left arm and a loud swooshing pounded in her head. She moaned and inhaled sharply, smacking her lips at the foul ashy taste coating her tongue. Her hands grabbed at the rough concrete floor, trying to steady her shaking core.

FIRE. I need to get out.

Sharp stabs pierced her limbs and head as she tried to shift, and her body flopped like a rag doll. *Where am I? What happened?*

The details flashed through her mind like a silent picture show — the brilliant flare of sunlight ... the silhouette of a tall black stallion appearing through the open barn doors ... the cloaked figure in red Cossack pants. It had all transpired so fast. Who was he? Why did he attack her? Was he still here?

FIRE ... RUN, KATARINA, RUN. YOU'RE GOING TO BURN TO DEATH.

1951, MUNICH, GERMANY

Peter tapped the newly filled nib on the fresh page to encourage the ink to flow. When the anticipated blue dot appeared, he turned back to the diary and reviewed the Gothic script once more before continuing. Aside from the readability of the font and the fact that Katarina had written in multiple languages, her fine scrawl was sometimes challenging to decipher. The complicated quadruple task — reading, translating, interpreting, and writing — was more tedious and time consuming than he'd initially predicted. Too often, it required reading between the lines and composing from his imagination. That would have been easier to do if he had known her history a bit more.

He berated himself for dismissing and shutting her down when she'd tried to relay her life's stories to him. He'd been such an arrogant youth.

He scanned the text again.

The sun was in my eyes. I couldn't close the doors. I didn't see the horse. I turned and ran. There was a whistling noise ... a hard knock to the back of my head ... I fell, then everything went black.

He pushed on the pen to bleed the next sentence. 'Her heart raced as the pain coursed through her limbs ...'

The image of the shadowy dark stallion passed through his mind. He stopped writing and lifted the tool off the paper. Was this the childhood trauma that had terrorized Katarina?

I've been shot ... the man on the horse shot me. I'm bleeding to death. First person accounts were difficult to navigate. Had she been shot, or did she only think she had been?

He pictured his mother as a naive fifteen-year-old girl at the mercy of blood-thirsty villains — helpless and terrified — lying unconscious on the cold gravelly slab. The image triggered his own memory of getting mugged in the park that fateful summer when he was only nineteen.

The horror of the moment — the fear of death — the crushing pain as the hard boots drove into his kidneys, and then — the heart throbbing torturous seconds when his breath stopped, and he faced the dark space between body and spirit. The awfulness of being utterly helpless and alone at the very end — the denial of dignity and the finality of it all; could there be anything worse? Did she feel it too?

The recollection was still too vivid. The agony too real. Could he write from that wounding and make it hers? Or were her own words sufficient?

Peter shook his head, trying to push away both the memory and the haunting shadows. He increased the pressure on the nib until indigo dots beaded on the leaf. He interpreted her prose, rewriting the script to make sense in his head: '*She envisioned herself lying in a pool of blood. She tried to lift her head, but it wouldn't move. She screamed but heard no sound from her voice.*'

He peeked back at the text. Why was this so hard? He wanted to throw the pen and the books across the room. Toss them in the garbage. He was stupid to even think he could craft his mother's story. It was the romantic dreamer in his soul convincing him to embrace such a massive assignment. He gritted his teeth and forced himself to keep reading.

Katarina's utterance shouted from the pages. '*I'm dying. Jesus. Where are you? I'm supposed to see you, aren't I? A preacher in a black suit with a Bible just flashed before my eyes. Am I going to hell? Jesus, save me. I'm too young to die. Help me. Somebody, help me. In that moment, I was convinced I was dying.'*

The pen slipped out of Peter's hand and rolled off the narrow desk, onto the floor. A hard lump formed in his throat as he stared at his mother's handwriting, the awareness of her predicament slowly dawning. *She wrote this ... my mother's words ... she was so scared.* He swallowed, but the constriction wouldn't release. A wet droplet fell on the page. He swiped it with his index finger, smearing the new ink into a muddy blue trail.

Peter looked up and across the room where his wife, Heidi, bustled with her back to him, busy with cooking in their small kitchen. He swept the back of his hand over his hot cheeks. How long had he been crying? Had she noticed?

Rattled by his own emotion, he set the book aside, walked over to the window, and stared at the trickling raindrops on the windowpane and the rivulets flowing along the street below. The gloomy weather beckoned to his soul. He bit his lips and turned away.

He had been so unfair to Katarina. She *had* understood. But it was too late now. He could never make it up to her. He took a deep breath and forced the lump down. As the wave of guilt washed over him, he hid his face behind his hands and sobbed.

1915, CHORTITZA

Breathing hurt. Katarina gasped and flailed, cracking her head against the concrete floor. A whistling sound from her lungs exacerbated the knife-like spasms in her chest. Moving onto her left side triggered a searing pain in her shoulder. She rolled to the right, sucking the air in loud gulps, then holding her breath to stop the burning dagger. She coughed and uttered a throttled cry as the waves of agony crested. Her hands — bloody and grated from the fall — searched for support from the damp roughness that reeked of horse urine. She wanted to get up and run, but strength eluded her.

"Katarina! Katarina!" Familiar voices called from the encircling whispering buzz. A gentle stroke on her arm and a calming squeeze to her hand affirmed her safety. She stopped punching the air and opened her eyes to a blurry haze. Pinching them shut, she tried to focus again. Kerchiefed profiles hovered above her in the dim lantern light. She turned her head. Anna's cornflower blue eyes met hers.

"She's awake." Anna's head turned to the levitating faces.

"Where's that blanket?" Lena snapped. "Don't move Katarina. We'll wriggle this under you. Don't help. Just stay still."

Tears coursed down Katarina's cheeks. Her body vibrated with uncontrollable tremors and electric shocks joined with searing stabs when she moved. She felt cold, then hot, then cold again. The sweat poured from her skin. She cried out, rebelling against the strange physical sensations, fighting the gentle hands that guided her head and body as they positioned the blanket beneath her.

"Back now. Steady now," Lena instructed. "Grab the corners. One. Two. Three. Lift."

The six women gripped the edges and ends of the coarse wool blanket and lifted Katarina from the concrete bed. At first, the weightlessness felt like a cushion of air, relieving the pressure on her torn muscles and broken bones. The reprieve quickly ended when the irregular transport jerked and bumped against the women's hips as they shuffled towards the house.

Katarina held her breath, praying they wouldn't drop her, and bit her lips to keep from screaming out from pain. But when the jostling movement elicited an agonizing swarm that stabbed and pulsated through her body, she protested violently.

"Careful," Lena scolded the team from somewhere behind Katarina's head. "Let's slow down so we don't trip and drop her ... Katarina, don't move about. You'll make it worse .... and stop hollering. It won't help the pain."

Katarina groaned. The convoy reminded her of a funeral procession. *Six. Like pallbearers carrying a coffin. With Mom as the funeral director.*

Lena's prediction materialized when the tormenting waves crested. Katarina's howls spurred a hormonal rush in her body which further aggravated her discomfort and triggered another round of violent emotions. She felt disconnected and out of control.

Insanity reigned. It was as if some strange machine had taken over her body and was pushing her out. She could only watch from the sidelines. She wanted to run away from this *thing* that whispered lies of death and danger, flee or fight. Rage shifted to fear and back to rage, disbelief argued with reality, and sense and reason were elusive. Her body felt like a prison.

Unable to control or understand the dance of trauma, she laughed, then cried, then screamed. She wanted to dismiss the horror like a bad dream. Maybe tomorrow, when she woke up, life would be back to normal.

"Hang on Katarina. We'll be in the house in a minute."

Doors slammed. Her body tilted upwards. A door squeaked. A familiar scrape of the worn kitchen door on the old plank flooring, the clicking of heels on stairs, and the pungent aroma of garden-fresh dill confirmed she was safely ensconced in the house. Despite the throbbing pain, she relaxed, allowing organized hands to do their work, trusting even Lena's direction.

"To the couch. And get some pillows," Lena yelled. "And a blanket."

Katarina squinted at the bright light. She shivered. *I'm so cold. Why am I so cold? It's a hundred degrees outside.* Her heart felt like it had a mind of its own, racing with the panic that ebbed and flowed, overpowering her with uncontrollable shock waves.

A weighted covering floated on top of her.

No, no blankets. I need to breathe. I need air. Why can't I stop shivering? She moaned and kicked at the added layer. She didn't need wrapping in this heat. Her tight clothes were already suffocating her. She just wanted to be undressed and lying in her own bed. Couldn't they figure this out? The padded wooden bench was too hard and uncomfortable, the pillows too many.

Confusing physical sensations competed for attention. Raising her throbbing head caused a shooting pain in her arm, forcing her down. Her racing heart demanded more air, but deep breaths induced sharp stabs through her chest. A burning fire raged along her bare skin. Her heart acted like it was running a marathon and her internal temperature setting was out of control. Nothing worked as it should.

She punched the air and screamed, "Why doesn't my body work right? Everything hurts. What's wrong with me? Somebody, please make it stop. I can't stand it anymore."

The smell of alcohol wafted past her nose. "Here, Katarina, take a sip. This will help." Someone dribbled a few drops of a strong-tasting liquid on her tongue.

"I knew this medicine would come in handy," Maria's voice bubbled above her. "There was a reason the men weren't supposed to drink this tonight."

A chorus murmured in agreement.

"We need the doctor," Lena said.

"The bandits might still be on the road."

"We can't risk anyone else getting hurt."

A sudden heavy metallic clang had the dual effect of interrupting the musings in the room and jolting Katarina upright. Her reaction caused a knife-like sensation to slice through her arm and she shrieked.

Lena settled her back onto the pillows. "Good grief, Justina. We have an injured woman here. Don't be scaring us like that."

Katarina blinked. *Mom just called me a woman.*

Justina puffed into the room holding up two cast-iron frying pans. "I have weapons, and I have Jesus. No weapon formed against me shall prosper. I'm going for the doctor. Who's joining me?"

Seconds later a posse of five armed with frying pans and kitchen shears braved the dark night in search of medical help.

Lena lowered herself into the wing chair beside Katarina and slid her feet onto the embroidered footstool.

She looks worried. "Mom, it hurts so much. Am I going to live?"

"Of course, you are." Lena reached over and patted her arm. "You're going to be just fine."

Katarina winced at the touch. "Did he shoot me? Is there much blood?"

69

Lena chuckled, "No sweetheart. He didn't shoot you. You have a few scrapes and bruises. I think your arm is broken. That heavy fabric protected your skin. I'm impressed. The good Lord sure knew what he was doing putting that material in your head."

Katarina wiggled her head into the pillows, allowing the downy softness to cradle her sore head and neck. "What happened to me?"

"I'm not sure. But you cracked your noggin pretty good."

"I saw the man on the horse. He tried to kill me." Rehearsing the event set her heart racing again. Panic resurfaced, and she broke out in a cold sweat.

"Relax, Katarina. Your imagination is running away with you. The villains were all over the yard. No one wanted to kill you. Your accident was just that — a mishap. They just wanted the hams and sausage from the smoke-house ... it's all replaceable. We're not the first farm to be robbed. They're harmless boys enjoying a day of trouble-making. Don't worry about it. Now lie back. The doctor will be here soon."

Harmless boys? Mom doesn't believe me. She didn't see what I did. They'll be back ... for me.

6

RECOVERY

1915 CHORTITZA

Doctor Neufeld grimaced, "It's a bad break. It may not heal straight. There's considerable swelling around the shoulder joint, too. Torn muscles, I suspect. We'll keep the splint on for at least a month. Now, young lady, it's important to keep the arm immobile and get lots of rest. I'm warning you that failure to comply comes with a big price: pain for the rest of your life — and we don't want that now, do we?"

He took a bottle from the black bag, opened it, poured a spoonful and fed it to her. "This here is powerful medicine. It's both addictive and deadly. So, I'm only giving you enough for a few days. You must learn to use your mind to control pain." He handed the bottle to Lena. Turning back to Katarina, he added, "Your breathing will get easier when the ribs heal. You were fortunate today. It could have been so much worse."

Katarina grimaced at the foul-tasting prescription and gratefully accepted the glass of water that Anna immediately offered. The drug worked quickly, and she sank back and closed her eyes. As the women and the doctor left the room and the voices faded to a melodic hum, she drifted off to sleep. The hard couch morphed into a warm, comfortable cushion that hugged her throbbing body in a protective embrace. She was home and she was safe. In that moment, that was all that mattered.

Relief from the euphoric pain-free cloud waned as the black stallion twisted and turned through her dreams — the laughing rider cracking the whip as the horse reared in front of her and a split-second side-show of the gaudy wide red pants with the sweeping braided belt.

Katarina cried out and woke with a start. She brushed the sweat from her brow and held her heaving chest. Her heart raced as if she had just run a marathon. The flickering yellow glow of the kerosene lantern caught her attention. Was someone in the room? Or was it just the breeze? She held her breath until she spotted the intruder — a moth darting about, amplifying the shadows in the moonless night.

She pulled the thin blanket up to her chin and tried to go back to sleep. But every time she closed her eyes, the day's events replayed in a never-ending loop. She moved onto her side to avoid looking at the fluttering phantasm. The increasing ache in her arm and ribs and the dull throbbing in her head encouraged her to shift again. A glass of warm milk would probably help. She tossed the cover aside and contemplated getting up, but that would require disturbing Anna who slept on a blanket mattress on the floor beside her. The day's fuss had likely exhausted her, too. She didn't want to wake her.

She glared at the insect. The annoying flyer zipped through the golden luminance and bounced off the wall with astounding regularity. Both frightened and fascinated, she lay with her head angled to the light, her eyes following the mesmerizing movements in a trance-like state until she noticed that her heart rate and her breathing had returned to normal. The pounding in her head eased. She yawned and repositioned herself on the pillows, allowing her mind to wander, praying the hideous dream would not return.

As she drifted, she considered why she wasn't lying in her own comfortable bed. Earlier in the week, she'd agreed to join her older cousins in the hayloft, allowing her siblings and their youngest brood to spread out using both her bedroom and the spare rooms. But the upset had turned an entertaining event into a nightmare, and now she was lying on a padded wooden bench that felt as hard as a mortician's slab. This made her rehearse the day again. And she wondered about her narrow escape.

Katarina slid her hand along the bottom of the settee, searching for a reassuring touch. Anna's arm rested against the scalloped edge of the divan. Their hands connected. Although the physical contact confirmed the sisterly bond, it also increased the apprehension of losing her biggest advocate and champion. She squeezed tighter as the tears welled. Writing letters would ease the ache of physical distance, but Katarina needed more. She resolved to pursue Regier's invitation, with or without her parents' approval.

During the first two days, Anna refused to leave Katarina's side. Her new husband stopped in frequently to check on Katarina's progress. Although concerned, David kept asking Anna when she would be ready to leave for Halbstadt.

"Not until Kat stops taking this horrible medicine," Anna insisted.

"Your mom will take good care of her, Anna. There's no need for us to stay," David pleaded.

Katarina guessed her new brother-in-law thought her situation a dire nuisance. Despite the recurring headaches, the debilitating nausea, the constant ache in her arm, and the violent nightmares, Katarina knew she couldn't expect Anna to sacrifice her happiness. She sensed her sister needed her permission, so on day three, she gave it.

"I'll be fine. Honest I will," Katarina said, despite her deepest fears that she wouldn't be. "Look, I've got both Mom and Katya here. The doc said the splint needs to stay on for a month, and you can't stay forever. You need to go start your marriage. Don't worry. When school starts, I'll be right as rain."

"I'll miss you so much. I promise I'll write every day."

"Me too."

"And you'll visit when you're better?"

"When Katya goes home for her winter break, I'll have her bring me on the train."

"I'll get your room ready."

"Make sure it's comfortable with down blankets and feather pillows. Because I might stay awhile."

"Enough said. I'll even paint it blue for you."

Katarina sat on the window bench and bawled, watching the carriage disappear down the dusty road. Although she knew the house would feel empty when Anna left, she was unprepared for the accompanying and sudden despondency. No letters could replace the missing late nights of girlish laughter or warm the cold blankets. There was no one to help dismiss her mother's abrasive tone, share a knowing glance, or dramatize poetry readings. Her only companionship in the big red brick house was the much-too-busy housekeeper, Katya, and two old and boring parents. She wanted to run away.

By the end of the week, loneliness pushed Katarina to join her parents for supper. Her eyes swept over the sparse offerings. "There's no sausage."

"It's all right. Katarina. We butchered a lamb yesterday. We can pretend it's Easter."

"But ... there's still no sausage."

"Don't fret, Katarina. Until the pigs are fattened, we're relying on the generosity of our neighbors. We're making do."

She forced down a bowl of the milky bean and potato soup. "It's not the same without sausage. Can't we get some from the butcher in town?"

"Have some lamb, Katarina."

She cried herself to sleep, feeling the lack of sausage was her fault somehow, even though she knew it wasn't.

At night, the black stallion's terrifying visits fragmented her rest. His hooves pawed at her back, knocking her down, and his malodorous belly added heaviness to the suffocating summer nights. At first, fear of the apparition's return kept her from falling asleep, until it became a reminder that she had won the war against death. If the horse didn't visit, she searched for it — anticipating it hiding in wait for her. Next time, she vowed to strike back first. But each nightmare took

75

her by surprise, and she'd awaken in the dark to sweat-soaked sheets and a racing pulse. She wondered if the fright would ever leave.

The scary dreams confused her thoughts and muddled her emotions. One minute she felt invincible and the next paralyzed with fear. She tried to describe the sensations to her mother, but Lena only gave a sympathetic smile with a dubious reassuring comment, "You'll get over it."

This made Katarina miss Anna even more. During their younger days, the two would have analyzed the dream for hours and Anna would have reassured her that the threat was gone. But the fact stood that since she was now alone, she had to figure it out by herself. Growing up was insufferable. She needed a good friend right now. Someone just like Anna.

As the headaches eased, the nausea stopped, and the anxiety lessened. A week after the night of terrors, as Lena so aptly named it, Katarina hobbled to the back porch for the first time.

She stood by the supporting pillar and gazed at the quiet farmyard. The baby sparrows chirped from their nest under the eaves, the black-eyed-susans were in full bloom, the crows pecked at the ripening fruit on the apple tree, and the brilliant cerulean sky whispered promises of a pleasant sultry afternoon. There was no sign of the previous week's chaos. The world seemed restored and pristine.

She looked across the yard at the open barn door and noticed the silhouetted figure moving inside. Dimitri. Her stomach tightened. When Dimitri rang the bell and announced the fire, all the men had evacuated the farm. This left the women and children unprotected. Was the farmhand involved?

At supper, she braved asking her father, "What happened to the mill?"

"Burned to the ground. We'll rebuild."

"What will we do in the meantime?"

"We're making arrangements with the Jews." He reached over and patted her hand. "Don't you worry your pretty little head about it. It's all under control."

She bristled at the dismissal and bit her lip. "Was the fire connected to the raid?"

"Undoubtedly."

"Who's behind it?"

"Everyone knew about the wedding. Someone tipped them off."

"Do you think they involved any of our servants?"

"Katarina, when it comes to the locals, we must be wise. They protect each other, so we can't know if they're telling the truth. However, we must trust those who work for us." Johann raised his knife to make his point. "I'm not saying they're trustworthy. Be cautious. Be friendly, but don't make friends with them. Guard your words."

"At the wedding, I overheard talk that the locals are turning against the German colonists and us too."

"There's spillover from some crazy ideas in the cities. Nothing to worry about here."

"Is the war getting worse?"

"Yes, but it's not here." Johann speared the meat with his knife.

"Who were the raiders?"

Johann stopped eating, gave a heavy sigh through his nose, and regarded her with his eyebrows raised. Katarina's skin prickled. She knew she was asking too many questions, but she was desperate for answers and conversation.

Johann shook his head and sawed through his meat. "Who knows? Some local gang, I suppose. The police and the mayor will investigate. The criminals will be brought to justice." He snorted. "Everyone needs to eat, but not everyone wants to work to feed themselves. These radicals look for easy pickings and egg each other on. They have too much time on their hands."

"Is this related to the war?"

"No. But these nutcases are forever seeking opportunities. They know full well that when the government's preoccupied with other things, local issues get ignored. There's a lack of respect for law and order these days." Johann pointed to the bowl in the middle of the table. "The world is full of fools. Pass the potatoes please."

A sharp pain jabbed Katarina's shoulder as she picked up the glass dish. It clattered onto the table, spilling the potatoes.

"Katarina," Lena scolded as she jumped up to clean the mess. She signaled to the skinny young girl with the braided brown hair standing in the doorway. "Well, don't just stand there. Bring me a wet rag." When she disappeared, Lena mumbled, "Honestly, what does she think we pay her for? Lazy. They're all lazy. It's impossible to find good help these days. This one doesn't deserve to sleep in the kitchen."

Katarina cringed at her mother's sharp rebuke and groaned in embarrassment at her own silly mistake. Why did Lena always project her frustration at others? Katarina assumed it had something to do with her mother's need for perfection. Nothing and no one were ever good enough. It was as if she expected everyone to strive for the moon as hard as she did. Instead, all Lena accomplished was setting impossible standards and putting others on edge.

Johann smiled and winked at his daughter before pushing another forkful into his mouth. "Don't fuss so much, Lena. It was an accident. Katarina hasn't yet learned to operate with one arm."

Katarina rubbed her face and mumbled an apology for the starchy disaster. She suddenly realized that in her moment of distraction when she picked up the bowl, she had forgotten the injury. The doctor said she had to learn to manage the pain with her mind. Was it that simple? If she focused on something else, could she make the ache disappear? She gritted her teeth against the new flare-up and tried again. "Dad, do you believe the riots in Russia are staged to inflame the peasants?"

"Of course, they are."

"And the raids?"

"To incite fear among those who have, and pressure them to give to those who have not."

"So, it's all about money?"

"Money and control. But mostly greed. These radicals don't recognize that the secret to a good life is hard work. Happiness comes through diligence and discipline. Just look at our prosperous villages and our peaceful lives. Because of our success, we can provide the locals with good jobs and decent pay. If they followed our example, they, too, could overcome their poverty. Instead, their jealousy consumes them. They drown their sorrows in drink and gossip.

"It's all sin, Katarina, the devil's lies. We must pray for the continued prosperity of our communities and the salvation of souls in the country. Revenge belongs to God. Be patient and wait for divine justice. When we look at our past, we can see how God makes beauty from ashes. Our people went through so much worse."

They stopped talking when the new young maid returned with the peach pie, set inside Lena's hand-painted Prussian serving dish. The girl scanned the table before setting the fancy plate on the buffet. Katarina was unaware that her mother had hired a new servant. She glanced at Lena. Her eyes were wide, her face frozen in a shocked expression. That plate was her grandmother's. Even Katya didn't dare touch it.

The girl turned to the samovar and poured the coffee into the traditional glasses, then placed them inside their filagree metal holders. Using both hands, she delivered the full cups to the table one at a time. After removing the empty serving bowls, she exited the room.

Lena's shoulders relaxed, and she blew a long sigh through her mouth. Katarina knew she would deal with the girl later.

Since Katarina hadn't seen the new maid before and didn't know her name, she wondered about her. Was she related to any of the other employees? How old was she? Twelve? Had she ever gone to school? If she couldn't read or write, Katarina could teach her. And it would be nice to make a new friend — someone different from her self-right-eous and nosey comrades. Although ... her parents would object to a friendship with a local. Still ... she could justify the teaching as 'good works'. Surely, God would be pleased.

She made a mental note to ask Katya about the girl. As the head housekeeper, Katya knew everything. But when Katarina reflected, she reckoned the idea was wishful think-ing. Lena would probably dismiss the child within a few weeks anyway. Katarina just missed Anna.

She turned back to her father. "Dad, were we ever

poor?" She pushed her plate away. Lena stood up and began clearing the table.

Johann held up his hand in a stop signal and jerked his chin at the platter in Lena's hand. "Lena, more lamb, please. Katarina, do you remember the stories about my great-grandparents?"

Lena dished out the last piece of lamb onto Johann's plate and put the dish on the buffet, then sat down and crossed her arms. The dessert would have to wait until Johann was ready.

Katarina turned away to avoid chuckling at the impatience registering on her mother's face. Lena hated politics and history, and she loved pie. But Lena also prided herself on the art of submission. She would never disagree with her husband, especially in front of a family member. In her opinion, duty superseded personal desire. Or, as she often said, "To do right is more important than to be right." If that meant she needed to wait for pie because her husband wanted to talk to his daughter about something Lena had no interest in — well then, that was just what she would do. But Katarina could tell from the twitching of her mouth and her flickering eyes that Lena loathed every second.

And because of that, Katarina encouraged her father to continue, "Are you referring to the move from Danzig to here? That's more than a hundred years ago." She avoided Lena's stern gaze by staring at her water glass and thumbing the beading humidity.

"Yes. But even before that. Three hundred years ago our ancestors fled Friesland because of persecution. They were promised religious freedom in Prussia, but they still had to prove themselves." Johann chomped on his meat. "They were only allowed to farm the mosquito-infested flood plain along the Vistula. So they drained the swamps and built windmills and dikes and turned the area into prime agricultural land. In time, they became respected farmers.

"Unfortunately, promises of freedom are never permanent. And there are other ways that persecution raises its ugly head. Back then, the Orthodox church leaders feared that our peaceful religion might corrupt the masses. And bigotry against us rose again. Then, when the war with Turkey threatened Russia's southern borders, God intervened on our behalf.

"Catharine the Great recognized our expertise in farming and offered us this land to grow crops for the vast nation of Russia. Because things weren't going so well for us in Prussia, we grabbed the opportunity to move here and expand our peaceful society. And Mother Russia was thrilled. In some ways, our peaceful presence protected an entire nation."

Katarina snorted. "How can a few farmers protect an entire country?"

"Before the steppes were settled, they were an open invitation to enemy aggression. After the Crimean War, Russia needed to solidify their military strength along the southern border. Our settlements gave Russia a good excuse to increase their defenses."

"Dad, why should I care about that? What does Russia's history and our ancestors' struggles have to do with the uprisings in Petrograd or the violence here today?" Katarina hated when her father went off on a lengthy tirade. She could almost sympathize with her mother right now.

Johann pushed his plate away and leaned back in his chair. "History always repeats itself, Katarina. Mark my words. What our ancestors went through in Prussia may very well happen again here. Wealth invites persecution because success and privilege cause jealousy. The poor see only their pathetic past and cannot envision the road to change without attacking the very hand that feeds them. And today, we are a finger on that hand, and the locals want to bite it off.

"But know this — regardless of what happens — God always provides a way out to those who follow him. We are not a forgotten race[1]. One day, someone will dig up our ancestors' graves and wonder about us. And they will feel ashamed by the truth. But always remember — God saw it all. And He has blessed us more than we could ever imagine. Everything we have today is because we worked hard and stayed true to his word. Never forget this." He pushed the dishes at her, "Please pass the beans to your mother. I've had enough. I'm ready for pie."

"I'm tired of potatoes and beans. Supper is not the same without sausage."

"Child, you complain too much," Lena snapped as she scraped her chair back. "If the world continues to rot, one day lamb will be gold on your table. Life always gets worse —"

"— before it gets better." *Today, I'm a child. Last week, she called me a woman.* Katarina rolled her eyes.

And then, they all ate pie.

---

1. At one time, the word "race" was used more broadly than to denote differences in skin color, similar to how we use the word "culture" today. Many Mennonites saw themselves as a distinct people, specially chosen by God. Therefore, their "race" was unique.

7

LETTERS FROM THE HEART

SEPTEMBER 1, 1915 CHORTITZA COLONY

Dearest Anna,
Thank you for your letter. I miss you terribly. How are you?
How's married life?

Thank you for asking about my progress. I'm sad to say it's
not going well. My nightmares and sleeping problems
continue, but less so. Maybe it's only because they don't
upset me as much anymore.

I walked into the stables last week for the first time. Immediately, I started shivering and my breathing became tight. I
got dizzy and started to heave. My heart raced and panic
rushed over me. That dusty mix — of manure, hay, and
horses — gives me a headache and an unrelenting sneeze.
Doc Neufeld says it's an allergy. It may go away with time. I
have an unexplainable angst that accompanies these strange
reactions. I doubt I will ever ride again. Dad says the sooner

I get back to riding, the faster I'll recover. But I prefer to skip this challenge.

As far as the arm goes, it didn't heal straight. And it's very weak at the shoulder. The doctor says there is nothing more he can do. Because of the constant ache plus the ongoing headaches, I won't be returning to school this term.

I'm keeping my eye on Dimitri. I still believe he was connected to the raid. He sneers at me with his squinty eyes. Dad dismisses my suspicions and Mom says it doesn't matter anymore. We should forgive and forget. That's easy for them to say. They didn't get hurt.

Milica will leave after harvest. Dad says we can't afford three house servants over the winter. Since Katya is young and strong and has proven herself, Dad assigned her to assist Dimitri in the barn AND manage the house. When I objected, Dad said that since I'm not in school this term, I can work. I told him I can't go into the barn because of this new allergy. And my arm is too weak for heavy work. (The doctor says it's a torn muscle and I shouldn't strain it further.)

Anyway, I'm slotted to house duties with another new maid — Oksana — the third new one this summer. They don't seem to stay long. But working in the kitchen, I get to know them a bit. Their stories are always sad. This one is an orphan. And she can barely read.

My vareniki dough is still too hard. It's tough to mix with one hand, but I'm trying to improve. Mom is patient with my learning, but I insist that this is not one of my spiritual gifts. (I have no desire to become a cook.) Father says my soups are tasty. Except for peeling vegetables and fixing the seasonings, soups are easy to prepare. I only need to watch one pot on the stove.

Katya takes my cooking to the stables. She says Dimitri appreciates it. I doubt that's true. My anger fuels each time I hear his name. Thank goodness he never enters the house. The stink would never leave. I already sneeze whenever Katya and Dad come in from the barn. By the way, Dad says we need to keep our eyes open for more trouble.

I miss you so much. Did I tell you that already? I pray for your continued happiness and safety.
Love always, your sister, Katarina.

OCTOBER 15, 1915 MOLOTSCHNA COLONY

My dearest sister Katarina,
Thanks for your letters. I miss you too. I'm doing well. Married life is wonderful, although sharing the house with David's brother and sister-in-law (J.D. and Agatha) and their four children requires plenty of patience. The construction of their new home is ongoing, and it should be completed by Christmas.

Our housing plans changed. Instead of us moving to the smaller, older house by the peach orchard, David's parents relocated there. There is ample room for all here, but they want their own quarters. According to David's father, when there are too many under one roof, things go missing and tempers are raised. It is better to have less space and enjoy peace. They insist that we need comfortable surroundings for our future family, too. (I'm excited to begin!) Thankfully, we get along well, and they come here for supper most nights.

One may think that we should live happily-ever-after in a house with sixteen rooms, but it's not as spacious as you'd imagine, as one wing is slotted for the senior servants. There's Olek (the stablemaster), and Alyona (she carries the weight of two jobs: Head Cook and Head housekeeper), and the old butler and his wife who care for David's parents, and Agatha's Mennonite nursemaid, Ruth Schmidt from Baratov. Our future au pair will have her own privacy, too. These helpers are all quite spoiled to have their own bedrooms. I've never before seen such decadence.

I've been busy learning the how-to's of managing the household staff and domestic agendas. Agatha hovers a bit too much as she teaches me, but I'm trying to be a good student. Now with the harvest season upon us, I'm looking forward to sausage-making as soon as the grain is stored for the winter. As at home, David's huge extended family will join us for the slaughter and grinding the meat and stuffing the casings. Many hands make light work, as the saying goes. Since this is the first major celebration since our wedding, I expect we'll catch up on dozens of missed birthdays.

My social calendar is full each week. I must attend every church and school function so that the community gets to know and accept me as David's wife and a member of this important family. Already, carriages arrive for Saturday tea, and I'm learning to be sensible about invitations for Sunday afternoons. The hectic schedule is exhausting. Thankfully, I have many servants, so I mustn't complain. We have love and so much more.

I'm so sorry you're still suffering. My goodness, this is taking a long time. I'll keep praying for your healing. A long visit with me should fix you right up. I'm getting your room ready. You're welcome anytime.

Mr. Regier from the newspaper dropped in last week and inquired about you. He says the job offer is still open if you are interested. What an amazing opportunity! You could live here, go to school, and pursue your writing talents, too. Now, I know what you're thinking: Dad will say this is temporary until you marry. Although our fate as women is unchangeable, I believe a higher education helps encourage one to be a better wife and mother. No matter what happens with your arm, take comfort in your intellect. It will help you attract the right future husband.

On a sadder sidenote: there are problems with hiring field-workers. The war has caused a shortage of supplies and the locals are restless. I'm not sure what that means, but David says inflation is chewing a hole in our pockets. Money doesn't buy what it used to, and conscription is inevitable. It's all very scary. All the able-bodied men will be gone soon. I fear for David.

A word of advice, Kat. Don't obsess about the orphan help. At twelve, they leave the orphanage to work in the real world. They move from place to place to learn their jobs. There's no point getting attached to them. It's just the way things are done. I'm surprised you never noticed this before.

Praying for you. Hugs. Your sister always, Anna.
P.S. Hug Mom and Dad for me. Tell them I am terribly
homesick.

OCTOBER 30, 1915 CHORTITZA COLONY

Dearest Anna,
Thank you for your letter and your prayers. I miss you
terribly.

Dimitri stopped showing up for work. I told you he can't be
trusted. I'm trying to forgive, but my grudge won't leave.

The shoulder weakness remains, but thankfully the pain
and nightmares have lessened.

Dad's reconsidered firing Milica because of the shortage of
fieldworkers. He regrets posting the 'help wanted' notice too
late — after the last conscription letters arrived. And he
complains about costs. What is inflation?

He's hired local women to stoke grain, pitch hay, and glean
the fields, but they come with their tots in tow who run
roughshod. Guess who keeps them in line? The small pack-
ages bring joy to my otherwise dismal days.

Rabbi Z from Vitebsk sent over two ten-year-old Jewish
boys to help on the fields. Father thanks the Jews for their
understanding and support and promises to return the
favor. They also have a shortage of good workers. But of
course, they won't slaughter pigs or make pork sausage.

What awful timing! How can we get everything ready for the winter? In the past, I've looked forward to the pressure of the season. But this year, I'm overwhelmed with the tiniest tasks. I'm jumpy and cry for no reason. Mom says I should pray more. The pastor says I must forgive and put this behind me. How can I do so when I'm still suffering? How can I forgive someone I've never met?

I admit to the anger in my heart. May God forgive me. But I fear another attack. I don't want to leave the house by myself. My heart races when I do. Then, when I am outside, I keep checking the horizon for signs of trouble. Dread follows me everywhere. Mom and Dad say I'm exaggerating and there's nothing to worry about. No one understands.

Are the concerns about war as dire on your side of the river? I miss you terribly. Father says I can come when the snow falls. I can't wait to see you.

I pray for you daily. Love always, your sister Katarina

1951 POST-WAR GERMANY

THE GRAY CAT ROSE FROM ITS POST ON THE BULLNOSE edge of the oaken desk and squinted at Peter, its yellow eyes analyzing him with a suspicious glare. It arched its back and yawned, displaying large canines. After directing another piercing gaze at Peter, it curled up, resting its chin on its paws.

Peter tucked his feet under his chair and watched the cat nod off to sleep before continuing, "There are very few entries for the following year, except for a few paragraphs about the complex political landscape. Several pages are missing ... torn out, it seems. The letters were stuffed in the middle."

Reinhart leaned back in his leather chair, crossed his knees and rubbed his chin. "Any clue about those missing pages?"

"No idea. The letters are fairly mundane, although conflicts between the locals and the Mennonite business owners are obvious. I'll need to research elsewhere, I suppose. Women knew little about the political upheaval and the men shielded them. Most of their news came from the female gossip mill, so the truth was easily distorted. Remember, this was in the day before modern conveniences like telephones and radios were common. The local newspaper was the best source of information, and even that was censored. When the reality about the war hit ... they were stunned. I doubt they ever dreamed their lives could be turned upside down so quickly."

"Yes, I've gathered as much. Do you think this is why Katarina fixated on the emotional brunt of the accident? I understand it was a frightening experience for a young girl, but in the wider scope of things, it seems minor. What's your take on it?"

Peter rubbed the back of his neck, "Well ... it was the start of the war for her ... or rather her first inkling that there was a crisis brewing."

"What's that funny look on your face? I sense I just struck a nerve." Reinhart moved a notebook and a pencil to his lap. "Or is there a problem with the cat?"

"The cat? Oh, no. It's not that." Peter waved off the remark and fidgeted in his seat. "I was reflecting on Mom's reaction to her accident. It reminds me of my own when I was nineteen."

"Really? Tell me, I'm all ears." Reinhart uncrossed his legs and put the writing tools on the desk. "What happened?"

"We — Mom and I — had a fight, and I ran out. I sat by the river to think. It was getting late, and the bums were restless. They decided they needed my coat and shoes more than I did." Peter flexed his hands. "They roughed me up and left me for dead. A cop found me and took me to the hospital."

"Oh, Peter. I'm so sorry. I had no idea."

"*Ja.* It was '37, before the war. My injuries were serious, but I didn't suffer mentally as much as Mom seemed to from her misadventure." Peter tapped the chair arm. "It's odd that we both started our war journeys in the same way. I've never noticed this before."

"Lots of people have accidents, Peter. Life is crappy at times. Don't read so much into things. Mulling over the divine reasons for our calamities only causes us to get bogged down. It's best to move on."

"I suppose. That night we were sitting at the table and she was rehashing one of her war stories. I tried to divert her attention to something else, but it was no use. Then she told me about her missing son, Jacob. Do you remember I told you about him in our phone call?"

Reinhart nodded, "Yes, I do. Such a tragic situation. But not unusual for those times, I'm sad to say."

"It was news to me. I'd never heard about him before. Even Dad never told me. I was dumbfounded. When I recovered from the shock, I blew up and called her awful names. Then I left the house. We never spoke about it again. Now, here I am—fifteen or so years later—wanting to understand the past. Except, there's no Jacob, and there's no Katarina." Peter stared at the sleeping cat. "I don't know where to find either of them. These notes are the only clues I have."

Reinhart nodded slowly, with his hands folded over his paunch, his mouth pursed, and a sympathetic expression on his face. After a long, pregnant pause, he answered. "One can't bury a missing body, Peter. It's an emotional grave with no headstone. There's nothing to mark the grief."

"Exactly. At least, now I can empathize with her angst. Her soul couldn't heal until she knew. Much like how I'm struggling today."

"Meaning?"

"She never gave up on finding him. I don't want to give up on finding out what happened to her, either. The military record only said, 'presumed dead.' That's not definite enough for me."

Reinhart nodded. "Well, you can't go into Russia and investigate any of this. Maybe one day you will. For now, I advise you to stick to what you can control. Writing is the best tonic. Allow the words to bleed onto the paper. It will all make sense eventually."

"Except the wound is so deep. I'm not sure I have the stomach to dig up old bones. And writing it out makes it feel so bloody real. Like I was there."

"You were there ... for the worst of it."

"Yes, but I was a little kid. We arrived in Germany when I was three. My memories are fuzzy."

"The best part about playing with puzzles is finding the missing pieces. This will all come together, Peter. Trust the process." Reinhart rested his elbows on the desk and smiled. "When I reflect back on the second war, I remember we all carried on as ordinarily as possible, until we couldn't. We held our breath waiting for the bombs and then sighed with relief when they passed. We held on to the promise of peace. It was the hope that sustained us. Do you think it was any different in Katarina's world?"

"Looking back and being in the middle of it are two different perspectives. Here, in her diary, it sounds like her life was spiraling out of control."

"No doubt she was terrified, Peter. War was disrupting her dreams and future goals."

"Yes and no. These letters suggest she suffered ongoing nightmares and panic attacks. Then, sometime over the next year, she began living at Anna's — which is exactly where she wanted to be."

"Hmm ... she strikes me as a strong-willed young woman." Reinhart picked up the sleeping cat and pulled it into his lap. "And this leads me to wonder ... how did the journals and letters end up in the rubble of a bombed complex? And you found them just before they cleared the debris? That's a strange coincidence. I get the feeling there's more to this story."

Peter shrugged, "That's crossed my mind. But my guess is they were in the back of a closet somewhere. I just happened to be scouring that corner that day. But now that I have the books, I'm preoccupied with what I have, not how I received it."

"Touché. There are many rabbit trails in this saga. It's best to stick to the main road. Tell me, do you know how the diaries survived through the revolution? Didn't they run from the house with the clothes on their backs?"

Peter shrugged, "I can only guess. About a month before the June battles my grandparents packed their belongings and fled the country. It's possible the books and letters were in their possession and shipped to her later. Although ... Mom stayed in touch with a few Russian friends. They could have mailed them to her here in Germany later. But I think the contents would have been censored by the NKVD first. If they passed through official hands, there would be signs of tampering."

"Ah, true enough. And the mail wasn't very reliable in the early years following the revolution, either. So that signals a later delivery or a different route." Reinhart nodded slowly as he tapped the pencil on the desk. "And your grandparents?"

"They eventually went to Canada to join my uncles and aunts there. The refugee life was chaotic. Everyone moving from place to place — trying to re-establish themselves after the war. According to a letter from my sister, my grandparents have passed on now. Mom wanted to go to Canada, too — but the pull to stay in Germany was stronger. Staying here kept her physically closer to Jacob, in case they reconnected. The unknowing possessed her."

"So tragic. And you said your dad's death unhinged her?"

"Like a light switch. After she processed his death, she became frantic, determined to find shreds of Jacob's existence. She threw herself into her job as a translator and jumped at the first chance to travel to Poland — hoping it might bring her closer to him. She forgave me ... eventually."

"For finding the identity documents?"

Peter nodded.

"I'm curious about something else, Peter. Help me understand ... If they ran through fire and water, how did they arrive at the camps with those papers intact?"

"Ah. Now that question, I can answer. Waterproof sashes. They were like money belts with large pockets."

"Very practical."

"And essential. Mennonites were like modern-day

survivalists — very frugal, creative, and always prepared for the inevitable."

"And ingenious. Who would think to sew a waterproof sash to keep valuables? Any idea on the process?"

"Beeswax, I presume. They raised bees and manufactured sunflower seed oil."

"I remember you talking about their cold-pressing invention."

"Yes. They owned many successful factories in the region — farm implements, machinery, brickyards, tree plantations, and mills of all kinds — lumber, flour. They were astute entrepreneurs and inventors."

"It's not surprising they were the targets of the anarchists."

"And worse. Lenin's land reforms removed their right to own farmland, factories, or hire help. These were confiscated and then placed under government control. Things got even worse under Stalin."

"Stalin is a brutal pig. I heard parents ate their own children during the Great Famine."

The cat opened his eyes and looked over at Peter and blinked, as if seeing him for the first time. Peter rubbed his lips together, pulled his feet underneath his chair, and crossed his ankles. He then cleared his throat. "That period is a bit vague. The horrible truth remains locked behind Stalin's iron curtain — to be uncovered by future historians. I'm aware the government took grain at gunpoint and sealed regional borders to prevent peasants from escaping. Millions of Ukrainians died, including many Mennonites, although not to the same degree.

"It's not surprising those regions most resistant to the communist changes during the Revolution were hit hardest by the Holodomor.[1] In my opinion, Stalin's genocidal approach to gain political control seems comparable to Hitler's. But, without the capability or permission to go in and assess the dead, we don't know the full extent of the tragedy.

"The Mennonite survivors said their frugal nature and their Christian lifestyle of helping one another kept them alive. When Germany arrived during the second war, the remnant welcomed us with open arms. And that's also when we found out about Stalin's brutality."

"Once again, Germany was their savior."

"Yes, and as the German army withdrew, many left with them."

"But despite knowing the threats, some still chose to stay?"

"Yes. To their detriment. They were exiled to Siberia and Kazakhstan; others were imprisoned or murdered."

"And the factories shut down or destroyed. Huh. Well, it's Russia's loss and the world's gain, I suppose." Reinhart placed the cat on the floor, then swiped his hands over the side of the chair. "Tell me, I'm puzzled by something else ..."

"What's that?"

"You said the Mennonites considered themselves German, and they were German loyalists, but they supported the White Russian army. However, Germany and Russia were at war. This seems contradictory."

"Not at all."

"No? Please explain."

"The Mennonites considered themselves politically neutral. Their beliefs — in non-resistance and in the separation of church and state — prohibited them from engaging in warfare. After 1768, a political maneuver by Catherine the Great — to protect the southern steppes from the ongoing aggression with the Turks — granted the Mennonites religious freedom and military exemptions in exchange for settling and cultivating the virgin land. They were granted a special peasant class and treated as a distinct society by the Imperial government but were technically never Russian citizens. They had their own laws, policing, educational systems, and hospitals. And institutions for the mentally ill and elderly.

"With their insistence of remaining separate from the secular Russian society and their strange religious practices, they never fit in with the culture at large. Their use of the German language and their distinctive ways labelled them as ethnic Germans. Their identity became fuzzy during the war and they tried to bury their heritage under claims of Dutch ancestry — for obvious reasons. When the Czar's government fell, Lenin eliminated their previously held rights and privileges.

"After a century of respectful relationships with the Imperial government, acknowledging their political responsibility to the Czar was the right thing to do. I guess you could say they supported both sides but cheered for none."

"Tough spot to be in."

"Yes, but they trusted God would reward them for following the path of peace."

"Incredible blind faith."

"They were prepared to die for their beliefs."

"Yes. And we can learn much from such struggles. But for a young woman stuck in the middle of a changing era, it must have been confusing." Reinhart scratched a few lines on the paper and checked his watch. "So, fill me in on the timing of this part of the diary. While Katarina's running away to Anna's, what's the military situation?"

Peter planted his feet flat on the floor and took a deep breath, then exhaled slowly. "This will take a while to explain, so please bear with me. It's important to appreciate that Ukraine was in a tug-of-war between Germany and Russia, and at the same time Ukrainians wanted their own voice. This put the country in a very delicate and potentially explosive spot. When Russia began imploding, Germany progressed inland, and resistance inside Ukraine increased.

"To fully grasp Katarina's life story, we must know who was in charge when. Without understanding this, we'll be confused later. So, let's keep in mind that Germany doesn't progress into the south until '18. Between '16 and '18 political chaos holds both Russia and Ukraine in strangleholds. Russia's losing the war and the Imperial government's in a mess. The Czar abdicates in March of '17 and Kerensky's provisional government takes over in July — and that's another political disaster. This opens the door for Lenin which leads to the October Revolution. It's a domino effect with profound implications for the German colonists.

"At the same time, in Ukraine, the ugly fight for independence leaves the country in disarray as various political factions struggle for power. While Russia has its hands full with its own problems, it doesn't have time or money to deal with Ukraine. So, the country becomes a convenient chess piece in a bloody game between Russia and Germany."

"And local tensions increase." Reinhart tapped the pencil nib on the paper.

"Correct. Ukraine becomes lawless. Anarchists and Nationalists rise up. Fear runs rampant. These new power-hungry activists quickly amass their own armies. But they all need an ongoing supply of money, guns, ammunition, and food. The logical targets are the wealthy landowners and German ethnic farmers." Peter looked up at the clock as it chimed four.

Reinhart continued scribbling, "As we learned in Germany, when the engine of political gain becomes the most imperative goal, lives are lost, and culture is destroyed. It's a bloody high cost for lofty ambition."

"Except each believes they have the key to a better society."

"Hindsight is always twenty-twenty. The world continues to shudder at the communist progression. In every generation, idealistic youth get wrapped up in impractical theories with no comprehension of the full impact. They want change, but they underestimate the complicated and often dangerous process."

"Exactly."

"I'm sorry, Peter. I went off on a tangent there. You were about to tell me about the local gangs and their affiliations."

"Yes, but then I'll need to go ... I'm to pick up beans from the market." Peter tapped his fingers on the armrest. "Heidi's making stew. Not as good as my mom's, of course."

"Naturally. A wife can't compete with her mother-in-law," Reinhart chuckled. "So tell me quickly. How did the political situation fit with Katarina's life?"

"Regionally, it was a mess. Peasant armies with conflicting politics sink in the mire between Russia's Red and White. Ukrainians want independence, but Russia won't let them go easily. And every faction has a plan on how to make it happen. When the Great War pushes into the region, the country implodes."

"How did Katarina's life change because of these upheavals?"

"Economic pressures mount. Imported goods become rare and expensive. Inflation is out of control. But as always, the Mennonites are self-sufficient — growing their own food, recycling goods, and minimalizing. They believe they can survive anything."

"Again, demonstrating their amazing ingenuity."

"Yes. But things got worse with conscription. When duty called— the able-bodied left and the old men and women ran shop. In the summer of '17, Makhno was freed from prison and his anarchist army expanded with breakneck speed."

Reinhart leaned back in his chair and flicked the pencil back and forth through his fingers.

"And I imagine that's when all hell broke loose."

"That's right."

---

1. The Holodomor—also called The Great Famine—was a period of genocide or ethnic cleansing that officially occurred during 1932-33 under Stalin. The horror originated with Soviet policies against Ukraine as early as 1918 which led to collectivization in 1929-30. An estimated eight per cent of Mennonites in Ukraine died from starvation during this time as well as thirteen per cent of Ukraine's population. See this informative personal blog for more info. https://gerhardsjourney.com/2018/04/06/ep-30-holodomor-the-bad-years/# and this resource: https://cla.umn.edu/chgs/holocaust-genocide-education/resource-guides/holodomor

8

ANNA'S HOUSE

SPRING 1917 RUSSIAN UKRAINE—
MOLOTSCHNA COLONY

Anna scooped the fragrant herbs into the hand-painted ceramic pot and added boiling water from the samovar. She leaned over and sniffed the tea. "The lemon verbena still has a good head."

"Let's hope this year's will be good, too." Katarina winced while reaching for the delft cups from the hutch. She grabbed her shoulder and quickly turned her back, hoping Anna wouldn't notice.

"You should go see the bone cracker. Your arm doesn't seem to be improving."

"I doubt twisting my neck will cure it. Besides, I saw the doctor in Chortitza. He said it's not fixable. I must learn to live with it." Katarina set the cups on the table, then angled her chair so the brilliant spring sun radiating through the window could warm her back.

"Still, a second opinion wouldn't hurt. You never know. Maybe a bone in your neck slipped out of place. You don't stand straight. That shoulder is lower than the other." Anna pointed to Katarina's left side.

"Fine. I'll stop in after work next week. Now stop being my mother. Let's talk about the garden."

Anna bit her bottom lip. "Sorry. You don't have to act so tough. And please don't snap at me. It's very obvious when you're hurting. I'm just trying to help."

Katarina rubbed the knot in her neck and gave her sister a dirty look. "You were saying about the garden ..."

"Right." Anna carried the cozy-covered teapot to the table. "We need a cool, wet spring like we had last year. Not that we can do anything about the weather. Mint gets leggy fast in the heat." She pointed to the sugar bowl. "Help yourself. Our supply is restocked. Olek and Alyona cashed in the ration cards this morning."

"Oh, thank God. Now we can bake some sweet rolls."

"Yes. My mouth is watering already."

Olek was Anna and David's personal carriage driver and the stable manager — although judging from the burly man's articulate speech and refined demeanor, Katarina guessed he was educated. It led her to assume that the middle-aged man likely had other duties. He was a true gentleman in every way — not coarse or rude like other drivers she'd known. In fact, he made a real effort to get to know her, and she found him quite likeable and easy to talk to.

Alyona was different. Although a typical cook and kitchen manager of a large estate — fully devoted to her job and exceptionally competent — the older woman's personality left a bit to be desired. Despite being polite and respectful, her speech was crude and simple, her mannerisms abrupt. She wasn't someone that Katarina would choose to gossip with over a cup of tea. Nonetheless, the woman had served the family well for decades, so Katarina was confident that in time, they would get along well.

Katarina plopped a sugar cube in her mouth and sucked it between her teeth as she sipped her tea. She closed her eyes, enjoying the sticky sweetness melting on her tongue. "Mm. Did you set some aside for David's parents?"

"Yes, their butler took it over earlier."

"Well, I'll be sure to thank the others for giving up their allotments for us."

"Thank them?" Anna scoffed, "There's no need to thank servants. Besides, it's wartime. We must all make sacrifices." She eased herself down in the chair, keeping a hand on her swollen belly. "I can't wait to get back in the garden after this baby comes. I'm craving sorrel soup and fresh rhubarb juice. Say, what do you think about creating some new recipes this year? Let's put our heads together. You could write about it in the newspaper."

Katarina considered challenging Anna on her small-minded comment but thought better of it. Her sister was obviously uncomfortable in her pregnant state. It was best to let it go. "Unfortunately, my current assignment is more serious."

"Such as?"

"Cataloguing births and deaths and visiting graveyards."

"Eww! That sounds grave." Anna poured the tea and slid a cup across the table.

"Ha-ha, funny." Katarina accepted the cup and raised it to her mouth. "It's about collecting vital statistics."

"Oh. And why is that important?"

"Regier says it's necessary for both census reporting and keeping track of our relatives. And it helps us understand our history. The churches record important milestones like births, baptisms, marriages, and deaths, but when their members move to new communities or change churches, those files don't go with them. In the past, family Bibles completed the ancestral pictures. But with the increased emigration, this knowledge could disappear after a few generations. The government demands access to these facts, too."

"How do the graves help?"

"Years ago, few burial markers had names. Plots were identified with stones or simple crosses unless the people were important. Today, we inscribe the monuments, but even so, many are of poor quality and they fade over time. I use the churches' lists to verify gravesite information. It's tedious, but fascinating. You could say I'm quickly becoming a bit of a genealogist."

"It sounds obsessive. But I still don't get why this is important."

"For a couple of reasons. First, remember when we were children, the church that burned down in Ziegenfeld?"

"*Ja*, vaguely."

"Well, the church records were destroyed too. Finding out who died in the fire was a process of elimination and knocking on doors. Lately, the colonies have slackened on their chronicling. God forbid another fire should happen; but if it does, my work will help identify bodies and families."

"What's the other reason?"

"Not everyone gets buried in the church cemetery."

Anna pursed her lips, "Right. Tradition held they shouldn't be mentioned."

"Surely their families deserve to know their burial locations. Even if they were unrepentant or died by their own hand."

"I'm content to leave that for the church to deal with.

It's above my theological understanding." Anna brushed a blonde strand from her face and tucked it behind her ear. "Anyway, this digging into families' histories seems creepy ... even intrusive. What is *The Post* doing with this private information? And what do the church leaders say about this?"

"Regier explained that *The Post's* dossier only provides a back-up of the data the churches already compile or should have collected but didn't. With all the violence going on, nothing is safe or sacred anymore. Not even the houses of worship or the graveyards. There's been several cases of grave-robbing in the outlying villages."

Anna shivered. "This is a bit too spooky for me. The possibility that war could come to our town ... I pray it never happens. In fact, I'll add this to my daily prayers."

"We can't predict the future. But as Oma used to say, 'We hope for the best but prepare for the worst.'" Katarina plopped a sugar cube into her tea and stirred.

"I suppose. We pray for a hedge of protection. If God's plan is for us to go through the fire, then we ask for strength to endure it. Then again, if all repent, God will be merciful. Isn't that what the Bible teaches?"

"*Ja.* Last Sunday, Pastor Friesen said that God will provide a way of escape. We only need to trust him."

"Then we have nothing to worry about. 'Though a host should encamp against me, my heart shall not fear; though war should rise against me, in this will I be confident.'"

"Psalm 27:3." Katarina slurped her tea. "I know my Bible, too."

"Good. We can quote this together if we find ourselves surrounded. So, tell me, will Regier allow you to write anything else?" Anna fidgeted and caressed her abdomen with slow, smooth circles.

"Well ..." Katarina made a face, "I submitted an article on the quilt-making project at the Brudergemeinde church in Rueckenau, and my bean soup recipe. But Regier said Mennonite women already know how to cook and quilt. They don't want or need lessons from a newspaper, and certainly not from an unmarried woman. According to him, I should write on more relevant topics."

"What subjects does he consider important? Are you supposed to report on grain prices or politics? Women don't know about such things. Do you?"

"I'm learning. I read the latest reports and eavesdrop on the men. That's all they talk about these days. But if I were to write on that, he'd say I'm just a young girl and shouldn't pretend to know as much as a man." Katarina made quotation marks in the air and scrunched up her nose. "Find something else."

"Oh, rats. I just spilled." Anna held up the teapot and pointed to the puddle on the oak table.

"I'll get it." Katarina jumped up and retrieved a towel.

"Well, maybe he wants you to focus on more academic pursuits or Biblical guidance for young people. You'll be teaching in a few months. Perhaps he's holding you to a higher standard."

"I suppose. But I want to write about food. I enjoy tweaking recipes to create something altogether different." Katarina mopped up the spill and refilled both cups.

"Mm. Yes, we can all learn something new. You and I compare recipes every day. I'm sure others want to see how well you cook."

Katarina scowled and snapped the towel. "Thanks a lot. I could say the same about your quilting."

"You could always call it *A Cook in Training*."

"Hey, that's not such a bad idea. I'll present it to him."

Anna rubbed the side of the teacup. "Isn't it uncomfortable being the only woman in the office?"

"A bit. But the men are very polite and keep their distance. They are *frindschoft*, after all."

"Second and third cousins, perhaps. Not that close. I think Jacob Kroeker is marriage material."

"Oh, please. His mother checks in on him twice a day. And the other two are married. Their wives check on them twice a day, too. Honestly, I spend more time visiting with the women than working."

"Aha. So that's why he hired you — so the women would stop interrupting the men at work. Or..." Anna held the ear of the teacup between her thumb and two fingers, "... the women are checking up on you ... a young woman in the workplace is rather scandalous."

Katarina snickered. "When school starts, I won't be there so much. The tongues will stop wagging then. Except Mr. Regier might miss having a clerical slave, not to mention my eagle editing eye."

"I'm sure your integrity is above board, and you're very good at your job. But Katarina, male-female relationships are complicated, and one must exercise caution in these waters. Women judge. And men misinterpret and overstep their bounds." Anna tapped the side of the cup with her fingernail. "I realize you're different from other young ladies, but people don't know you that well yet."

"Huh," Katarina scoffed. "They can see I'm smarter than most. Haven't I proven that already?"

"It's not about you. You must tread carefully. Never let the men know that you're brainy. You don't want to insult them and make them feel inferior. Instead, be clever. They need a gentle education, Miss Schoolteacher. When they try to dismiss your intelligence, make them believe your ideas are theirs."

Katarina bit the inside of her cheek. Where was Anna going with this? Lately, she asked a lot of questions about the men in Katarina's life and offered what Katarina inferred as being unsolicited romantic help. Whether Anna was digging for information or trying to educate her about marriage, Katarina wasn't sure. Either way, the discussion was uncomfortable.

"I suppose. However, I have yet to learn your fine art of manipulation. Besides, I want credit for my brain. Why should they get all the fun?" Katarina snapped as she fingered the knot now spreading into a tight band across her shoulders. Maybe she should see the bone cracker. However, the idea of a man putting his hands around her neck felt weird. She shivered. A sugar cure was a better idea. She dropped a second cube into her cup and gave a vigorous stir.

Anna kept nattering as if she didn't notice the insult. "Personally, I don't see your attraction to working in a man's domain. Most women are content raising a family, managing a household, and doing church stuff. You can't continue after you're married you know. You'll have to give it all up. So, what's the point?"

"It's just not for me, that's all," Katarina pinched the tight muscle again and stretched her neck, "I've told you a hundred times. I want to be a teacher and travel the world. My goals haven't changed just because I've grown up." Had Anna forgotten the reason Katarina had moved to Halbstadt?

"Well, it's just that ... a woman pursuing a man's sphere seems unsavory. It doesn't fit in our way of life."

"Listen, Anna. The world is changing. One day women

and men will be employed side-by-side. Look at the Russkye women. They all have jobs outside the home. They even do factory work."

"But they're not Mennonites. Let's remember we are separate from the world. We're not to copy them." Anna nudged the spoon to the edge of the saucer with the bottom of the cup.

Katarina crossed her arms over her chest. "Does being separate make us better than them? What does work have to do with it? Did Jesus say women can't work? I don't think so. What about Lydia, the maker of purple cloth?" Katarina was dismayed. Anna was supposed to be her advocate, but at the moment she was being as critical as their mother.

"There's a bigger picture here, Katarina. We rely on the wisdom and leadership of our church fathers who spent their lifetimes studying the Bible. But since you brought it up — if you want to use the Russky as a measuring stick — therein lies a reason this country's in so much trouble. Between the mothers slaving in the fields and factories and so many absent fathers, their children are left to parent themselves. There's no guidance or discipline. It follows that they stoop to criminal behavior like joining gangs, committing thievery, and hurting innocent landowners."

Katarina rolled her eyes. "Young boys often get into trouble. Parents or not, it's human nature. But the war isn't connected to broken homes."

"No? How do you know?"

"Papa said war is about greed and politics."

"Tell me, do the men at the paper discuss the war news?"

"Yes ... and it's all very dreary," Katarina sighed. "From what I'm hearing there's little chance it will end soon." She put her elbow on the table and toyed with her teaspoon.

"Educate me." Anna folded her hands over her belly and sat back in the chair. "Bring me up to date. Pretend I'm your student and you are explaining current affairs to me."

Katarina smirked. Anna had decided to stop pushing the guilt button and was proposing a peace treaty. But she wanted proof of Katarina's dedication to her craft. Well, she could recite the details. Everyone in town gossiped about the latest royal scandals in Petrograd. And when it came to the war, she read the daily Russian news at Regier's office. And she eavesdropped on the men's political discussions. Putting the pieces together was easy.

"Well ..." she tapped a fingernail on the table. "With the abdication of the Czar, Russia now has a provisional government. The Soviet's in a bit of a disarray with Bolsheviks and Mensheviks creating coalitions to prevent laws from passing. And these parties encourage strikes and social unrest.

"Here at home, Ukraine seeks self-government. There's talk that we'll become a republic and our currency will change. But with Russia in crisis and without strong political leadership here, it's anyone's guess what will happen next."

Katarina paused and reflected on recent headlines as she spoke. The latest news seemed irrational and sensational. Even she had trouble believing it was true. "I've seen reports about looting and rogue gangs in the villages. It's happening all over. There's no safe place anymore. Businesses complain of corrupt police and irresponsible authority. There's dread in the air — as if everyone's waiting for the next shoe to drop. Mr. Regier says the country is unstable because of the politics. No one's enforcing the ever-changing laws. It's hard to tell who's in charge anymore. He's afraid of printing details as the church might accuse him of fearmongering. He couches his words. It's nerve-wracking."

"Indeed. Do you think the war between Russia and Germany is part of the upheaval?" Anna picked up the teacup and held it by the ear between her thumb and two fingers, with her little finger sticking straight out like a pointer.

Katarina bit her lip and redirected her gaze to the clock on the wall above Anna's head. She didn't dare laugh out loud at Anna's pretense of tea-drinking like a snooty royal. It was clear Anna had picked up a few new habits from her in-law's high-class practices. She wanted to make fun of her but thought better of it. Anna might insist Katarina copy her to fit in better with the snobby crowd. It was best to avoid going down a rabbit hole towards hurt feelings.

She put her elbow on the table and palmed her chin. "I'm sure it is. I've heard vagrants are drifting in from the war front. Caravans of families in oxcarts moving through the countryside. And disheveled characters soliciting work. Squatters camp out by the river and in the fields. Beggars in the city. Mr. Regier says the news is concerning. I wish I knew more details, but the men are so hush-hush around me. Every morning they huddle in Regier's office behind a closed door. I strain my ear, but I only hear bits and pieces. It's like it's all a big secret," Katarina toyed with her spoon.

"Oh, they're just trying to protect you from grisly details."

"That's for certain." Katarina straightened her posture and snorted. "But I learn a lot from reading the news articles. I'm beginning to think everything fits together like a giant puzzle. I just haven't figured out the pieces."

"Some things are not meant for our ears, Kat. Men tend to be quite crass when they're by themselves. As women, we need to stay pure in thought. If we contaminate ourselves with the world's affairs, we're pulled away from our more important duties."

Katarina laughed, "Well Russia doesn't seem to agree with that opinion. The government is encouraging women to join the war and bear arms. I'm all for education and working women, but even I think that's going a bit far."

Anna gasped, "Insanity. Women and guns? They must be desperate."

"*Ja*. Between the war, the politics and the local dissension, it feels like everyone's waiting for a powder keg to explode."

"Maybe it's the end of the world."

"Pastor Friesen says Jesus is coming back soon and we best prepare."

"Yes, I heard him say he wishes Christ would hurry up. We are to escape the tribulation, not go through it."

"But first we must go through the fire of purification."

"Yes, we must ..."

Katarina went to refill her cup, but discovered the teapot was empty. She walked over to the samovar, added a heaping spoonful of lemon mint into the pot and filled it with boiling water. At the half-way mark, the boiler dribbled. She sighed and touched the kettle. It was still hot. Had they drunk so much tea already? The morning must be almost gone.

As she wondered whether she should have the samovar refilled, she looked around for Alyona or the scullery maid. From her stance, she could see down the long hallway and into the formal dining room. Where was everyone? It must be almost time for lunch. This lack of promptness was unacceptable. If the kitchen wasn't buzzing with activity by the time they finished this last cup of tea, she would find the cook and reprimand her for her tardiness. Katarina fumed as she carried the half-full pot back to the breakfast table and refilled their cups.

Anna didn't seem to notice the late time nor the servants' absence as she swirled the sugar in her cup with an absentminded expression on her face. It was obvious there were other things on her mind.

She tapped the spoon on the side of the cup and then added a footnote as casually as if she was speaking about variations of mint. "Since you're so up to date, I suppose you've heard about the latest political activism in the city."

"What do you mean?"

"Remember those bombings ten years ago?"

Katarina flashed back to the conversation around the wedding reception. Her skin prickled, "Vaguely. I was just a kid then. I heard talk. Didn't that happen in Ekaterinoslav?"

"Yes. There was a Russky in Gulai-Poyle who organized a regional *Union of Peasants*.[1] They wanted to confiscate all the land that 'rightfully belonged to the peasantry' and to reorganize it into free communes." Anna made quotation marks in the air. "To accomplish this, they set out to inventory and redistribute local wealth. There were armed attacks against the Mennonite and German businesses and estates around Tokmak."

"Right." Katarina flashed back to the wedding and the moment when the men's discussion stopped. "There was gossip about the widow Trudchen. Her husband was murdered and buildings set on fire. Apparently, she never got over it and the estate went to pot."

"I don't know if that was the same gang, but the one responsible for those bombings is now out of the Moscow prison and back in Tokmak and stirring up trouble. They call him Makhnovsky."

"Oh?" Katarina felt the blood drain from her face as the image of the black stallion rode though her mind. Goosebumps formed on her arms and the hair on the back of her neck bristled. She picked up her cup, then sneezed.

"Careful." Anna's eyes widened.

"What?"

"You're spilling your tea."

"Oh." Katarina set the cup down, pulled out a handkerchief from behind her waistband, and blew her nose.

"Are you alright? You're shaking like a leaf. And you're as white as a ghost." Anna frowned and shifted sideways.

Katarina pushed away from the table and walked over to the stove. "All this talk about criminals, trouble, and war. I can't help but think about the attack on the farm. I know it's not connected but ... this news just makes my stomach sick." She flexed her fists over the warmer.

"Good grief, Kat. I thought your newspaper had the bird's-eye on the latest gossip. Didn't anyone write about it?"

"If they did, I missed it." Her mind raced for an explanation.

Anna grinned a sly smile and blew on her tea. "David told me they're shooting up the sky and encouraging protests. The farmers told him these troublemakers have a small army of local fans. I guess it pays to have a husband in the know."

Katarina thought back to the men's huddle around Guenther's — the new reporter — desk last week. She had strained to eavesdrop. When Regier looked up from the conversation and caught her curious eye, he moved the meeting to his rear office. Later, she felt a chill in the air. The men met her questions with abrupt answers and paper shuffling. The weird reactions rattled her.

The next day she approached Regier and asked if she had made a mistake or done something improper. He assured her the office was dealing with a serious news item. It was nothing she needed to worry about.

After this, Olek mysteriously arrived with the buggy at six o'clock every night, using the excuse he was in town running errands, or insisting it was too cold for her to walk the five *versts*. She sensed a conspiracy of overprotection.

"I wonder if there's been trouble that Regier doesn't want me to know about? And he's worried about me because of the raid at Mom and Dad's."

"Oh. Of course." Anna stared at Katarina with a blank face. "He wouldn't tell you for fear of upsetting you. I hope I didn't. You're not still having nightmares about that, are you? That was almost two years ago." Anna floundered. "I thought you were over it by now ... besides, there's no correlation between a ten-year-old crime and the attack on our farm. The criminals that committed those bombings and attacked widow Trudchen were in jail until now. I just told you that. Plus, our felons weren't very sophisticated. There was only a handful of them. 'Juvenile thugs,' Dad called them. Anyway, I'm sure Dad knows who pillaged the farm. He hasn't told us because either we don't need to know, or he thinks it would upset us. These men who just got out of jail are far more dangerous."

"Unless dear Mr. Regier knows of a link. You know how the men keep things from us. How did David find out?"

"He overheard the new field hands. Then, when he attended a meeting at Lentz's factory, Abe confirmed it. There's been grumblings about more strike action at the mills, too. And something about politics in Petrograd reverberating here. And to add what you said earlier, David also mentioned the protests for Ukraine independence."

"*Ja*, I heard the Bolsheviks are trying to push through some policies that will hurt the farmers and businesses. Do you know ... are these local protestors for or against Russia?" Katarina frowned. An icy sensation tickled her back. She shivered and rubbed her arms. There was something sinister about this news, but she couldn't put her finger on it.

"My understanding is neither of them. David isn't sure what they're up to, but this Makhnovsky is apparently quite charismatic and manipulative. And he has friends on all sides. Lentz said Makhno worked for him back in '05 as well as on a few other Molotschna estates. Back then, the criminal's rebellious attitude needed severe disciplining. Rumor is he now wants to even the score against the Mennonite farmers. David says there's bound to be trouble. They're keeping an eye on him."

"Hopefully, he'll meet someone who can out-finagle him." Katarina squeezed her eyes, trying to erase the black stallion from her mind, and reminded herself that there was no logical connection to the raid on the family farm. And yet something about this story gnawed at her.

"To add to this, David says we're losing our strongest workers to conscription. He's worried. Without labor, how will we farm the fields? It's driving up the cost of every-thing. We must sell grain at higher prices to cover our expenses. But Russia's refusing to pay more. To protest, we may need to stockpile it. But where? If it doesn't get milled it will rot in the barns. David says the economy of the entire country's in trouble. Now, add in troublemakers like Makhno ... it sounds to me like the threat of losing our hams and sausages is the least of our concerns."

Anna's insight astounded Katarina. Her sister understood the crisis as well as she did. "What's his biggest worry?"

"This estate, of course. We can't afford to lose any more help. We're one of the biggest properties in this part of the country. If these *khokhols* decide to target us ... God only knows what could happen," Anna tapped her index finger on the table.

"Like what?"

"I don't know. But if this Makhnovsky is seeking a vendetta against our people for some past sins ... and if the locals see him as some kind of savior, it won't take much encouragement for him to do something rash."

Katarina frowned. She felt she was missing something. David's wealth could more than offset any interruption in production. "I don't understand. Money buys protection and loyalty. Why doesn't David just increase wages? The workers need to eat. Pay them more and they'll stay, *and* they'll protect the farm."

Anna stroked her stomach. "We don't know if that's true anymore. You know how rumors spread. Even our own people are restless, talking about the need for change. Few are satisfied with the status quo."

"*Ja*, there seems to be a lot of dissension."

"Most of these locals hail from Tokmak region — where Makhno's support lies. If they quit on us, from where will we find help? We can't import qualified labor under the current war regulations. David says we need to tighten our belts and our boundaries but increase output. The work must go on. It's a quandary."

"What about the migrants drifting through? They're trying to escape the war and they need to eat."

"We can't rely on unscrupulous hobos who are here today

and gone tomorrow. Besides, they probably don't have the right papers. David says they can do odd jobs to work for food, but they can't stay here. We don't want them dying on our property. And we don't want trouble with the authorities."

A heavy gray cloud passed over and blocked the warm sunlight from streaming through the window. Katarina rubbed the goosebumps from her arms.

"Anyway ... it's not for us women to worry about. The men are meeting at church tonight to discuss solutions. And they're trying to come up with a plan to protect the villages." Anna shifted and straightened her blouse, "But I can guarantee we'll be paying our own way to get out of this mare's nest."

"It sounds to me that almost everything's contingent on what happens in Petrograd. And with the Czar removed from power, the government is in disarray. Kyiv's also confused. If there's no legal direction anywhere, then there's no law and order everywhere. That allows every regulator to make up the rules as they go along. Which means there's no true authority. And as we speak, Russia's drawing lines in the sand. But if our people choose to be on the wrong side ... what happens?" Katarina mused.

Her words hung in the air. Two years ago, as an innocent and carefree young woman, Katarina expected a promising and fun-filled future with the freedom to pursue her dreams. Then, politics and war were abstract concepts. The black stallion had changed that — making her aware of unpredictable sinister forces and diabolical political intent. She sensed the scary event pivoted her into an invisible intersection and she'd made a wrong turn. The dark horse wasn't her biggest problem; it was only a harbinger of evil that hung a dense, dark curtain over her destiny. She wanted to run back and correct her course. Except she couldn't.

She tugged at her wool shawl and walked over to the window, staring at the moving clouds and the sloppy, spring yard. The adult world was far messier than she had ever imagined. She had moved here to get away from the violence, not walk into more of it.

---

1. During 1905-1908, social change and political upheaval dominated Russia. There was a national movement to establish unions and create a more egalitarian society. Although women received the vote, some local revolutionary peasant committees trampled on the wealthy, confiscating their wealth, property and land. Some estates in southern Ukraine were attacked during this time. https://en.wikipedia.org/wiki/All-Russian_Peasant_Union

9

FEARFUL HORIZONS

KATARINA SHIVERED AND RUBBED HER ARMS. THE OLD oak pointing its leafless tentacles to the dark, snow-filled clouds looked as naked as she felt. Exposed. Vulnerable. Could an attack happen here — in this serene, contemplative setting tucked between fruit orchards, nut groves, and a mixed tree plantation?

The expansive estate, surrounded by golden grain fields and bordered by the murky Molotschnaya River, offered extensive natural barriers to unwanted visitors. The privacy alone led one to conclude that the property was exceptionally safe. In sharp contrast, their childhood home with its proximity to the main road and its cluster of smaller buildings was an obvious target for insurgents. But two recent armed raids at nearby farms caused her to second-guess this theory. What if the estate's isolation meant they were actually more defenseless? If a criminal element penetrated the boundaries and held them at ransom, they could be trapped for days. And if David was gone and Olek was murdered ...

She shook away the *what ifs* and took a deep breath to relieve the tension in her chest and cleared her throat. As she turned around, she noticed Anna's odd posture — holding her head with one hand and her stomach with the other.

"Are you all right?" Katarina asked, before noticing Anna's pale, sweaty face.

Anna shook her head. "Please, get Alyona."

"Why? What's wrong?"

"Please, Katarina," Anna sputtered. "Get Alyona."

Katarina frowned. Anna's sudden and dramatic shift in demeanor coupled with her flushed appearance suggested she was ill — which didn't make sense since she'd been fine until now. In fact, Anna had been exceptionally energetic all morning. And she didn't resemble Katarina's mental picture of a woman in labor. She'd seen farm animals give birth before. This didn't look like that. She shook her head. "Was it the tea? Did you eat something bad?"

Anna doubled over and groaned. "Get her now. No time." A bloody fluid dribbled to the floor underneath her chair.

This was obviously no upset stomach, Katarina realized as she stared at the developing scene. "But it's too soon."

Giving voice to the thought helped Katarina to grasp the seriousness of the matter, and she dashed down the hall to the front porch where the gray-haired cook was sweeping the steps. "Alyona," she called. But with her back to Katarina, the woman didn't seem to hear. Katarina raised and sharpened her voice, "Alyona, I think Anna's in labor."

Alyona looked up and set the broom against the wall. "What? In labor? *Nyet*. It's too soon."

"I know. But it's happening," Katarina tapped her foot impatiently. "You must come right away."

"It's her first. She doesn't know. It could be false labor or indigestion. But … you best find Olek and tell him to get the midwife, just to be sure."

Katarina gaped; her eyes widened. Did a servant just *order her* to run an errand? The nerve of the woman. She stood motionless and stared back in disbelief. "I'm not walking through that wet slop." She pointed to the muddy yard with its mounds of melting snow. "You go tell him. I'll take care of Anna."

Alyona put a hand on her hip and tilted her head. Her mouth tightened into a wrinkled circle and her brown eyes flashed. "Do you know anything about birthing babies?"

Katarina stepped back and hung her head. Her chin dropped to her chest. "No." Alyona had a good point. Anna had never given birth before, so she probably didn't know what to do herself. So how could Anna advise anyone on how to help?

Katarina looked beyond the old oak tree to the massive red brick stable, with the upper panel of its blue Dutch door flopping in the breeze. The buggy was parked beside it. Olek was most definitely inside and that was the last place in the world that Katarina wanted to enter. She hadn't been inside since …

"Go," Alyona interrupted her thoughts. "He's probably in the horse barn." She pointed to the building, then scurried past Katarina into the house.

The gravity of the situation spurred her onward. "Right. She'll help Anna. Someone must get Olek. Alyona can't do everything."

She studied the long building again and scanned for signs of life from what she could see of the rest of the property. *Where is everyone else?* "Why me?" she muttered. She turned back to the door to ask Alyona, but the woman had gone indoors. "I'm sure we can wait until one of the other

servants shows up. Babies take hours, sometimes days."
What if Anna can't wait?

A gust of icy wind whipped around the corner. Katarina rubbed her arms. She needed a warmer shawl, or maybe a coat. Her sister wouldn't want her to catch cold. She ambled back to the door, then stopped and scolded herself. "It's a two-minute walk, Katarina. What's wrong with you?" *Anna needs help.*

She traipsed to the stairs and stared at the slushy yard. She pictured her ankles sinking in the muddy water holes. "I should get my winter boots." And again, she turned around.

Staring at the messy challenge made Katarina reflect on Alyona's demand. And the more she thought about it, the more irritated she became. Who was working for whom? She fumed. Katarina was no child to be ordered about by a senior servant. Her family was paying the woman's wages. Alyona was required to take orders from her. She would march inside and tell ... no, she would *order* that woman to find someone else.

She reached for the handle, opened the door and called out, "Alyona, I'm not walking through that slop. Someone else can go. Where's your helper? Isn't she working today?"

There was no answer. She poked her head inside. A weak wailing that sounded like Anna's voice from somewhere deep in the cavern of the house indicated that the situation was escalating. She closed the door and turned to face the stairs. *Do I dare go inside and get my coat and boots, or should I just run straight to the barn? My things are in the mud room by the back door. I'll have to walk right past Alyona and Anna. Anna will be disappointed in me. And I can't face that fierce cook again.*

She appraised the melting snow and mentally traced a

clear path through the puddles to the stables. "It's not that cold. It's just a short dash. I can do this. Less than two minutes to the horse —"

Horses. She sneezed. Once. Twice. Three times. Her heart jumped and her pulse quickened. She wiped her nose and swallowed while she stood at the top of the stairs, staring across the mucky yard. How long had it been? The summer of 1915 seemed like a lifetime ago. Since then, she hadn't been inside any barn, much less ridden a horse.

The door slammed. "Here. Catch," Alyona yelled as she tossed a heavy wool shawl at her. "Run fast and you won't be cold. There's no time to waste."

Katarina's cheeks warmed as she caught both the covering and the servant's stern stare. Her stomach tightened. There was no way out now. She felt like a child who'd been busted with her hands in the cookie jar.

She suspected Alyona thought she was a spoiled rich girl, unwilling to dirty her hands with a little sweat or manure. Alyona probably didn't know about the accident. Or, she didn't realize Katarina had developed an unusual allergy of horses and a terrible fear of tight buildings. Getting into a carriage while it was under control of a trustworthy person was one thing, but approaching an untethered large animal in confined quarters was an entirely different matter.

Until now, the availability of servants had made it easy for Katarina to disguise her weakness. She hadn't dared to admit this to anyone except her folks and Anna. Her parents had snorted at her confession, and Johann had told her to 'Get over it.' Only Anna was sympathetic.

Katarina could hear the voice of logic in her mind, but her queasy gut fought back. Why hadn't Alyona called someone else? Oh yes, two were in the laundry shack. And the others? Everyone was busy in the morning hours. David was involved with the construction of the new grain storage facility on the far side of the estate. He'd appropriated all the available able-bodied help. There was no one else on site. Katarina despaired. She should have insisted that Alyona run across the yard while Katarina waited with Anna. Would two minutes have made any difference?

Since Alyona hadn't yet called off the emergency and she'd used the words *no time to waste*, Katarina knew the situation was serious. "You don't have a choice, Katarina. Just do it. Anna needs your help," she scolded herself and grimaced as she stomped down the stairs. Another frigid gust of wind urged her to hurry before things got more desperate and she became colder.

She tightened the heavy wrap around her shoulders, took a deep breath, and blew it out through her mouth in a long, slow stream. "Alright Katarina. Don't be such a princess. Just take one step. Go. Come on. Don't be such a coward."

Her hand tightened on the railing. She dropped two more steps, then stopped and studied the barn again. If she went to the entrance and yelled loud enough, Olek would hear her. Where was he at this time of day? The tack room? She took another deep breath and exhaled with a long hiss, then lifted her skirt and stepped into the ankle-deep glop.

"This is for Anna. Just do it." She gritted her teeth. As the wet snow sloshed over her laced walking boots, an icy pellet melted over the tongue and dribbled to her instep. The freezing damp trigger woke her resolve. She shivered and picked up the pace.

Reaching the barn, she stood in front of the gabled door and touched the lower edge, pulling herself to the orifice. The familiar stench of horse sweat and manure permeated the air. She turned her head and took a deep breath of the less pungent breeze behind her, then twisted back and yelled with as much gusto as she could manage. "Olek. You are needed."

Clear, firm direction should carry the message. She placed her hand on the thumb latch and listened for a reply from the murky, malodorous belly. What was she waiting for? If the man was in the far end, he wouldn't hear her. Surely, she could walk into the barn like when she was younger. What was so hard about that? She should go to the tack room and ring the bell, rather than standing here freezing her feet.

Except ... she glimpsed into the filmy, dark cavity and shivered. The image of the black stallion galloped through her mind. She shook her head. That was such a long time ago. There was no danger here today. The mirage danced again. She pushed it away and chided herself. "Just open the door and go in. Do it." She tightened her grip, but her thumb refused to obey the simple command to press down. *Why can't I do this?*

A gust of wind whipped one corner of the shawl off her shoulders. A handful of straw dropped from the open hayloft door and dumped on her head. She swore under her breath, stepped back, and dusted herself off, rearranging the shawl to cover her hair.

Her nose tickled. Before she could rub it, a raucous sneeze exploded. "Achoo! Achoo! Achoo!" She caught her breath and searched for her hanky. "Good grief." Another sneeze escaped. "Achoo! Oh, for the love of ... horses. I hate you."

She wiped her nose and approached the door again, staring into the misty darkness of the chamber. Perhaps Olek didn't hear her the first time. *Call again, a little louder this time.* She opened her mouth, but her voice caught in her throat. She gagged on her words, coughed, and sputtered. *What's wrong with me?*

The clickity-clack of horse hooves across the cement floor moving in her direction told her she'd been heard. Light from the air vent reflected on the gray mare walking towards her, while a shadowy figure moved in the rear bay.

The tightness in her chest joined with a wheezing sound from her lungs. *This dank air will be the death of me.* She tried to shake away the memories of the black stallion and the Cossack rider, but the picture continued to surface. She replaced it with her sister's face. Then added a baby. She gulped. *We're having a baby. Anna needs me. I can't let her down.*

Olek still wasn't replying. He clearly didn't understand the urgency of her call. And she couldn't run away from this task. There was too much at stake.

She cleared her throat and tried again. "Olek. You are needed." Her voice sounded strangled and tired — as if she had been yelling for hours. She barely recognized it.

"*Da, ya idu.*" The stableman shuffled from behind a bay.

The seconds for the man to emerge after saying, 'Yes, I'm coming' felt like hours. Katarina stomped her feet and rubbed her hands, trying to keep warm in the damp cold. He waved and tied the mare to the crossties before walking to the door. Her lungs rebelled as she spat the message through a hoarse whisper. Talking threw her into another coughing fit. Her knees weakened and her legs shook. She gripped the frame of the lower door to keep from falling.

Concern resonated on Olek's round face as he watched and waited until she finished barking. "I'll get her. Go home. Get out of here before you drop dead on us."

Now oblivious to the cold and only aware of her challenged breathing and her racing heart, she nodded and turned to tramp back through the glop. Her legs shook beneath her as she strode towards the house. Despite there being no strength left to run, praise rose in her heart. While praying that she wouldn't collapse in the mud, she also thanked God for her personal triumph. She flopped on the stairs and waited for her racing heart to settle and her strength to return before running back to Anna's side.

Katarina stared across the muddy landscape and smiled at her success but wondered about her irrational fear and her intense physical reactions. Twenty months had passed since the attack on her parents' farm. All this time, she'd imagined the villains stalking her, waiting for her behind those dark doors. Even the horses held sinister intent. She'd avoided the barn at all costs, allowing her imagination to fuel her fear. Instead, only a cordial Russian — whose kind personality shone with trust and safety — greeted her there. It was almost like God himself had encouraged her to step out and embrace life again. But she needed to take the step towards healing.

Then she wondered about Alyona. Did she know about Katarina's fear after all? Perhaps she too, was acting on God's direction. In that moment, Katarina sensed that God could use anyone at any time to accomplish his plans.

"Fear is not from God," she whispered. "The Bible says, 'be strong and of good courage.' Today, I embraced courage. I was almost in the barn and it didn't kill me."

Her skin tingled and a new energy flowed through her body. Even though her voice was still hoarse and her throat tight, her lungs felt ... *clean*.

Katarina closed her eyes and marvelled at the word *courage*. The definition was facing and overcoming great fear. In her short life, she had never needed it. But now that she'd experienced it, the achievement was … exhilarating. She wanted to capture this feeling and save it in her bosom.

Maybe she could call it up when she was ready to get back on a horse. Riding was so much fun when she was little. She'd love to ride again — without being afraid. Maybe Anna could go with her one day — when she wanted to take a break from mothering. All mothers tire of their babies once in a while. They could leave the infant with a nursemaid and ride together as they did when they were children.

She pictured the two of them riding through the forested trails and along the riverbank, sharing a picnic lunch and skinny dipping in the swirling eddies. The war couldn't stop them from enjoying the simple pleasures. There was a new baby on the way. And Katarina had just birthed courage. Life was getting better, not worse. She had to believe that.

She leaned back against the stairs, inhaled deeply of the crisp, spring air, and let the warm sun toast her face. And silently celebrated her victory.

10

BABY MARGARETHA

SUMMER 1917 (THREE MONTHS LATER)

KATARINA WAS FURIOUS. THE CONDOLENCES FROM THE women were uncaring, insensitive, and just plain rude. Had they no shame? Couldn't they hear their own words? Whatever happened to the phrase 'Think before speaking?' They were all old enough to know better. She crossed her arms and hid her clenched fists under her armpits.

"I'm so sorry dear. I know it's hard, but there'll be other children." Maria Marten's comment drew a waterfall of tears from the grieving mother.

"My sympathies, dear Anna. This grief shall pass. Life goes on," said another.

"The next one will be stronger."

"The good Lord needed this child in heaven. It's all for the best."

Katarina wanted to slap Aganetha Janzen when she saw Anna's shoulders buckle forward and raise the handkerchief to her face. What possible good could come out of this?

"This sickness has taken young and old alike, Anna.

There was nothing you could do. You are not alone. Be thankful God gave her to you for three months."

"God bottles our tears and turns them into joy."

"Margaretha will always be with you. Embrace her memory."

Katarina narrowed her eyes and gritted her teeth. Butting into the conversation would only make things worse. However, when another of Anna's sisters-in-law uttered a similar condolence, she'd had enough. Searching the room, she spotted her mother standing beside the dessert table with a plate in hand. Katarina pushed her way through the small crowd.

She touched Lena's elbow and whispered into her ear, "Mama. These people are not helping. They're upsetting Anna with the mean things they're saying. She's beside herself with grief already. Why don't they leave well enough alone? They're making it worse. Can't you stop this?"

Lena Rempel stopped mid-bite and looked at the wall above Katarina's head. When she finished chewing, she pivoted to face her daughter. "Child, what are you complaining about? I thought you would have learned by now. Death is a part of life. None of us know how long we have on this Earth. Yes, we all miss this baby now. But we take comfort knowing God has everything under his control. He allowed this for a reason, and we must trust him."

Child. Two years ago, you called me a woman. Katarina felt her cheeks warm at the insult. She blinked away the brimming tears and swallowed. *Ignore it.* "But Mom, their sympathies are condescending and disrespectful."

"Katarina, listen. I know it's sad, but the reality is children die, and sometimes mothers do too ... and lately even fathers. We don't know why, but we must have faith ... accept this loss and move on."

Bile rose in her throat. Why couldn't her mother understand her feelings? She bit the corner of her lip and swallowed. "What are you saying? Just accept it, get over it, pretend like its nothing? Aren't we allowed to cry, to grieve? Does God want us to be cold and unfeeling?"

Lena chomped on the honey and cheese filled pastry. "Today we mourn. But such pain is temporary. We must not hold on when God says to let go." The gooey filling oozed onto her hand and she raised her palm and licked it off.

Katarina pointed to the women in the room. "If we have permission to mourn today, why are they talking to Anna as if she has no right to cry? It sounds like they're telling her to get over it."

"They mean well, child. They understand. They've either passed through the fire themselves or seen enough of it during their lifetime. They are trying to provide reassurance to Anna."

Again, with the child. "It doesn't feel very supportive." Katarina toyed with a sugar cookie.

"Anna's exhausted and very emotional now. She's been through a lot. When she has time to rest, she'll reflect and gain strength from the words."

"Are you saying she's overreacting? Her baby just died. Can there be any worse pain?"

"Losing a child is always hard and it's impossible to prepare for such a loss if you've never experienced it before. But it's a learning lesson. She'll be better equipped with the next one."

"Are you blaming Anna for Margaretha's death?" Katarina scowled. Lena was being far too flippant. And there was an unfamiliar emotion brimming in her mother's voice.

She tried to put a finger on it. What was it ... guilt? Was she feeling bad because she wasn't available to help Anna?

"No, of course not. I'm sure she did all she could. Babies get sick all the time. Unfortunately, some don't survive. If you weren't so busy with that job of yours, you could've helped her more. Then she wouldn't be so tired. With more rest, different decisions might've been made."

Katarina's eyes widened, and she raised her voice to a loud whisper, "So it's my fault?" She crossed her arms and glared at Lena. Now she understood her mother's reactions. She was projecting her own guilty feelings onto Katarina — turning it around — blaming her. Katarina squeezed her fists.

Lena popped the rest of the sweet pastry into her mouth and brushed the crumbs from her hands. "Katarina, part of the reason we agreed to let you live here was for you to help your sister, not selfishly parade your worldly ambitions. You are to learn how to be a suitable wife and mother and position yourself for potential marriage proposals. When we know our place, then life is ordered. We must be cautious to not cause hardship for others."

If Lena had slapped her across the face, it would have hurt less. Katarina raised the glass to her lips and gulped the water to swallow the lump forming in her throat. She wiped her mouth with the back of her hand and tried to steady her trembling chin. "Mom, I didn't create hardship for Anna. Margaretha's sickness was not my fault. Nor her death. None of this was my fault." Her voice rose to a controlled squeal.

A nearby trio stopped talking and turned to observe the confrontation.

"I know what's expected of me. But I'm only seventeen.

And if this is any sign of my future, I'm not interested in marriage or having babies."

"Now you're being dramatic, Katarina. Of course, you'll get married. Sometime in the next five years you'll be starting your own family. And just like your sisters, you'll be a good wife and mother." Lena pasted a stiff smile on her face and nodded to the gawkers. They turned away.

"Mom, I don't want to be like everyone else. And I don't want to live in the land of the Mennonites forever, either. I'm becoming a teacher so I can travel. I've told you that a million times."

"Settle down, Katarina. I'm not having this argument with you now. This is a funeral. Good grief, must I explain how to behave? Look around. Can't you learn anything by observing others?"

"The others? They seem like cold fish. Where is their heart, their compassion? Why are they here? To make themselves feel good? Or pretend they care? Or because it's expected — just the way we do things here in our corner of the world. No, Mom. Life must be more than duty." Katarina brushed away the tears slipping down her cheeks. *I hate funerals.*

Lena turned her back and began rearranging the dessert squares.

Katarina raised her voice. "Mom, I wish you would stop treating me like an invisible child. I'm not some flower that you can rearrange in a vase. I'm a human being, with thoughts and feelings —"

She sucked in her breath and took a step back as Lena twirled to face her. Her mother's eyes widened, and her jaw clenched, her mouth tightening into a white slash.

Be courageous, Katarina. Tell her how you really feel. She gulped. "Just like Margaretha was supposed to become.

Instead, she's dead and they ..." Katarina gestured to the room, "... they can't even say her name. They just call her *child* like she didn't matter. Well, she did. Even though she never said a word and the world didn't know her, she was still a real person. She made a difference to me ... and to Anna and David. She should've had a full life. Instead, she's gone — snuffed out like a candle. We barely got to know her. I was looking forward to playing with her, maybe even teaching her at school in a few years. Yes, I'm angry. You should be, too. You lost a granddaughter. I think everyone should be crying with Anna, not blaming her, or minimizing her loss. Instead, it feels like we're being told it's wrong to be sad. I'm hurting too, you know."

Lena placed both hands on her daughter's shoulders and looked her straight in the eye. "That's enough Katarina. What exactly do you want them to say? These women, including myself, understand the depth of this pain. Everyone is quite willing to listen and give advice. Anna only needs to ask. In time, she'll learn that crying won't make the grief go away. Besides, tears should be shed in private, not public. Anna can cry in her husband's arms at night. As for you, you need to be the strong sister. Next time it will be your turn. It's your job to provide her with sympathy and affection. Don't be crying in front of her. It won't help her." Lena squeezed Katarina's shoulders.

Katarina winced and tore her gaze away. "But it hurts so much," she sniffled as she palmed the tears dribbling down her chin.

Lena's eyes narrowed and her voice dropped to a stern whisper-shout, "You're hurt? This wasn't your child. You have no right to focus on your own feelings right now. This day belongs to Anna and David, not to you. Put your tears away. Stuff your feelings inside your blouse and go do something useful. You can't change the past. But you can make the best of today. Here." She shoved a bowl of sugar cubes at Katarina's chest and waved her hands in a backward motion. "Go fill the sugar bowls. Help pour coffee. See if the men want more cheese, meat, or buns. Go be useful. Help the situation. Stop whining about it."

Katarina grimaced, but accepted the dish as she jerked away. A sharp pain shot through her arm. "This is all so wrong. Life shouldn't be so cruel." *Old people die. Not babies.*

"A controlled life isn't cruel. It's predictable." Lena grabbed her by the shoulders, spun her around and pushed her towards the door. "And predictability is comfortable."

And therein lay Lena's answer to life, Katarina thought. If one lives by the Mennonite rules of order, chaos cannot reign. But what if it was the other way around? If war came to their doorstep, could the rules survive?

She looked at Anna sitting in her pretty floral lady's chair, fumbling with her teacup — her handkerchief tucked in her buttoned sleeve. She admitted that Anna was everything she wasn't. It was clear that their mother wanted Katarina to become more like Anna, but that would not happen. War or not, she would succeed in her dream.

Katarina wondered how her sister stayed so composed under the circumstances. She knew Anna well enough to know she was grappling with her personal battlefield, fighting both grief and fear. But Katarina questioned if denial and suppression were the right weapons to use. Do bad feelings dissipate if you wish them away or pretend that they don't exist?

Since Katarina didn't know the answers, she wiped the tears from her face with the back of her hand and swallowed the large lump in her throat. She'd take her mother's advice for now. But one thing was certain — she needed to learn how to stop Lena from pushing her buttons. Anna had figured this out. Katarina filed away a plan to ask for advice. Except not today. Today required obedience and silence.

Lena's chastisement burned in her stomach like a sour orange at Christmas. Seventeen marked the age of experience — mature enough to marry and start a family or become a schoolteacher; but, according to her mother, not wise enough to understand life.

"One day, I'll be old enough and smart enough that they'll come to me for advice," she vowed. She popped a sugar cube into her mouth and muttered under her breath as she squared her shoulders and stomped down the narrow hallway. "Life is so unfair. How can a baby's death be God's plan? Where is the justice?"

When Kiva, the scullery maid, brushed past her with her arms laden with dirty dishes, Katarina stopped her. "Can you take this in there?" she nodded towards the parlor.

"I would, but your mom is watching. And I have my hands full." The maid jerked her chin towards the food table.

Katarina rolled her eyes. "She wants me to parade around to find a suitor. I keep telling her I'm not interested."

"Sorry, Miss Katarina, I can't help you. Pretty flowers are easy on the eyes. But no one wants the bad smelling ones," Kiva winked.

"Thanks for the advice." Katarina frowned as she turned sideways to allow the tall servant to pass by. *She has the most amazing hair. Thick and puffy. It looks like a giant brown mushroom with the stem wrapped in braids. Nothing like my straight blond that flies all over the place. I bet it's easy to plait.*

She stood and pondered Kiva's parting comment, then grinned. "Aha! This straightlaced Mennonite girl needs to find a dark side. Got it."

She found her father engaged in a serious talk with an elder deacon and her brother Dietrich — who recently returned from the forestry service for a short leave. Judging by their posture, she reasoned that her father would neither want her listening nor interrupting. If she created a disturbance, he would dismiss her. This should be easy.

She scanned the smoke-filled room. After the tobacco farmers plied their wares on the captive audience, the place took on the ambience of a seedy hotel. Although Katarina had never set foot in such a place, she'd heard rumors about them. It wasn't surprising that the wives refused to enter. She didn't want to be here either. The sooty air tickled her throat and burned her eyes.

If I'm respectful and polite, I'll be running errands all day. If I'm noisy, they'll kick me out, she reasoned. She rustled her skirts behind the men's chairs then moved to the serving cart and slammed the crystal sugar bowl on the teak. She rearranged the spoons and clinked the glasses, pitchers and bottles. A few of the male guests looked over and gave her a dirty look. But her father ignored her. Her scheme wasn't working.

She studied the room, noticing the prevalence of crossed arms and grim expressions, then spotted the twenty-year-old son of her father's second cousin — the veterinarian from Vitebsk. His head rested against the back of the settee with his eyes closed, the long legs stretched out and hands folded over his lean muscular frame. *Is that ... Peter? What's he doing here? It's a three-day journey from Vitebsk. It can't be. Unless ... maybe David bought new horses and Peter delivered them.* She frowned and shrugged. If her mother's ideas included that boy, at least Katarina could honestly say he showed no interest in her.

She tapped her finger on the wooden stand. Regier had said to watch, listen, and learn. Put two and two together, he said. She wasn't exactly sure what that meant, but she wanted to. She tried to describe the atmosphere as he'd instructed — like a gray cloud on a snowy day, she determined. It was neither animated nor mournful like the women's room.

She scratched her head. There was something else going on. Turning her back to the small crowd, she shifted strategies and quietly straightened the buffet while watching the interaction out of the corner of her eye. Within seconds, the hum of conversation returned.

"Grain prices are up. They're trying to encourage production."

"That's good for us. But without strong labor, how are we supposed to bring in the harvest?"

"Mennonite ingenuity. We have machinery."

"The country expects us to feed them, but they want to expropriate our land and machinery. How can we fight this?"

"Resisters will be shot or sent to Siberia."

"They can divide up the land all they want. There aren't any savvy farmers among those peasants. The locals know we'll gladly pay rent. They want wages, not land." David swirled the dark liquid in his glass.

"As long as the government allows us to continue hiring. But they may not."

"We need to figure out a way to deal with the squatters. They refuse to move, claiming they're entitled to the land."

"Enough with the fear-mongering. These political threats will all go away with time. When the food runs out, people will scream for jobs," Johann drawled and wriggled his mustache. "Let's remember — we control the economy. Not those yahoos in Petrograd ... as much as they'd like to think so."

"We can find creative solutions to the land grab and hide the machinery. Our representatives will develop a legal recourse to all of this in time. But we still need workers. Should we hire the vagrants under the table?"

"That's asking for trouble with the authorities. They don't have the right papers."

"Soon we'll be left with only old men and women."

"The Kleinrussen women are strong like bulls. One can do the work of two men."

Katarina's eyes widened at the mayor of Hierschau's put-down. Was he really comparing the local women to animals?

"Yep. Saw that over at Koop's. They're good workers. Strong and steady."

"Just keep them away from the men. They're loose."

"Who, the men or the women?" A guffaw rippled around the room.

"Unger had to referee a couple of fresh ones last week. He penalized them a day's wages for their immoral behavior."

"Got to keep 'em under control."

Katarina felt her ears grow warm. She wished men would keep their tongues in check. The sunny window bench beside the closet in a private corner provided respite from hearing further obscene details. She plopped down before noticing the oven-like heat baking through the open window. As the sweat beaded on her forehead, she gritted her teeth and wiggled her ankles, trying to avoid the temptation to eavesdrop on the repugnant conversation.

Finally, she could bear it no longer. *Regier said use your eyes and keep your ears and mind open. People often know more than they realize they do.* She pressed her ear to the wall. *Time to practice my observation skills. Maybe they'll say something about that rebel situation in Tokmak.*

"Had another problem with one of those boys last week."

"How bad?"

"I caught him stealing eggs. I should've fired him on the spot then. Now I know why production is down. I suspected as much. I gave him a break and fined him a day's pay. One more chance, I said. That's it."

"You gave the thief a second chance? That's mighty Christian of you. I would never be that charitable."

"Well, I caught my stable boy fooling around behind the cows again. These characters are perverts."

A chorus of moans erupted.

"God have mercy on his soul. How did you handle it, Martin?"

"I thrashed him until he was face down with his nose in the manure pile. Then I picked him by the back of his shirt and threw him against the wall. Not on my watch, I said. After that, I threw him into the grain bin and let him stew there."

"Yikes, Martin. That's a bit much."

"I gave him a good kick in the pants. Believe me, he deserved a lot more punishment than that."

The room erupted in laughter.

"If he was one of us, he'd be confessing in front of the congregation, thrown out of the church, and shamed."

"Like the Unger boy in Rosenort."

"Yep. Whatever happened to him?"

"Oh, he left the colony completely. He knew he'd never be allowed to marry one of our women. I think he moved north to start his life over."

"Probably married some Kleinrussen."

"Yep. The consequences for sin are severe."

"This younger generation is hell-bent."

"Don't these boys understand what a woman is for?"

"Did he hurt the cow?"

The room burst out in laughter. "Hank, you're so gullible."

"Well ... If he hurt her, it could affect her ability to calve."

"True enough. But there's always hamburger."

"Tina knows how to make a good roast from tough meat."

"Beef sausage works too."

"Isn't it very dry?"

"No, mix it with the pork and a higher fat ratio. It gives a smooth flavor."

"Is he staying on?"

"No. I can't trust him. He can't be working with my animals after this. I got him a job sweeping floors in the factory."

"Good plan. He'll find himself a woman there."

"Those women are all loose, anyway. They're probably used to such deviant behavior."

"They do have brothels in the city. God forbid any of ours set foot in that place."

Another roar rose in the room. Katarina's hand shot to her mouth in disgust. These men treated their livestock with more respect than the women in their employ. Surely her father didn't think like this.

Johann usually ignored the female servants. Except for Katya. He was always polite to her. In fact, she'd seen them share a private joke on occasion. As for this household, David treated Alyona with great respect. But then, she'd been with the family for two decades. Katarina hadn't noticed his interaction with the others. Overall, she concluded that the men in both families abstained from bigotry against their female domestics. But evidently, this was not the case in other homes.

As for the local men — that was another subject entirely. She'd heard they could be as wild as untamed horses. Her father had warned his daughters to give them a wide berth.

"Don't speak to them unless you are giving them an order," he said. "Look straight ahead and never look them in the eye."

Are they as distrusting of us as we are of them? Is it us versus them and them versus us, or is there room for us and them? Katarina considered her own accusation of Dimitri's involvement in the raid. She had jumped to conclusions, having no facts or first-hand knowledge of him, then realized she'd never held a genuine conversation with the fieldhand during his entire eight-year tenure.

Regier had said, "Don't judge a book by its cover. Research and test all data." She hadn't done that with Dimitri. Her conscience pricked with a tiny bit of guilt. She brushed it aside as her mind wandered back to that day. What was the final outcome of the attack? She hadn't heard if they'd arrested the marauders; so, until they did, she wouldn't trust the beady-eyed man if she ever saw him again. She wondered about his whereabouts.

She turned her attention back to the present. After listening to the vulgarity further, Katarina decided the men were toying with each other. Even though their crude, other-deprecating humor sounded strange to outsiders, they were upstanding, reputable leaders. As her mother cautioned — when it came to the opposite sex, she needed to develop a thicker skin and stop being so sensitive.

Katarina guessed the men knew she was eavesdropping, and the sarcasm was a ruse to throw her off. She decided to walk back into the room and capture — as Regier would say — a bigger picture, hoping they would entertain her with details about that character Makhno's latest exploits.

She wiped the sweat off her brow, took a deep breath, and waltzed to the serving cart, pretending to take a quick inventory of the food before surveying the room. An air of tension now replaced the joking. J.T. Wiebe nodded at her and poked the man next to him with an elbow. Another cleared his throat. She suddenly felt conspicuous, as if she had interrupted something. Were the men reacting nervously because there was a more concerning topic on the agenda they considered too racy for her ears? *Is it the war or the local unrest, or both?*

She glanced at the settee and noticed Pastor Friesen jostle his shoulder against Peter, the son of the veterinarian from Vitebsk. The young man sat up and pulled in his long legs and looked directly at her.

Katarina ignored him and shifted her gaze to David sitting on the blue floral wing chair beside the bookcase. He thumbed the side of his drinking glass and stared at the floor with a somber expression on his face. Whether he was listening or ignoring Thiessen's babble about grain prices, she wasn't sure; but she sensed his heart wasn't in the conversation. She wondered if he was missing his baby, too. Tired of the game playing, Katarina slipped out through the servants' side panel.

Katarina reflected on the odd fact that she had never witnessed David shed a tear, but then neither had she seen her father or brothers crying. This caused her to wonder if death impacted men the same as it did women. She remembered Johann saying, 'There's no point in talking about something that's already done. We can't bring the dead back to life.' In the male world, life was about the church, grain prices, land ownership, and politics. Everything else was irrelevant.

The church emphasized the differences between men and women being God's design. If this was true, then there should be a disparity, she reasoned. *Maybe women have more tears than men because we're uniquely created.* However, according to Lena, crying accomplished nothing, so tears should be suppressed — which meant the adage 'strong women don't cry' was contradictory to the divine order. It was clear that not everything could be explained so simply.

She bit her lip, reflected on Lena's point, and agreed that crying didn't solve problems. *I must control my emotions, stay busy, and bury the tears.* But she couldn't stop them from flowing. She slipped into the closet, dropped to her knees, and sobbed. She then made herself a promise. Tonight, she would lie in bed and cry an entire bottle of tears and ask God to collect them and bring them to baby Margaretha to let her know she was loved.

After this, I'll never cry again, she vowed.

11

DAVID'S DILEMMA

SEPTEMBER 1917

THE HEAVY DRAPES WERE NO MATCH AGAINST THE sun's powerful rays. A golden finger poked through the thin slit between the panels and toyed with Katarina's face. She punched the pillow and pulled the covers over her head, arguing with the light until dreamland eluded her. Now wide awake, she lay buried under the luxurious silk comforter, contemplating her to-do list. During the week, she appreciated the quiet of an early morning before the busy workday began, but today was Saturday. She had wanted to sleep in.

She tossed the blanket aside, swung her feet over the edge of the bed, sat up, and rubbed her face. While musing over the past week's challenges and next week's tasks, she stretched and flexed her stiff arm.

Her day's priority was to organize her lesson plans and figure out a new strategy to teach odd young George Toews to read. The child's struggle to learn was puzzling. He read backwards and wrote his letters upside down. Since he could repeat oral assignments verbatim, the problem wasn't that the boy was stupid, but that he had an unusual learning style. His need for private tutoring stole valuable teaching time from other students. Katarina sighed as the complexity of the boy's disability became clear. The school board had no budget for educating such children, so the only solution was to expel him.

It wasn't a decision she wanted to make, but her instincts said he couldn't manage public school. He needed more attention than what she could give him. His parents would be disappointed. But they could consult with the Institution for Mental Handicaps, or the Deaf School. Both had teachers that catered to special needs. Katarina wasn't giving up on him. He had other options. The Mennonites believed in education for all. If his parents chose to place George in one of those boarding schools, he would still learn to read and write.

An early start would help her put those pieces together. She'd draft a letter to the school board and another to the parents to discuss with the headmaster on Monday. Although she felt sad about the boy's dilemma, there was no point in feeling guilty about something she couldn't control. Her options were rather limited.

After finishing this task, she would help Anna plan the autumn church functions. Slipping a silk dressing gown over her cotton nightgown, she padded down the stairs in her bare feet towards the kitchen, bypassing the squeaky boards near the dining room.

The sweet earthen smell of boiling prips[1] wafted down the hallway. She filled her lungs with the tantalizing scent, envisioning a decadent morning with a steaming cup snuggled up in her favorite chair and writing in her journal.

She stopped short of the threshold to the breakfast room

as the sound of muffled voices broke her fantasy. Who was making such a racket at this time of day? It was too early for breakfast and — if Alyona had a visitor — she couldn't greet a guest in her bedroom clothes. She cocked her ear.

"You served four years before we married. And you paid the extra tax. They can't demand you to go again. I won't allow it." Anna's shrill tone was evidence of a discussion that had turned into an argument. Most likely it had been going on for a while.

"It's war, Anna. I don't have a choice."

Katarina's eyes widened. The lovebirds were having a fight. At the crack of dawn? She frowned. Had David been conscripted? If so, it was no wonder Anna was distressed. How would they manage without him?

Who would oversee the estate? Surely not his eldest brother J.D. That man had as much business sense as a Christmas cracker. There was David's father, but he was too elderly to learn the new complex regulations. He could supervise the fieldwork, but Katarina doubted he could manage much else. David's other two brothers were serving at the forestry camp in Berdyansk with her brother Dietrich. There wasn't anyone else — except the older servants. And they were either locals or Russians. David would never leave management of the estate to one of them. There must be some mistake. The government wouldn't conscript the only capable man in the family. Maybe she'd misheard.

She put her ear to the door.

"But you have an estate to run, a family, and a household to feed."

"The rebels are threatening our lands, Anna. If we don't stop them, they'll send us to Siberia. We could lose everything. The situation is tenuous."

"Can't you buy them off? Do something?"

"It's not that simple. Besides, the wounded need help and I'm a trained paramedic. I'll be on the hospital train. I'll be fine."

There was no mistake. The man was leaving. Katarina sympathized with Anna's distress.

A tap-tapping on the plank flooring in the breakfast room penetrated the awkward silence. Katarina flexed her hands and flattened her back against the wall. A cock crowed. Then, a solid crack split the air, followed by a dull crunch and the familiar hollow clunk of wood on wood as it hit the stack. The smoky scent of the fire, mingled with the baking of yeasty sweet bread, wafted through the open windows. Alyona and her assistants were already hard at work in the outdoor stone kitchen. Katarina's mouth watered, her head pounded, and her stomach growled. She needed coffee.

As she leaned against the doorway, she wondered when, or if, she should announce her presence. If she walked in too soon, it could make things worse. Or it would shut down the argument — in which case she'd miss hearing such juicy secrets that only eavesdropping revealed.

Judging by the silence, Anna was probably standing dead center in the middle of the room with her arms crossed and her mouth clamped shut. One foot would be extended outside her skirts, her toe smacking the floor. Her eyes would be shooting ice daggers at David. He'd react by putting his back against the wall and crossing his arms. Predictably, Anna would then uncross her arms, tighten her white apron, and chew her bottom lip while she considered her next words.

Katarina knew this routine. She'd watched the newly-weds disagree a few times. And she'd experienced Anna's controlling and manipulative defiance on more than one occasion.

She listened to the slow and steady rhythmic beat of the taps on the plank flooring. Anna was thinking hard. Then the tapping stopped suddenly — mid-beat. Anna had found another pain point.

"But I'm with child. What if I have trouble again?"

Katarina's jaw dropped. She assumed Anna's pale pallor, constant fatigue and despondency were because of Margaretha's death — not another pregnancy. Her sister had only just recovered her strength. A pang of guilt hit Katarina as she realized she'd been too busy to notice. It made sense now.

"My darling, Anna," David's voice softened. "You have your sister and my family here ... and half a dozen servants catering to your every whim and wish. And Alyona takes good care of you. Kiva's willing to pitch in whenever you need her. She may want more money, but so what? I'm not abandoning you to the wolves. I'm making business arrangements for the estate, so you don't have to worry about that. You're a strong, independent woman — adept at running the women's mission committee and overseeing the house servants. Come now, don't be silly. You can manage without me for a few months. You'll get through this. If it's the baby you're worried about, write your mother a letter. Ask her to come for a visit, or Olek can take you there."

"Write?" Anna's voice rose another octave. "Write my mother a letter? Do you know what she'll do? She'll demand that Kat and I go home so she can take care of us. I will not leave my house." Her voice softened. "I mean our house."

Katarina took David's unintelligible murmur as her cue to enter. She gave a loud yawn and stretched her arms wide as she waltzed into the room.

"Oh, I'm so sorry." Katarina clutched her chest and stepped back, pretending shock at seeing the couple. "I didn't expect anyone else to be up this early." Ignoring Anna's stare, she looked around the small room before ambling to the samovar. "Where's Alyona? Is the coffee ready?" She tapped the steaming kettle. "Oh, good. It's hot."

Using her good arm, she retrieved a cup from the overhead shelf, examined it purposefully and pretended to wipe off a smudge. After filling it with the steaming prips, she lifted the cup to her mouth and blew across the hot surface, then turned and peered over the rim at the stony-faced pair as she sipped. Anna's cornflower blue eyes narrowed and twitched. Katarina returned her sister's stare with a bold one of her own until Anna's eyes flickered.

Katarina smirked and strutted to the table, set down her cup, and plopped into a chair. She then picked up the notebook lying on the inset shelf beside the table, cracked it open to a blank leaf, and scribbled.

"So ... what's going on?" She forced her tone to sound normal, then coughed to clear the giggle sitting in her throat. "You two don't normally have breakfast at first light." She fidgeted with the pencil and flipped the pages.

"We have important things to discuss, and I think you should leave." Anna's firm tone left no room for misinterpretation. It was not a request.

"*Oba, nay.* This sounds serious. I think I should stay," Katarina raised her cup with both hands and put her elbows on the table, then looked over at Anna with wide eyes and blinked in a deliberate and dramatic fashion. Anna's eyes flashed, and her chin flexed. She bit her lower lip, repositioned her hands to her hips, and drew in her shoe.

It was hard to take the petite and delicate woman seriously. Especially when she stood next to her towering giant of a husband who resembled more of a cleaned-up version of a tough lumberjack than a business owner. The husky gentleness of his voice was at odds with his intimating appearance — he barely drew breath when he spoke.

On the other hand, diminutive Anna looked like a little girl dressed in grown-up clothes, and today, this adult-child was having a temper tantrum. Katarina was surprised David didn't resort to spanking her. He could pick her up with one hand to do it.

David cleared his throat and put his hands in his pockets. His gaze drifted from Anna to Katarina and back to his wife. "It's all right, Anna. Your sister might as well know. We don't keep secrets in this family."

Anna sniffed and flared her nose, then pursed her lips and glared at Katarina. A sharp grating on the plank flooring was followed by rapid clicking sounds from under the long skirts. Katarina sipped her coffee and smirked, while Anna shook her head side to side as if to say, "How dare you interfere in my life."

Katarina stood her ground. Rattling her sister's cage was more fun than decoding mysteries. "Well?" She pushed the next button.

"David's going to war," Anna blurted as she stomped to the table and plopped into a chair.

"Ooh. I'm so sorry." Katarina stopped teasing as the pain of the moment dawned. "What will we do without you, brother?"

"Thanks for the vote of confidence, Kat. I realize you'll have your hands full, but things will sort themselves out. It's your sister I'm most worried about. She's not feeling well," David sighed.

Anna traced a pattern on the table. "He means I'm with child."

"Well, that's wonderful news!" Katarina raised her cup in a toast, "Congratulations." She did a quick calculation in her head. "David, will you be home for the expected birth?"

"Doubtful," David replied. "It's wartime, on more than one front. Russia is not only fighting Germany, she's also in political turmoil with herself. They've called on everyone of fighting age to contribute."

"I'm guessing running an estate is not a contribution?"

"Not a valid one — at least in their opinion. Despite the shortage of food and their pleas for grain, they're shipping all the good men to the front. I don't know how they expect us to feed the country without the labor to bring in the crops. On top of that, we have little protection from these hoodlums running rampant. They've taken to razing the fields, trying to pull us under. Half the German farmers have already been pushed out." David rubbed his neck. "I don't know how the colonies are going to defend themselves ... or how the country will feed itself. But I'm required to report for duty."

"This is ridiculous," Anna spouted. "You already served once. You shouldn't have to, again. Besides, we are Mennonites. We are supposed to have freedom from military service."

"Ah, dear sister, this is where you fail to grasp the intricacies of politics." Katarina leaned back in her chair.

"And just what do you know about this war? Have you been listening in on the men again?" Anna scrunched up her face.

Katarina wiggled her hands in the air in a pretense of horror. "Actually yes, dear sister. I make it my business to read the newspapers and eavesdrop on the latest gossip. Would you like to hear what I've learned?" She looked at David, "My dear brother, allow me to explain to your beautiful wife the incredible dilemma of the great Russian empire."

David raised an eyebrow and chortled, "Oh, please Katarina. I'm sure your elder sister would greatly benefit from your expansive worldly knowledge."

The man's sarcasm was deliberate. Katarina's eyebrows shot up and Anna's eyes widened. Anna clamped her lips between her teeth and folded her hands in her lap.

The woman was obedient, Katarina acknowledged, and David had a wicked way of putting her in her place. Even if she didn't agree with her husband's decisions, she would never defy him, at least not in front of others.

At the same time, Katarina realized the mockery was directed at her, too. She hesitated to continue. She could drop the subject at this point and let David think he knew it all. Or she could embrace the challenge and prove she was as smart as any man. She was tired of being dismissed as irrelevant and treated like an ignorant child. Her gut burned to rebel.

But what if she flaunted her political literacy and it was wrong? She admitted she didn't know it all. So, what if a few of her facts were off? David would correct her and then beat his chest, making her feel like a fool. After that, Anna would gaze star-struck at her intelligent hero. Not that there was anything wrong with the adoration between a married couple — Katarina just didn't want to be a third player in that game. And she didn't want to give David ammunition to confirm his opinion of her as a stupid woman. On top of that, if Anna laughed at her — she'd be humiliated.

But what if she was right? She'd be validated and earn their respect.

She weighed the risks, inhaled a deep breath, and blew it out with a long exhale through her mouth. *Go for it.* "Well

... all right, then. It's like this. The Austrian-Hungarian Archduke gets assassinated by a Serbian. Germany backs Austria and invades Serbia, but since Russia supports Serbia, we get dragged into protecting both our borders and those of our friends as well. Then other countries decide to attack us too, for some reasons that are not very clear.

"I think of it as when two bullies fight in a playground, and a third guy gets involved, and then the whole school-yard joins in. It's insane. Instead of sitting down over a cup of coffee and talking it out, these grown men decide one death justifies more killing."

"I know this story." Anna rolled her eyes. "It's been going on for three years, and the entire world is involved."

Now Anna wanted to shut her down. That would not happen. Katarina stiffened her back and raised both arms in the air. "Oh ... it gets better. A group of political yahoos in Petrograd decide the Czar is making all the wrong decisions and is no longer capable of managing the war or running the country, so they force him out. While he and his family are exiled to the palace in Siberia, a committee of men — who think they know how to make better decisions than the Czar — are dictating our side of the global chess game and oiling the machinery of everyday Russian life. I hear they've elected a leader now, but it's a very discordant situation — to say the least.

"Shall I go on?" Katarina looked at David for approval and then over at Anna who was paying more attention to her fingernails than to the conversation.

David raised his eyebrows and grinned. "Please do." He planted his back against the wall and folded his arms across his chest.

Again, she wavered, trying to read into David's words and body language. Was that respect or ridicule? She wasn't sure. The grin said he was enjoying her flamboyant description. A nervous flutter passed through her stomach as she second-guessed her data. Was she describing it correctly? She'd never discussed politics with a man before ... except her father, and she didn't think that counted.

She took a long swig of the now lukewarm prips and cleared her throat. "So ... while all this chaos is going on, the Bolsheviks and the other Soviet political parties capitalize on the confusion, throw the government into disarray, and encourage people to rebel and workers to strike. There's not enough food or fuel to feed the country. To top it off, the army complains of a shortage of ammunition and weaponry."

"Well, they should quit then." Anna leaned into the conversation.

"It's not that easy."

"Seems easy enough to me."

Encouraged by Anna's shift, Katarina's keenness returned. "One. They don't want Germany to win the war. Two. They need a scapegoat for their financial woes. Three. These new parties want to change the balance of power by manipulating the working class to rise against the old guard and the land wealthy — like us. They consider us kulaks — greedy, arrogant, and undeserving peasants. We give them jobs, for crying out loud. But it's not good enough. Now the Soviet says we don't deserve to have so much. We must share the wealth with everyone else. So, some cornstalk who hasn't worked a day in their life gets to farm our land. That makes no sense to me."

"Nor me," Anna echoed.

"On top of that, the Soviet looks at us with the evil eye and accuses us of being in bed with the enemy because of our Germanness. The fact that we're Mennonites with no interest in colonizing a nation seems irrelevant. Because we came from Prussia, our loyalty is questioned. This, they claim, is why there are food shortages in the county. How this computes in their heads is beyond me."

David interjected. "I agree, Katarina. One reason for the food shortages is because there's not enough labor on the farms to harvest the crops. The military needs to eat, but those very same men who were in the fields two years ago are now carrying guns and dying on the front lines, and many have already died."

"Exactly. Our German background has nothing to do with it. But they accuse us of hoarding grain. The shortages are our fault, they say."

"Well, I suppose I should reframe that," David said as he stroked his beard. "We did hold back for a while when the prices were too low. But they're back up now. Unfortunately, we have no more grain to sell."

"*Ja.* But even their inspectors don't believe us. To prove otherwise, only our joining the military action will convince them of our loyalty. Sadly, this causes religious conflict in our communities and pressures our men to struggle with their conscience about violating their vows to God." Katarina flexed her fists. "The more I think about this, the more it upsets me ... it's clear to me that these politicians want total control of the economy. They believe they can run the farms and businesses better than a private citizen. Imagine what will happen if they succeed in this insanity." Katarina wanted to throw her cup across the room.

"Yes, I'm aware of all this. It's affecting all the colonies." Anna frowned.

"*Ja.* Well ... while the world and the motherland are sorting themselves out, we have this growing local problem. This character from Tokmak, Makhnovsky and his cohorts, are taking advantage of the political vacuum, adding their own spin to the chaos."

"Where do you think he fits in?"

"According to Mr. Regier's sources, he's not aligned with anyone. He's got his own little circle, pushing his personal ideas for an independent Ukraine —although how this is supposed to work isn't clear. I've read part of his manifesto, but it's confusing. The man's a bit nuts, if you ask me."

"The women were discussing this at sewing circle. He's a nobody with a criminal record and he's raising feathers all over the region. How is he amassing support? Is he connected to the armed bands in Galicia and those in the north?" Anna's brows knit together in a frown.

Katarina relaxed. Both Anna and David were listening to her ... talking politics. She was both pleased and amazed. "That I don't know. And I'm not clear on the connection to the national problem. It's true the Ukrainians seek independence, but each group has their own ideas. For example, what would a free country look like? Will we continue to depend on Russia? And then ... you're right about Makhno. Where and how does he fit into this scope? It's yet to be seen. His reputation as an instigator goes back to his childhood. We can only pray he'll be arrested before he causes too much trouble. I'm wondering why he isn't fighting in the larger war. His ability to get so many local supporters is mind boggling. Regier says most of his admirers are youths and defectors — men as young as, and even younger, than me — if you can believe it."

"Ladies, this man is scary. His gangs are robbing both the wealthy Germans and the Mennonites, attacking the farms and wagons in broad daylight. This estate is in his sights, I guarantee it. You'll need protection while I'm gone." David shuffled to the samovar and poured a second cup. "But don't worry. I've put Olek in charge. He'll hire the right people. He knows who can be trusted. You'll be safe with him."

Katarina chewed her lip. She'd heard the genial, old stableman was educated, although she knew little else about him. His articulate speech and multi-lingual abilities led her to suspect he was overqualified for his current position. If David trusted him to oversee the estate, then evidently Olek had other skills.

"Olek?" Anna asked. "Is there no one else? He's Russian. What if he turns on us?"

David winked at his wife. "Never. His loyalty is beyond reproach. Trust me."

It dawned on Katarina that David had considered the implications of his absence. She guessed he'd already talked to his family and the hired help before presenting the problem to his wife. Anna didn't realize that she was the last to know — not the first. At least he wasn't leaving them to the wiles of Makhno.

"How do you know Olek won't join up with this separatist nonsense? Can he protect us from this Makhnovsky character?" Anna's brows wrinkled and she pulled at her hair.

"Anna, please trust my judgement. There are other servants I'm concerned about. But not Olek."

Katarina interjected, "I hope you're right, David. The locals herald Makhno like a god with his vision for a new Ukraine. But why terrorize us? Does he see our Prussian ancestry as a threat to his political goals, or is it our support of the Imperial government that he doesn't like? Or is this all about money?"

"Greed blinds the eyes, Katarina. The locals don't see

how we can help them in their endeavors without violence. We could resolve all this craziness with negotiation. People don't need to die for an ideal." David put his cup down on the table and stretched his arms. "I agree with you. It's lunacy."

"I don't like the sound of all this." Anna pushed back her chair and crossed her arms and legs. "I may know nothing about politics, but I know this: freedom isn't free if you need violence to achieve it."

Katarina nodded. "Exactly. We know that. The Bible commands us to seek non-violent solutions, and to be forgiving and merciful. We're supposed to take care of the less fortunate, but we don't have to give up everything we own to do it. We should give people a second chance when they mess up and try to understand their motives, not judge them by their actions. If everyone lived like this, the world would be a better place."

Anna shook a finger in the air and nodded. "That's right, Kat. Russia has seen how we live. They know we're a peaceful people, model subjects of the Czar. We've always paid our taxes and co-operated with the Imperial governments. We negotiate our differences and appeal for understanding. At the same time, I know we're not living in the 1700s anymore and the Soviet is slowly ripping apart Czarina Catherine's agreement with us. Their demand for service under the current conditions is understandable. Thousands are dying. I get all that." Anna's tone shifted, and her expression softened.

"I just don't understand why — after David did his required four years as a medic in the forestry service — now they're demanding his return, but this time on the front lines — which is far more dangerous than Berdyansk. He paid extra taxes so he wouldn't have to serve again. But it's not good enough for them ... and I'm not comfortable with David working so close to the war front. He could be shot. Then what happens to me? Am I going to be a widow before I'm twenty-one? David, what will you do if you're ordered to use a gun? If you don't obey, you'll be labeled as a traitor."

David sighed, "I can't predict what will happen, Anna. These things are not in my control. I trust God will place a hedge of protection around me and I won't have to make that decision."

"Well, I doubt there's any room for conscientious objections on the front lines. Your superiors must know that our church believes that all killing is murder — even if it's in defence of life. You can't be placed in a compromising position. God gives life and only He can take it away. War goes against everything we believe in. Killing is murder, plain and simple ... what does the church say, David? We must resist. What are the church leaders doing about this?"

"I agree it's a dilemma, Anna. But David will be treated as a traitor if he refuses. This is a quandary for the church to figure out." Katarina clicked her fingernails against the side of the cup.

"Ladies, I think it's important to point out the church agreed to these alternatives during the last regime. The government is holding us to task. Each man must contribute. I can't buy my way out this time." David clasped his hands behind his back. "Anna, you're right. There are no guarantees I'll come home. War is an unpredictable animal. Being at the wrong place at the wrong time is a calculated risk."

Anna smacked the table. "Well, I think the colonies should decide who stays and who goes, not the government. Forcing every man to take part in war sounds like they are holding a gun to our heads. Plus, it violates the original agreements between the Mennonites and Russia. We're a self-governing people, separate and distinct from the masses. We shouldn't be involved in a global problem. They're dismissing our faith and chipping away at our rights. We as a people — the entire colonies — should protest."

Katarina cringed at Anna's vehemence, although she, too, was disturbed by the attack on their freedom and hoped the church could reason with the new government. Whether it was possible remained to be seen. The chaos in Petrograd was too confusing for anyone to know anything for certain. And the small Mennonite population lacked the political power to be heard over the din. Reason needed to prevail. Katarina could see that Anna's emotions were a twisted mess and she was grasping at straws to convince David to ignore the call to service.

She tried to explain it another way. "Anna, maybe the new government doesn't have a choice. Desperate times call for desperate measures. Regier said the Czar made many poor decisions with the world war. This new leader Kerensky searches for answers in ideological thorny bushes while the war with Germany rages on. The die is cast, and the caucus is split. The country's falling apart. The bread lines grow, and citizens are taking to the streets with swords and bullets. Innocents are murdered. The political division pits neighbor against neighbor, son against fathers. Neutrality is gone from reason. Everyone must choose a side. God help those who choose the wrong one."

"Exactly right, Katarina." David nodded. "Anyone who defects to the anti-government rebels are traitors. But the Bolsheviks will kill anyone defending the government. It's hard to know where to stand. There are factions for and against both sides and others for neither. And I'm sick about this local craziness. Makhno's gangs are fueling terror for the sheer thrill of it. There are rumors they'll kill anyone who doesn't support them or agree to hand over their property or money. As for the world war — it will sort itself out. It can't go on much longer."

Katarina pushed away from the table, strode over to the simmering samovar, and refilled her cup. "The country is imploding while every law-abiding citizen is being pulled in different directions."

David strode to the table and put his hand on Anna's shoulder. "My dear sweet, please understand. The government must get this situation under control. If I don't go, they'll brand me a traitor. Then we will have to run for our lives. As a Mennonite, I can't kill, but I can help in other ways. Their request is reasonable and I'm not violating my conscience."

"If the rebels find you in a government uniform, you'll still be shot." Anna hung her head and traced a pattern on the table.

"If this Makhnovsky is building his own Ukraine alliance, he won't care which uniform David's wearing. If his motive is money or revenge, he'll kill either way," Katarina added.

The room fell silent. David wandered over to the alcove, his hands hooked in his pants pockets. Katarina sipped her prips and contemplated the crisis. The confusing politics were frightening, but David didn't have a choice.

She sensed David felt guilty about leaving, especially in Anna's condition. For him to have peace, he needed his wife's approval. The discussion had helped them to better understand the complicated circumstances. Yes, there were risks to David's new job. He could come home without his arms or legs, or worse. She prayed it wouldn't come to that.

Regardless, the matter needed settling. The problem was obvious. Both David and Anna wanted reassurance. But this wouldn't happen unless ... unless she stepped in to be the peacemaker. That was risky. She could make the situation worse. They could both turn on her. Anna had an unpredictable temper, and she could be at the tipping point now — if she hadn't already blown up earlier – before Katarina walked in the room. Then what could she expect from David? She'd never seen him get angry, but she didn't want to, either.

Watching Anna sulk behind an untied messy blonde veil, her long fingers writing invisible letters on the dark oak, Katarina guessed her sister was now using the weapon of silence to build a wall ... or maybe she was just thinking ... or she was about to explode. Either way, it wasn't good.

As for David ... he felt torn. He wanted validation for his decision to serve; but Anna clawed him back. She needed his emotional support during — what she feared was — a precarious pregnancy in a worrisome political climate. Both sides had their points. The undertaking carried unknown dangers and there was no escape plan. David had little choice — unless he fled the country. But if he did, they would all have to leave. And how would that work?

Katarina rubbed her face. There were too many ifs, ands, and buts. Too many questions and too few answers. It was impossible to make rational decisions when the entire world was in disarray. All needed to trust that God's will would be done — regardless of what that meant.

She appealed to logic. "Look at it this way Anna. Our men are honest, loyal, and hard-working. The sooner this fight gets settled, the better. But unless someone on the battlefield brings the wounded to safety, more senseless deaths will happen. Too many have died already. The church is grappling with the growing number of widows and orphans. This can't go on. We need to do something. If we must sacrifice to end this, then so be it. Think of it this way — David isn't killing, he's helping the injured. God forbid, but if war comes to our home, we may need to do the same."

"*Eich*. God forbid." Anna brushed the hair away from her face, revealing reddened eyes and a frightened but somber expression. "David, is that possible ... might the war come here — to our home?"

"Yes." David rubbed his lips together, his voice grave. "It is definitely a possibility."

Anna's face paled and her eyes widened. She looked away.

Katarina looked over at David. "So, when do you leave?"

"Tomorrow, on the morning train."

"*Oba*. So soon," Katarina picked up the pencil and tapped the table. The government's new mandatory policy meant negotiation was impossible. If money could purchase delays, David would have done so. Katarina knew David didn't need their support, but he wanted it. As the head of the household, he was entitled to respect. As Anna's husband, he expected obedience. He had made his decision, and it was final. The women needed to accept it.

Katarina controlled the quaver in her voice. "David don't worry about us. Russia has called you to serve. God be with you. We'll figure out the details. We're not alone. That's a powerful thing about us Mennonites — we help each other. Between your brother Johann, your Dad, and Olek's supervision, the estate will be fine. And as for us, we have Alyona and the other servants. No one has abandoned us yet. Besides, there are other families in the same predicament."

Katarina could feel her heart racing as she tried to lighten the tension in the room. *At least, I hope we'll be fine.* "We'll sort it out. Anna's great at forming committees. Our parents will drive out when they have time. Mom will come to check on Anna's condition. Don't worry about anything. You go save the country. We'll be here when you get back. And. We. Will. Be. Fine."

Anna's mouth dropped open and her eyebrows shot up. Katarina turned her palms up in a silent question mark. Were there any untruths to anything she said? Anna closed her mouth, shook her head, and looked down.

Katarina hoped David wouldn't take offense to her tone. She wanted to ease his guilt, not add to it.

His response was unpredictable. "Katarina, you don't know this, but my father's not well. He may not survive until I'm back."

That's why he's not recovering from that flu bug. It's serious. "David, I'm so sorry. I had no idea."

"Thank you. I'm sure you can appreciate this makes it doubly hard to leave right now and I wouldn't if I had a choice. But nonetheless, I must ... and I appreciate your understanding. I'm thankful you're here to help Anna. I hate leaving both of you all alone like this ... this situation tears me up inside." David's voice cracked. A single tear slipped down his cheek. He pulled out his handkerchief and blew his nose.

Katarina picked up her cup, but the prips had grown cold and bitter. *We'll be all right, won't we?* For the first time, Katarina sensed the game of war was not child's play.

It was possible that David might never return. She feared for Anna.

---

1. Prips: a beverage like coffee made from roasted grain and used as a replacement for coffee when the latter was not available. It was sometimes referred to as coffee.

THE DOG'S BREAKFAST

EARLY OCTOBER 1917

"I THINK I'LL TAKE UP RIDING AGAIN. WHAT DO YOU think?" Katarina paced around the room in her bare feet. The constant clicking from Anna's knitting needles was driving her crazy.

"You haven't been on a horse in over two years. Besides, you're allergic. Why would you want to?"

"I wasn't always allergic. I managed fine when I was younger. We both rode then."

"We were little girls, then. Now we're women. It's not proper for us."

"Ridiculous. I'll talk to Olek. He can help me get back on the horse."

"You will not. I won't risk you having an allergic reaction or cracking your head again. I need you by my side. I'm an abandoned wife with a baby on the way." Anna continued knitting.

Abandoned? Katarina exhaled loudly through her

mouth, "Fine. In that case, I'm going for a swim. It's a hundred degrees in here. I'm dying."

Anna looked up; her brows furrowed. "What? What are you, a child? Don't be silly. It's October. The water is cold by now. Use some sense." She clicked her needles together. "And it's not a hundred degrees. Stop exaggerating."

"Well, it's hot enough that I'm sweating. And the stony pool under the bridge is rarely cold. I'll hang my feet in before I jump. If it's freezing, I won't take my clothes off."

"The leaves are falling. Someone could see you."

"There's no one around. Come with me. Let's have some fun. We could pretend to be little girls again. I'll let you push me in the water," Katarina joked.

Anna sighed and put down her knitting. "Kat, I know you're bored, but please find something else to do. Mature women shouldn't engage in such childish sports. Besides, I will not risk walking down to the river in my condition. It's not safe."

"Then I'll go alone." Katarina threw the towel in the air, pirouetted, then hooked it before it landed.

Anna rolled her eyes. "Oh, no you're not. There're too many scary vagrants passing through. They congregate on the riverbanks, squat on the fields, and rummage through the sheds. They could be sneaking around the yard for all we know. Olek says we need to be vigilant. He's caught the field masters sleeping on the job. We can't let down our guard."

"I'll be careful."

"Oh, you're so rebellious. Honestly, Katarina you have no sense ... all right. If I can't talk you out of it, take someone with you."

"Who?"

"Take ... what's her name? That one with the mousey

brown hair that looks like you from behind. I can spare her for an hour or two."

"Mousey? Do you mean Kiva with the puffy hair?" Katarina furrowed her brows. "She looks nothing like me."

"Yes. Kiva. That's her name. The tall one. Alyona's helper."

"Taller than you, I suppose. Not that tall. I don't see the resemblance, but whatever. I'll take her with me. If you insist."

"I do insist. By the way — keep an eye out for the sheep dog. Olek says he hasn't seen him anywhere." Anna pulled a strand from the ball of wool and clicked the needles.

"Do you mean Mopsy? Did the wolves get him?"

"Oh, yes. I suppose he meant that one. As for wolves — it's still too warm for them. Unless it was a rabid one. And the pens are intact."

"He's probably sick and hiding somewhere after eating too much fat when we rendered the pigs. He ate the trimmings."

"Uh, uh. He's old and a bit crazy. Not to worry. Olek's training the new pup." Anna yawned.

"He'll come running when I splash around."

"I'm sure he will."

Katarina kicked at the dusty ruts and glanced over her shoulder at the scullery maid trailing behind her. "Where're you from, Kiva?"

"Me? I live in Petrovka with my husband." The woman picked up the pace and drew closer.

"Does he work at the factory?"

"Yes."

Kiva's abrupt answers were annoying and Katarina's attempts at pleasant conversation were failing miserably. During the servant's daily interaction with Alyona, she was quick-witted and talkative. But Katarina had never been alone with her before, at least not like this. She wracked her brain for a good topic. The woman was a local. Perhaps she had insight into the recent uprisings. "Do you know Makhno?"

"I know of him. Everyone does."

"I heard he's a trouble-maker."

"He has ideas to free Ukraine from Russia."

"I see. Are they good ideas?"

Kiva shrugged, "I don't know." The maid's pace slowed as she shifted the picnic basket to her other arm.

Katarina sensed more resistance. She changed subjects, "So ... what's it like in Petrovka? I've never been."

Kiva snorted, "We live, we work, we sleep. Like everyone else."

"Do you have roses in your gardens? I like roses, corn-flowers, and sunflowers. I'm sad when summer is over and they fade into nothing."

"We don't have time for such things. In our free time, we celebrate with friends and families."

Katarina frowned. "We do that, too. And we enjoy our gardens."

"We don't have servants to take care of our homes. We take care of your homes, then we go home and take care of ours. You Germans think everyone has servants."

Katarina clenched her fists. She wanted to slap the maid's face. Anna would never tolerate such disrespect. However, discipline would only increase the animosity and make for an uncomfortable afternoon. She wanted to enjoy a peaceful walk and a blissful hour under the golden autumn sun by the water. A dignified rebuttal would put the maid in her place. "We're Mennonites, not Germans."

"It's all the same to us."

Katarina grimaced. There was obvious resentment in the cold tone. Had she offended Kiva? She'd always made an effort to get along with the help, but it wasn't working this time. She bit her lip. Maybe the woman hadn't slept well. That thin mattress under the kitchen table couldn't be very comfortable. Then again, not seeing one's family for the better part of the week would be tough for anyone.

Katarina wondered about the servant's family. Where was Petrovka? Would Anna be upset if she asked Olek to take her for a drive to see it? She shook her head. That would invite gossip from the sewing circle.

Her father's words flashed through her mind, "Don't make friends with them." She squared her shoulders. As much as she wanted to be liked by everyone, it wasn't proper to defer to the servants. Friendship was not a requirement of the job, but rudeness wasn't tolerated. She'd report the behavior to Anna later.

They traipsed past the grain bins and the machinery barns without speaking further and took the left fork into the tree plantation, past the neat airy lines of fruit trees, turned right by the walnut and chestnut groves, and meandered into the deep, structured rows of coniferous and evergreen trees.

The lush emerald forest of summer was morphing into veils of rusty tentacles draping into a spooky comb of shriveled brown fingers and a dry, warty bottom. She shivered at the thought of the upcoming long, chilly nights.

Her mind drifted to the war and the soldiers' requests for warm clothing. The women's charities concerned themselves with such things. Soon, they'd pack up holiday gift boxes for the men filled with cakes and dried sausages, knitted gloves and woolen socks, and other life-preserving necessities. An encouraging letter would be slipped into each box before it was loaded into wooden crates and shipped to the front by rail. She looked forward to taking part in the seasonal brigade.

Katarina wondered if David would be home for Christmas. Or Dietrich. If she and Anna went home ... no. That wouldn't happen. If Anna refused to walk on a beautiful day like today, she certainly wouldn't go on a trip to the other side of the river during bitter frost. It was going to be a long, boring winter.

She pictured the snow drifting over the evergreens and considered the seasonal change, then looked over her shoulder at the servant sauntering three paces behind her. "Hey Kiva, do you celebrate Christmas?"

"Of course. In January, like all Orthodox."

"Do you believe in Jesus, too?"

"Yes. We have the true religion."

True? "You mean, Christian — like us?"

"No ... I don't know. The Orthodox church says they are the true church. Started by Apostle Andrew." Kiva shrugged. "I suppose we all believe in the same God."

Is it the same God? We think our church is the correct one, too. Can both be right or is one wrong? That Russian leader wants to ban all religion. Does she know anything about politics? "Lenin says there is no God."

"Who? That communist leader? Oh. He can say what he wants. I don't care about his ideas."

So, Kiva knew who Lenin was. And she knew Makhno. How educated was the woman? Katarina probed, "He has many strange convictions. Do you think he'll change Russia?"

"Anything is better than what we have now. The people are tired of being slaves to the Czar."

Anything is better? Katarina wondered what was so bad about the Czar. The Mennonites appreciated the strict values of the old guard and they were aiding in the battle to restore old Russia. Was the system so unfair to the locals?

They turned the corner and exited the plantation along the western river trail. Katarina filled her lungs with the musty autumn air — the mixing smells of decomposing foliage and freshwater triggering memories of the earthy scent of her father's arms after a hard day's work on the fields. Recalling the innocent times in the pristine world of yesteryear caused her to sniff again to spark another child-hood image. Instead, a stinky whiff caught her nose, and the daydream screeched to a halt. Vagrants, she guessed. Rotting garbage on the riverbanks. She shuddered and prayed they were alone.

The lure of the sparkling river pulled them to the familiar bathing spot beyond the wooden bridge. Sunlight danced, embracing the water with a shimmering hug. The liquid stream answered with a faint mist rising from its rippling surface. Hidden beneath lay a hard-packed shallow sandy bar encircled by a stony ridge. The current swirled around it, creating a warm, natural pool — the perfect place to fantasize and wish the world away.

Katarina contemplated stripping down to her drawers to sit on the mound, or rolling her skirt up above the knees and wading in. A soft, cool breeze wafting across the water suggested testing the temperature with her feet. She plopped down on the bank to remove her shoes, gazing dream-like at the gurgling body with the remnants of summer floating along the surface, "Where do you go, river? How I wish I could go with you."

Katarina turned to invite Kiva to join her, but noticed the maid standing rigid with her hands clutching her chest and staring into the tall grasses on the bank.

"Kiva, what's wrong? You're as white as a ghost."

Kiva's mouth trembled. She shook her head and pointed to the marshy grasses under the bridge. "There."

"What is it?" Katarina crawled up the stony ledge and ran over to the maid.

The charred remnants of a fire and scattered animal bones at the edge of the stream suggested a recent resting spot for undesirable guests. She looked up into the bulrushes and swampy pit where Kiva pointed. Her eyes followed the trail of trampled grasses to a fetid, furry heap. A chill ran down her spine and her hand flew up to her mouth. "Dog ..." Katarina held her breath as she tiptoed around the fire pit. "It's Mopsy ..."

Kiva shadowed and touched her elbow. "Your sheep dog ... are you sure?"

Gagging on the pungent smell, Katarina removed her headscarf and tied it around her mouth and nose; she crept closer to inspect the bloated dome, "Black and white. The flies are buzzing. It must be days old."

"Look. There's a piece of wood with writing on it." Kiva pointed beside the carcass. "Be careful," she added as Katarina stepped into the brown river grass, "Snakes are still awake."

Snakes and what else? Katarina inched forward, bending each marshy blade with her foot. A river rat zipped out in front. She hesitated and scanned her surroundings. How did the dog die? Could it be that infamous rebel trying to make a name for himself? Anna said to watch out for bandits.

Her arms prickled with goosebumps and her knees

quaked as she crept down the bloodied trail. The rotting mass with a gash across the neck carried a deliberate message. The Cyrillic lettered board lying beside the animal left no room for misinterpretation. *Go home, Kulak. Next time it won't be the dog.* Katarina bit her lip to fight the brimming tears as she picked up the sign. "Kiva, we have to bring this home. Can you bring it to Olek, please? I'll tell Anna."

The maid accepted the board from Katarina's shaking hands and examined the lettering — tracing the patterns with her fingers. The color fell from her face as she looked up. "Miss Katarina, I am so sorry. It is no one I know."

The maid could read, but not well, Katarina noted. She swallowed the lump in her throat and jerked her chin towards the trail. "Let's go home."

The last swim of the year forgotten, the women grabbed their supplies and hiked back. The late afternoon sun flickered through the gloomy canopy and carved sinister outlines through the deep woods. Katarina kept a watchful eye along the forested path, her stomach in knots. "Kiva, why? You must know why."

"It's a warning."

"This is no caution sign, Kiva. They're threatening our lives. I want to know why. Why do they want us to leave? We have nothing to do with the war. Haven't we proven ourselves after a hundred years? We're a peaceful people and we've faithfully served Russia. We bear no grudges, and we try to get along with everyone. What are we doing wrong?"

"Your German ties make you an enemy." Kiva's voice was cold and emotionless.

Katarina searched for an explanation. "But we're not German. Speaking the language doesn't make us warmongers. It's the language of our ancestors. They came from Prussia."

Kiva scoffed. "You don't act like Russian. You keep your German ways and your precious churches — bullying our people like rich aristocrats and insisting on your own languages and your own schools. You don't try to become like us. And you steal our land."

Katarina stumbled on a rock. Neither the scorn nor the attitude made sense. "Steal your land? What do you mean? Catherine the Great gave us land and asked us to farm the steppes. We didn't steal it."

"Miss Katarina, have you ever been to one of our villages?"

"No, I can't say that I have."

"You should come and see. We don't live like you — your pretty little rows of perfect boxes with drawn lines around a piece of dirt that you buy and sell like expensive shoes covered in ribbons and colored jewels."

Katarina wrinkled her brow. "What does land have to do with any of this?"

"We have a saying here. God is our Father. The land is our mother. And nature is our teacher. Land is an eternal gift from the creator. It is a treasure to be shared, not owned and traded like a commodity. You Germans would sell your own mothers for land. You have no respect for the sacred." Kiva gestured to the trees with an upturned palm.

Katarina's mouth gaped. "The land is your mother? What kind of nonsense is that? Do you worship creation? I think you should talk to your priests. I doubt any Christian church teaches that. It's not Biblical."

Kiva rolled her eyes. "That's not what I meant. We honor the land the way God commands. Each person uses what they need."

"We take care of the land, too. God gave it to us to produce food so the world can eat," Katarina protested. Kiva's logic was confusing.

"To feed ourselves and our families, yes. However, when one has too much land, one needs help to take care of it. Like the greedy Czar, one falls into temptation to make slaves of the workers."

Katarina pondered the maid's statement. "Yes ... it's true that responsibility increases with ownership. But God requires us to be productive and to increase our wealth so we can help those who cannot help themselves. Besides, anyone can own land if they work hard enough."

"Own land? We already own the land. It belongs to us. All of it. You have no right to it. That's my point."

"But we provide work for you. We pay well. We developed the steppes and constructed the factories. Without us, you wouldn't have jobs or money."

"Jobs?" Kiva snorted, "Money? My dear Miss Katarina, I scrub your floors, and toilets, wash your clothes and decorate your tables with roses from your fancy gardens so you and your sisters can parade as ladies of leisure — knitting socks and organizing your committees — trying to justify yourselves when you serve the poor with a bowl of soup. Every night I go to bed on a thin mattress on a cold stone floor — with my knees bleeding and my hands cut — all for a loaf of bread. On my free days, I scrub my own floors, wash my husband's dirty factory clothes that stink of petrol, help him scour the grease from his aching body, check my children's teeth, and cook a good meal. I see my family two times a week. I'm thirty-five years old; my joints hurt, and my fingers can no longer hold a needle and thread. Now you tell me how I can work harder."

Katarina tripped over a root sticking up from the ground

and her bad arm flailed for support. The quick movement pinched. She bit her lip, steadied herself on a low-hanging branch and grasped for an answer to the verbal assault. *She talks as if we treat her like a slave.* "I'm sorry, Kiva. I didn't mean to imply you didn't work hard. I'm sorry about your life. I know the heart of my families. We don't want for your people to suffer ..."

"There ... you just said it. *Your people.* You see. There's a thick wall between us. Who will tear it down?"

Are we enemies? Is it us versus them? Fear knocked on Katarina's mind. How far would the rebels go to achieve their political goals? Was Kiva one of them? She reflected on her doubts about Dimitri. Could any of the servants be trusted?

They broached the perimeter of the pasture as the heat of the afternoon faded. The clammy silk undergarments twisted beneath her skirts, sticking to her sweaty legs in awkward folds. Katarina wished the rotting dog and the signboard had surfaced after the swim. It was too late to turn back now. She brushed the sweat from her brow. Her throat parched, she turned to the maid. "Kiva, did we bring water?"

Kiva set the disturbing placard on the ground. She opened the picnic box, retrieved a bottle of water, uncorked it, and held it up to Katarina.

Katarina realized she'd never studied the woman. The plaited coarse brunette hair, wrapped around her head in the traditional style of a young woman, belied the strands of gray peeking from the temples; the gnarled, scarred hands, the lines in her face, and the bags under her amber eyes all suggested a woman much older than her stated thirty-five years. Katarina had guessed the maid to be at least fifty. A pang of guilt washed over her. The woman deserved a better life.

Katarina toyed with the drops beading from the jar. If she had been born into a local peasant household, would she be any less worthy? She held the container up to Kiva. "Here. You haven't had a drink all day. You must be parched."

"Oh no, I can't," Kiva gushed. "It's not right."

"I insist." Katarina pushed the container at Kiva's chest.

The maid hesitated, then accepted and guzzled. She wiped her mouth on the back of her hand before offering the jar back to Katarina. "Thank you. Shall I put it away, or do you want to drink after my lips have soiled the jar?"

Katarina hesitated to take the dare. Anna would have a fit and probably send her to the doctor to be checked for contagion. Except Anna didn't need to know. She sensed the relationship with Kiva was paramount — although she wasn't sure why; she barely knew the woman.

Accepting the bottle, she wiped the top with her sleeve, and held it to her lips, sipping tentatively while Kiva watched. The smirk on Kiva's face widened. Not wishing to be scorned further, Katarina turned the bottom to the sky and gulped. Kiva's smile disappeared.

They completed the trek in silence until they reached the yard — at which point Katarina took the sign from Kiva's arm. "I'll go talk to Olek. Take the rest of the day off. I'll tell Anna that you're running errands for me."

Katarina found Olek training the colt behind the stables. Her throat tightened at the dusty smell and her lungs rebelled with a coughing fit. Olek yelled and waved her away. She held up the board until he tied up the young horse and walked over for a closer look.

"You shouldn't be here. You'll get sick." He grabbed the sign out of her hands. "Why didn't you get someone else to bring this to me?" He climbed over the fence, then grabbed her by her good arm and led her away from the dust cloud.

Although the senior servant's paternalistic approach was calming, her gut warned her to be cautious. As an educated Russian, he likely enjoyed the works of Lenin, Chernyshevsky, and Dostoevsky. The intelligentsia were rumored to support the Bolshevik policies. They wanted to change Russia by demolishing the old ways. Despite David's hearty accolades of the man, Katarina wondered about Olek's true loyalties.

They stood in the middle of the open yard while Olek analyzed the cryptic words. He sucked on his bottom lip and inhaled through his teeth. His face took on a sympathetic expression. "I'm sorry you found this, Katarina. It's not right. But it's not directed only at your family. The war is sensationalizing the anti-German sentiment. The rebels are trying to push all foreigners out of the country." He patted her shoulder. "Don't tell anyone about this. I'll add extra guards along the perimeter. They won't get in here. I promise. I'll keep you safe."

Katarina prayed she could trust him as much as David and Anna did. Olek held the proverbial keys to the estate. With David gone, the entire family's lives were in the stableman's hands. *But he called us foreigners.* She rubbed her face. Until now, war was a fantastical illusion happening in another part of the world. She never believed it would land on her doorstep. It was becoming much too real. For the second time since the war began, Katarina was scared.

13

A SPLINTER BETWEEN SISTERS

OCTOBER 1917

THE DOG'S VIOLENT DEATH AND THE CONVERSATION with Kiva rattled Katarina's confidence and plagued her with shame about her heritage. For the first time, she questioned how being a true Russian was different than being a Russian Mennonite. Was there more to the divide than just class, language, religion, and politics?

Or was the animosity — as her father said — all about money? They were considered rich agrarians — the monied class with vast agricultural holdings and social ties to the Imperial Government. The poor served them. The class differences were obvious.

Perhaps some anger was about land, as Kiva had pointed out. The lower peasantry had little, some had none. The maid seemed convinced that all land should be divided equally. Did Kiva support the ideas of the Bolsheviks or of Makhno? The distinction between the two was sometimes blurry.

And then there was Olek — possibly from the intelligentsia class. He'd used the word foreigners when he saw the sign. Did he object to the Mennonites' presence? The intelligentsia supported Marxism and now Lenin. How did he end up as a stableman in charge of the estate? This puzzled Katarina. Did his political or religious beliefs impact his job?

Katarina wondered about the political controversies and how, or if, faith fit into the picture. What was wrong with some having more than others? Although God loved and cared for all, and God was no respecter of persons — according to her father's interpretation of the Bible — all were *not* created equally. He'd explained that each was born into their particular position for a specific reason that only God knew. One should therefore be content with their lot in life and do the best with what they had. Since Johann studied the Bible together with the male church leaders, and men were only one step away from God on the religious hierarchy, his answer had to be true. And yet, Katarina questioned the wisdom. At the same time, she felt guilty for doing so.

She reflected on the communal make-up. There were few wealthy expansive estates in the colonies, rarely more than one per village. Most Mennonites were working class peasants who owned a house and a cow, and labored in the same factories, mills, and estates as the Russky. However, these Mennonite workers were viewed more positively because of their common culture and language and they usually received slightly higher wages than the locals. The favoritism showed in the disparity in treatment.

Was this the reason for the increasing reports of theft, assaults, and ambushes by bandits? Except, she reflected further — there were clear evidence of deep bigotry and antagonism by the locals towards all Mennonites — not just the wealthy. No, the enmity was about more than money. The Russky didn't like *them*. Despite living in Russia for more than a hundred years, they were still *foreigners*. At what point did this label go away?

Katarina tried to brush away the gnawing awareness of the stigma by delving into her work and taking on additional projects. When the school day closed, she raced to the newspaper office to help Regier with proofreading and continued to compile the genealogical listings until sunset or until Regier implored her to go home. Fearful of being criticized by her family or confronted about any perceived religious violation by the community elders, she dutifully attended the Wednesday and two Sunday church services, assisted with the community dinner preparations on Saturday, facilitated the women's charity luncheon on Thursdays, and attended the unmarried women's sewing circle on Tuesdays. She opted to forgo the youth group on Fridays, feigning she had grown out of such childish activities, while believing no one would notice if she missed a few weeks.

Adding further pressure to her hectic calendar, Regier began dropping hints about needing more help. When an advertisement in the storefront brought no qualified applicants and Regier added a second pair of spectacles on top of his already thick windowpanes, she couldn't say no. The pressure built to a breaking point. Unwilling to admit she couldn't manage the workload, she felt incompetent at both posts, and worried that her inadequacy showed. Then she busied herself further. She knew that her haystack was piled far too high and one measly gust of wind would blow it all down. Although she knew she needed some guidance to reorganize her schedule, she was afraid to ask for it.

Today, the timetable loomed. She rushed through breakfast, slathering a generous amount of lard and salt on her bread — enough to stop hunger from knocking on her appetite for several hours. "I'll be late again today. The men are busy gathering war details. I'm editing their reports," she announced between bites.

"How long will you work two jobs, Katarina?" Anna scooped the raspberry preserves from the Flemish crystal dish and tapped the jelly spoon on her plate twice, then picked up the short knife, spread a thin layer on her zwieback, and lay the knife crosswise on her plate. She lifted the rusk to her mouth, looked across the table, and raised an eyebrow as if she was scolding a child.

Katarina sensed her wealthy sister had an unpleasant agenda for this conversation, but she'd play along for a few minutes. "It's a bit hectic right now, but everything will slow down once the snow falls. I can manage."

"You're going to burn out, Katarina. How can you continue to prepare lessons, teach school, help the newspaper, and chair the women's mission relief committee? Not to mention church. I've watched you fall asleep during the services. You're exhausted and your schedule is insane. It's time to slow down. You can't find a good husband like this."

"Meaning?" Katarina gulped her coffee.

"You're not attending the young people's social evenings. How do you expect to meet a good man if you don't make yourself available?" Anna took a sip from her cup, then set it down and cleared her throat. "Katarina, men are intimidated by a strong woman who works at a man's job. You're only going to attract the lazy ones who don't want to work." Anna peered across the table with a concerned expression. "I worry about you."

Katarina laughed. "Stop. The men can look elsewhere. I'm only seventeen and I don't have a house to look after. There's no need for me to have a husband. Let me live my life. If my circumstances change, then I'll adapt. But right now, this works for me." Katarina gave a back handed wave to dismiss Anna's maternalistic urge. She finished her breakfast and pushed the plate aside.

"You know, you could do something a bit more respectable, like helping with the widows fund, or the orphanage, or even at the hospital. They need nurses there. Our family can take care of you. You don't need the money."

Katarina raised her eyebrows and gave a wide-eyed stare to the table. *Something more respectable?* Lately, Anna's snobbery had lost its juvenile appeal of special privilege; instead, it grated on Katarina like the cock-a-doodle-doo of a rooster call on a weekend morning.

Her jaw muscles tightened, "That, my dear sister, is your work. The perfect job for married women without children — organizing the household help, sewing quilts, crafting, making baby blankets, jelly making, hosting bake sales, babysitting — it's all wonderful, godly stuff. I appreciate your life is full, but so is mine. Please understand, my interests lie elsewhere."

Anna squirmed. "The women talk, you know. They say you spend too much time with the men. They imply that your morals are a bit loose."

"Bah, humbug. Those judgmental old hens have nothing better to do than spread gossip. Please tell them to mind their own business."

Anna sighed. "My dear sister. If you don't change your ways, you may become a spinster."

Katarina rolled her eyes. "So, what if I do?"

"That doesn't bother you?"

"No. It does not." Katarina grimaced. *Here we go again. Now she'll spout the importance of conforming to the community image. Why do my decisions matter so much to others? Why can't I be myself?*

Anna nodded. "Tell me, do you remember the story of old Henrietta Wiebe, the spinster? She refused to move to Canada with her family during the last emigration. A fierce, independent woman who never married. When she became sick, she had no husband or family to provide for her. Of course, the community pitched in. But the poor woman was so embarrassed to fall into such desperate circumstances and having to accept help from the church coffers. Many blamed her for causing her own problems."

"Why didn't she marry?"

"I'm not sure, but I heard she had offers. At one time, she was quite attractive, but eventually, she became too old. Men want young, child-bearing women."

"There were no widowers needing a mother for their children?"

"Yes, but she refused every offer. She said she didn't want to be ordered about by a man or look after someone else's children."

"Smart woman."

"It was unnatural."

"My guess is there was more to that story."

"Perhaps."

"Didn't she work?"

"Well, yes. She did typing duties at Lentz's — hiding away in a dark little office slaving over a typewriter with one lightbulb hanging over her desk. I doubt she ever saw the light of day except on Sunday. Everyone talked."

"Shame," Katarina sipped her coffee and drummed her fingers on the table. The fact that the woman worked was not a shame, but the perceived need to hide a working woman was, although Anna — being the conformist icon of the community — saw things very differently.

"Yes, it was shameful. When she died, her friends — and she didn't have many — looked after all the details. Imagine having to write your friend's family to let them know their daughter and sister died." Anna embraced her coffee cup with both hands, "She should have been surrounded by family — children, or at least a husband. Instead, she died all alone. With no one to love her."

Katarina sighed. "Anna, why is this important? I'm not sick, I'm not dying. And I have you to look after me."

"It's wartime, Katarina. Anything can happen. What if something happens to me, to our family? If you had a husband ..."

Katarina burst out laughing. "Yes, it's wartime dear sister. You are so right. Anything can happen. If I had a husband, he could die in war. Then I'd still be alone. Only, in your eyes, a respectable alone."

Anna's mouth opened and closed like a fish searching for air. Katarina grinned while she refilled her coffee, waiting for the comeback. She accepted that the argument was nonsensical, but the rivalry was delicious. Allowing her emotions to release felt as comforting as taking the lid off a boiling pot, or rather how the pot might feel if it could.

Anna composed herself, straightened her shoulders, and sputtered, "But if you had a husband, you'd have children. Then you wouldn't be alone. They'd grow up and take care of you when you're old."

Katarina softened her voice but kept her tone firm. "Anna, I appreciate your concern over my long-range future. But you must know all the good men are helping with the war effort. And I refuse to marry some old widower with ten little ones. I'm doing my part by working two jobs until the good men come home. Which, I might add, are both poorly paid jobs — barely enough to pay rent if I had to do so — which, by the way, thanks to your generosity, I don't need to. I'm not sure how I would manage otherwise."

And that, Katarina admitted to herself, as she stirred the cream into her morning coffee, was the more concerning issue. She honestly didn't know how she could ever take care of herself without the financial support of a man or her family's generosity. The story of Henrietta Wiebe was admirable. The woman had spunk. Katarina wasn't sure she could fight tradition in like fashion, nor if she wanted to, at least to that extent. She guessed Anna would get her wish at some future date, just not as fast as she wanted.

Anna stared across the table with her eyebrows raised and arms crossed and bounced a restless leg under the table. Katarina noted the irritated body language, but the stage was set. Even though Anna had raised the subject, Katarina would not allow proprieties to suppress her feelings any longer. If she couldn't be honest with her favorite sibling, then who would understand? She wanted to appeal to the woman's common sense, even though she suspected her words would provoke more heat than light.

"And that brings me to the next pebble in my shoe, Anna — the unfairness in a woman's working wage. For some reason — I suspect because of some twisted scriptural interpretation — men have decided that a working woman must be paid less than a working man. I don't understand this thinking. If I do the same job as a man, why is my worth less?"

Anna slapped the table and stiffened her spine. "Because your primary job is to raise children and take care of a man."

"Bah. What if I don't want to do either?" Katarina

raised her voice. "What if I choose to live like Henrietta Wiebe?"

"The Bible says we are created to be companions to our husband. That is our primary role. So, we must be content to be under a male covering. If not your husband's, then your father or your brother." Anna composed her posture and folded her hands on the table. "Henrietta still had family, only not here. I'm sure they sent her financial support."

Katarina narrowed her eyes. "Suppose she received no assistance ... or I didn't. If I stay single and when my father and brothers die, what happens to me?"

"Then the rest of your family helps out," Anna replied in a matter-of-fact voice.

"And if I have no family?" Katarina pushed the subject to irritate her sister further. Even though she knew the answers, niggling Anna was a game she didn't want to lose.

Anna caught on and called her bluff. "This is ridiculous, Katarina. You have a family that loves you. Why are you asking such absurd questions?"

Katarina grinned. *I'm winning.* She changed her tone copying Anna's matter-of-fact style. "Follow me through, Anna. If I had no father, no family, and no husband, would I get paid any more in the workplace?"

"Well, I have no idea. A working woman is simply not natural." Anna sounded puzzled, as if she had never thought of this dilemma.

"You mean a paid working woman. You work at all kinds of things, but you don't get paid," Katarina explained.

"Yes, but I do women's work. And I am under a man's covering." Anna scrunched her eyebrows together and cocked her head.

"Exactly my point. You do women's work and don't get

paid. Our culture doesn't value your contribution to home or society in the same way as a man's."

"Katarina, this is insulting. Of course, I am valued."

"You are not being paid," Katarina shouted.

"Life is not about money, Katarina ... whether or not one is paid. It is about relationships. Each contributes to society, to the best of their ability, in whatever capacity God calls them." Anna stood up and placed her palms on her hips. "Money is a worldly tool, Katarina. It is not a god to be worshipped."

"We all need to eat, Anna. And money buys food and clothing. Should I have less because I am a woman? Am I inferior because I was born without a penis?" The spiteful, yet bold words flew out before her hand reached her mouth. Her heart stopped in her chest and she swallowed hard, wondering whether she should apologize or continue. She reflected on her statement and decided she had spoken from her heart. *The truth is ugly, but that doesn't make it less true.*

Anna flinched and gripped the wall, "Katarina, that's enough. You are displaying unjustified anger."

Katarina punched back. "Unjustified? You think my anger is unwarranted? I see so much unfairness, Anna. People are being murdered in their beds. Young women become widows overnight and struggle to feed their babies. Fractured families — all because of this stupid war. I'm searching for answers, for meaning in all this chaos."

Anna's voice softened. "There is a bigger picture, Katarina. God sees all the despair. He knows the end from the beginning."

"Oh, well, that's fantastic," Katarina snorted. "God knows, so we should just trust and accept. Is that it? We do nothing? While fools run the world and murder each other, we twirl our thumbs and sing *Silent Night?* Somehow, I rather doubt this is all God's will."

"Katarina, you are being very disrespectful."

"Of whom?" Katarina spat.

"Of God. And of our culture. And me too."

"Well, I'm sorry, Anna. No disrespect to you intended." She softened her voice and looked up to the ceiling. "And as for God. Please forgive me for my overt expressions. Although I won't repent for my anger, which I believe is completely justified. And I'm sure God understands the pain in my heart. As to our culture, well, maybe it needs shaking up a bit," she seethed as she gulped the last of the tepid coffee.

"Please, Katarina, don't repeat these words in public. You'll bring shame to the family," Anna pleaded.

"Perhaps a little shame would change a few things." Katarina glared at her sister. "The Mennonite culture is a little too high and mighty these days. Perhaps some Bolshevik religion might level the playing field a bit."

"You are exasperating, little sister!" Anna threw up her arms and scraped the chair into the table and turned to leave the room.

The game of words was over. Katarina raised her eyebrows and lifted her coffee cup in the air. "I salute you, big sister. But this time I won."

Ignoring Anna's gaping mouth and dumbfounded expression, she threw her shawl over her shoulders, picked up her bag, and walked out the door.

14

CHESS GAMES

LATE OCTOBER 1917 AT *THE POST*

Regier circled the room with his shoulders stooped, one arm across his chest, his other hand stroking his newly trimmed beard. In the past few weeks, Katarina had noticed her mentor's worried looks, the vacant stares, and his cheerless disposition. Wide, white streaks replaced the former sophisticated salt and pepper sideburns blending into his thinning crown and added to the picture of an old man carrying the weight of the world on his shoulders. The recent dark circles enveloping his droopy gray-blue eyes and the lines around his lips furthered the somber appearance.

Katarina wondered if the man had problems at home or if he was aging from the worries of war. As much as she was dying to know, Anna had insisted it was impolite to inquire.

"Katarina, if he wants you to know, he'll tell you," Anna said when Katarina asked for her advice over breakfast that morning. "Otherwise, just do your job and don't ask questions."

Now, watching him pace in figure eights around the

wood stove in the middle of the room, she could tell he needed to talk, but was thinking about his words. Katarina bit her lip and re-assessed. Was it the constant negative news getting him down, or was it her? Had she done something wrong?

She feared hurting their growing relationship. They were getting along so well — at least she thought so. Perhaps she should apologize. For what? Anything. She must have done something to upset the man this much. Was he getting ready to let her go? She straightened her spine and tucked in her chin. Whatever it was, she could bear it.

Truth could be scary, but it was better to ask and know than to stay silent and guess. Her father's voice echoed in her head, *Apologies are humiliating, Katarina, but admitting a mistake shows character*. She rubbed her lips together, and her throat tightened. With only the two of them in the office today, now was as good a time as any. She took a deep breath, tapped the pencil on the dictation pad, dated the entry, then casually asked, "Is something wrong?"

Regier stopped pacing, crossed his arms, and stared at the floor. He stroked his beard, and grunted, "Yes, there are a few things on my mind."

Katarina froze, holding the pencil in mid-air, and gulped. *What did I do?*

Regier adjusted his suspenders, put his hands in his pockets, and sighed. He glanced at the Teletype machine in the corner. "I'm waiting for particulars about a shooting in Schoenfeld ... do you know the village?"

"A shooting? ... Ah ..." she stumbled for a response. "Yes, it's on the eastern side ... near Chernigovka, I think ... but I've never been... I don't have family there." *It's not me.* She breathed a sigh of relief. *But ... a shooting? How? Who?* She leaned forward, anticipating more details.

The thick eyeglasses slid down his narrow nose as he stared at her. The gray-blue eyes flickered and scanned her face. "Good. I mean it's good you don't have any close connections there. I don't either — at least I don't think so, but nonetheless, I hate to upset you. You'll hear about it soon enough. It's highly disturbing — although the details are sketchy. Heinrich left on the morning train to find out more. There are rumors about multiple deaths. But as I said, it's not confirmed." He dropped the news in slow bites, stopping to gage her reaction between sentences. Then as soon as he concluded, he pivoted and began pacing in the opposite direction.

The pencil slipped out of Katarina's hand and dropped on the floor as she jolted back in her seat, her mouth agape. She stared at Regier and blinked rapidly, trying to comprehend the newsflash. "Multiple deaths?" *Makhno?* Had the radical man and his friends gone beyond threats and farm raids? The possibility sent shivers up her spine and triggered memories of the black stallion and the dead dog. She placed a hand over her mouth and looked across the room at the sink, hoping she wouldn't need it. She stared wide-eyed at the editor, waiting for the gruesome details.

Instead, Regier waved his hand in a dismissive gesture. "Oh, never mind. You don't need to know this now. We'll find out more by the end of the day."

Don't need to ... then, why did you mention it? Katarina shook her head at the incongruence, swallowed the acidic belch, and breathed away the queasiness in her stomach. She leaned over and picked up the pencil from the floor.

The editor continued as if he had just announced the sky was blue; except his tone shifted and took on an irritated edge. "On top of this, I have another problem. Jacob's left for Kyiv to ... can you believe this? Assist the Sich Corps.

He said they're pushing back against the Bolshevik buildup forming there. He'll write as he's able. I hope he lives through it —"

The second stunning revelation felt like a punch in her stomach, "What?" *Jacob's enlisting to fight? To kill? But we don't …*

Regier nodded and threw his hands in the air. "Yes, it's a shock to me, too. I didn't know the man could shoot that well. I guess winning all those contests went to his head. He joins the other scattered sheep abandoning their Mennonite roots. May God protect him. I'm praying he connects with the Ukrainian Press on the way. He's an excellent observer, a real head for details. It's a shame to lose him."

He resumed pacing and toying with his beard. "Be that as it may, this leaves me a man short to help with editing, typesetting, and getting the weekly paper out on time. Katarina, I feel bad for what I'm about to ask you. You've pitched in so graciously over these past few months. I hate to make further demands on your time, but until I find another body, I'm at a loss."

Katarina frowned. There were too many threads in this conversation and Regier was jumping all over the place. First, he wasn't firing her — he needed her help. She could stop worrying about her performance. Second, Jacob had left rather suddenly. Had he been conscripted, or did he volunteer? Regier needed more reporters. And third, this bombshell news about *shootings and multiple murders?* No wonder the man was agitated.

Regier's pacing around the center of the room spoke volumes, although his tone — in her opinion — was much too casual. If she was in his shoes, she'd be lashing out. Then again, he was sort of dumping his cares on her. No man had ever talked to her like this — with such openness.

There was no anger or other emotion directed at her. Women talked to each other like this — but never a man to a woman. It was unusual. She wasn't sure how to respond, so she waited for him to continue.

"Katarina, I'm sorry to throw this at you. This is my dilemma, and you shouldn't feel obligated. You're already swamped with the school and the women's committees. I'm hoping you might have some ideas on how I might reorganize and maintain efficiency under the circumstances. Conscription is taking all the good men, but the war news also demands more reporters and more print here at home. I'm in a bit of a pickle." Regier stumbled over his words.

Katarina jumped at the opportunity to discuss her own worries. "Oh, no apology needed. I'd love to work here full time, but there isn't an empty space in my calendar. The pressure's enormous. The government's new mandates are so restrictive — I feel like I'm handcuffed."

"I understand, Katarina. The recent change in regulations have placed a lot of pressure on the school board as well. Finding qualified teachers has become a problem."

"Yes, exactly. With pastors now banned from teaching, and both local and German students integrated into one school, my workload's ballooned. The colony's teachers are meeting weekly to contrive solutions. And add to this the language changes in the curriculum. We must now teach in Russian instead of German, but few of our students speak it fluently. On top of this, the Ukraine dialect is forbidden — which compromises the locals. I seem to be the only educated person who can speak five languages, so I've become both translator and teacher. You're right, I'm overwhelmed and I'm about ready to quit. I'm happy to give you all my free time because I enjoy this job, but my first commitment is to the school. I can't be in three places at once."

Regier chuckled, "Yes, they're fortunate to have you as a teacher. I don't know anyone who possesses your talent for languages. I'm surprised you haven't yet learned Polish or Czech."

"Give me time. I'm still young. With enough study I'll learn at least a dozen more by the time I'm your age," Katarina sassed.

"I don't doubt it. There are few who could compete with you, except me. I think you and I could collude in colloquial espionage." The elder's eyes crinkled as he smiled.

Katarina sat back, stretched out her legs, and crossed her ankles as she felt the man's mood lighten. If he only needed some chit-chat to help him relax, she was more than happy to oblige. She needed it too.

Regier stopped pacing, leaned against his desk, and hugged his arms. "I'd like to help you out at the school, but obviously, I can't. The only linguists I know are old men and they're busy caring for their absent sons' businesses and family farms." He scratched his graying beard. "These changes have really thrown a wrench into the system."

"I agree. It's confusing." Katarina nodded as she repositioned the pencil and notebook.

"Katarina, I'm aware that teaching is a thankless job. When the clergy were in charge, their intimate knowledge of every family meant they could intervene promptly when life became unmanageable. The church held the community and school together like a well-oiled machine. This process has worked very well for us for hundreds of years. What is it that the Bolsheviks don't understand?"

"They seem to think it's their job to reinvent the wheel."

"Yes, and now they're poking their nose in our business, booting the church out of the school, and imposing their educational imperatives without any regard to our moral and spiritual values. Without properly educated teachers, I doubt few schools can meet the standards they want."

"That's so true. The teacher's college will need to change their curriculum to graduate teachers who can."

"The churches want input on this legislation. I can see the wagon train to Petrograd already. The expenses will pile up as we fight this. It sounds impossible. Katarina, I appreciate the mountain before you. I do. If I could help you, I would. Which brings us back to the original problem — mine. What can I do?" Regier scratched his balding head and shuffled to the window. "I wish I could think of a qualified elder that could teach so you could work here."

Katarina felt a warmth spread through her core as she basked in the compliment. She cleared her throat. "As you said — most of them are busy running the farms and training the children in the fields."

"Yes. And old men tend to have poor eyesight." He tapped his thick eyeglasses. "Which means they're no help for either of us. We need a young and intelligent eagle eye with time on his hands who's willing to take on a new challenge."

"Hmm ..." Katarina tapped her chin. "I'm sure this is completely irregular, but you know our stableman Olek is highly educated and speaks at least five languages — if not more. Would he be acceptable?"

Regier raised his eyebrows, "Absolutely not. He's a Russky with questionable values. The church would never agree. Besides you need him on the farm. He's far more than just a stableman."

Far more? "Whatever do you mean?" Katarina pulled

her feet under her chair. Olek's new duties included monitoring the fieldwork and reporting irregularities. Although she sensed that to be an unusual duty for a stableman, David trusted him enough to place him in a managerial position. However, she had no knowledge of the man's work history or his relationship to the family.

Regier twirled to face her, "You don't know, do you?"

"No? I don't know ... What?"

"The man's background. Listen, Katarina, Mr. Olek was a bodyguard to the senior Grand Duke. The Duke's cordial relationship with the Penners gave them rare special privileges. The great elder Penner helped the Royal with business dealings in the colonies and in turn the Duke granted the family additional acreage among other favors. In the good old days, vacations to Petrograd to have dinner with the Czar were common. The connections are legendary. When the Duke left for France, he lent Olek to the Penners to help with security concerns. As you know, the Duke passed and Olek thus became a permanent fixture on the farm. He's comfortable with the horses and those duties provide a good front to his real job."

Katarina felt her eyes were about to pop out of her head. "What? I had no idea," she blinked rapidly trying to grasp the information. "With such credentials, under the current political strain — if the locals find out — our lives could be threatened." *The sign by the river ... were they threatening Olek or us?*

"Oh, I suspect the locals know. You know how word gets around. Don't underestimate Mr. Olek. He may seem to be a kind man, but he carries a heavy stick. He can be quite intimidating. The locals give him a wide berth. He's the primary reason the estate hasn't been vandalized. The guards that patrol the perimeter were carefully chosen and report directly to him."

A shiver passed down Katarina's spine. "When I told him about the dead dog and showed him the sign, he said he would add more guards. I didn't think he meant real guards. What, with guns? Surely not?"

"It's best we don't know the details." Regier put his foot on a chair and rubbed his forehead.

"So, the Penners have...."

"History, influence, and connections. Your sister married into a prestigious family. Who else could afford two weddings — one on each side of the river? Their affluence bombards the average Mennonite's sensibilities. Why do you think your parents were so agreeable to your move here after the attack on their farm? They know you're protected now."

"I'm shocked. Although, to some degree comforted. My parents said the Penners were very important. I didn't realize what that meant," Katarina reflected. "But now, based on what you've just said, I don't know if I should worry more or less. Does it mean the war will come to the estate? Can we put all our trust in Olek? Will the Bolsheviks attack us because of the family's imperial connections?"

"Katarina, the German front is moving closer. It's bound to trigger panic among the Russky and encourage violence against the colonists. As far as Olek is concerned, I don't think you need to worry about his loyalty."

"But our safety, dear cousin? We're safe now, but ... how can anyone know for certain? The violence in the region seems to be escalating. When I think back — the fire on the mill, the raids on the farms — there was no warning when we were attacked. Two years later, we still don't know if servants were involved. The recent uprisings and strikes at the factories have injured and killed workers. Businesses are scrambling to keep things together. They can't even trust their own employees. Here at home the dog and the sign are threats that all is not as it seems. The violence is getting personal. And now there are murders in the east. Is it all linked?

"And Olek aside, under these conditions, how can we trust any who work for us?" A shiver ran down Katarina's back. "My stomach is tied in knots." The implications of the situation were frightening.

"Yes, Katarina. The overall picture is disturbing. But when it comes to the Penner estate, let me reassure you that everyone who works for the Penners was chosen for one of two reasons: they either have a family connection or they owe a debt to someone in the family. They work until it's paid and then they keep working because it's paid. Few would revolt easily. The most senior servants would more likely turn on each other before they would cross the family."

"Unbelievable."

"Well, believe it. Now back to your suggestion of Olek teaching at the school. It won't, and it can't happen. Do you understand now?"

"Yes, I guess so." Katarina rubbed her face. If only she could erase the growing fear as easily.

15

THREADS OF CHANGE

KATARINA SCRAPED HER CHAIR BACK, WALKED OVER TO the sink, and turned on the new brass tap; she stared at the crystal liquid as it gushed from the faucet and bubbled into the glass. *Running water is such decadence. How did we manage without it? What do the Bolsheviks say about this kind of progressiveness? Will they institute running water for all? Who will pay for it? Is it possible to lift the poor from the gutters without tearing apart the fabric of social order?*

Our world is changing too fast. Katarina thought as she gulped her drink. She returned to her desk, picked up her pencil and notepad, and waited for Regier to continue.

"Shall we get back to generating creative solutions for our more immediate problems? What's your next idea?" Regier resumed pacing around the stove.

Katarina scrunched her eyebrows together and blew out a steady stream through her mouth. "Well ... I usually get the older children to tutor the younger ones, but right now many are away with the fall harvest. When the snow falls, I can spare a couple to help you with the more menial tasks. Other than that, I'm at a loss too."

Their problems were like tangled balls of wool, she thought; they simply weren't pulling on the right thread. She yanked on a possible solution. "How about this? I'll talk to my sister and her sisters-in-law, and I'll also raise the issue at the women's mission meeting next week. As far as the school goes, I can't do anything without clearing it with the Board. Technically, they still have control for staffing, even though all changes require the stamp of approval from the new Russian government. And they'll understand these latest regulations better than me."

She scratched her head. Right now, she desperately wanted to pull down her tightly wound bun and re-braid it. Plaiting her hair helped her to think. She could do that at home, but she didn't dare do it here. It would send the wrong message. She tucked the loose strands behind her ear, checked the pins on her black roses embroidered head covering, then picked up a pencil and doodled. There was no obvious solution. The more they talked, the more complex the situation seemed.

Regier shook his head and pulled on his beard. "We can't sacrifice education for the sake of the press. There must be another answer. Let's think this through. We've got mandatory changes in the curriculum — the language changes, and compulsory attendance to the age of twelve. This affects us how?"

"Classrooms bursting at the seams, frazzled teachers —"

"Yes, yes. Think broader. You need help in the school. I get it. The farmers rely on the children for seasonal help. Now that's reduced because of the age limit. Add in the war at large. The young, strong men are gone." Regier's eyes widened as if a light bulb had turned on. "There aren't enough bodies to go around ..."

Katarina nodded. "Yes, that's what I was saying earlier. But it's more complicated than that."

"More so? What do you mean?"

"Our entire education system is being revamped and turned upside down. Under the new regulations, all teachers must be re-certified to meet Russian standards. This will be an additional strain on the classroom time until we are all credentialed. I'm not certain I can even qualify under the new rules.

"Until now, teachers were trained according to the church curriculum. The government has eliminated that religious mandate and replaced it with Bolshevik dogma. If we don't obey the new rules, the government will appoint their people to teach. What will this do to our credibility? The church's influence in education is being eroded."

Regier pulled on this beard. "Yes, I fear we risk damaging young minds with all this liberalism. Community standards will eventually suffer. Morals will decline. The world is becoming like Nero's Rome."

"As a teacher, I'm caught in the middle. I'm waiting to see how this plays out." Katarina tapped the pencil on her leg.

"Well, not all is lost, yet. I'm sure the overseers are planning further discussions with the government. Let's pray they come to a better arrangement. Although ... this new government is quite forceful, not as amiable as the Czar. As long as his lackeys received their bonuses, we could do what worked. In the old days, money could buy anything." Regier pulled out a chair from behind the desk, put one foot on the wooden seat, then rested his elbow on his knee, and cupped his chin. "I guess those days are gone."

Katarina frowned. "I'm sorry. My dilemma doesn't help yours. It makes it worse."

The corners of the elder's mouth crinkled with a downward smile, and his gray-blue eyes drooped. Discouragement resonated on his face as he tapped on his chin with his index finger. Suddenly, his eyebrows shot up and his eyes widened. He put his foot down and he snapped his fingers. "Say, Katarina, has the government said how many hours a student must go to school?"

"Umm. I'm not sure."

"I wonder if the school day could be shortened." He beamed, then grimaced. "Oh dear, I didn't mean to sound selfish."

"I think it's a great idea. I'll explore that possibility. That makes me think of something else."

"What's that?" Regier looked up with great interest.

Katarina bit the inside of her lower lip. Did she dare suggest an alternative without checking with her superiors? They might not agree. She shrugged her shoulders. Regier could ask and credit himself with the idea. Wasn't that what Anna said about how to handle men? She cleared her throat. "I don't believe there's any law that says education can't include co-operative work."

"Whatever do you mean?"

"Well ... you need help typesetting. Some aspiring children may need to learn this skill in preparation for future work. The older ones can help with cleaning the building, delivering newspapers, and filing. At school, I can focus the writing class on storytelling. If they're good enough, they could polish their craft here."

"Juveniles in the office would only slow me down. I don't want a bevy of crabby little ones dipping their fingers in my ink. The paper would never get published. And our records must be one hundred percent accurate. A child could never do that."

"Huh. I disagree. I know a few studious ones who could manage these tasks. I can personally guarantee they won't be a problem. Trust me, I'm the teacher." Katarina wriggled her eyebrows and nodded with assurance.

Regier threw his hands in the air. "Well, I suppose I'm at your mercy. Anything is worth a try at this stage. But ..." he shook a finger in her face. "Any trouble ... and I mean any trouble ... and those brats are gone."

"I understand completely. But you know I can't approach the headmaster on this. Or the Board."

Regier stared at her as if he didn't understand. Then he nodded. "Of course. I'll stop by his house on the way home. With luck, we should have an answer by daybreak."

The whizzing and clacking of the Teletype stopped the discussion and they both turned to stare at it. Regier pointed with his chin. "This must be it."

They simultaneously rose and strode to the machine. Regier ripped the paper from the feeder in one quick swoop, angled the page to the light, and pushed the thick, wire-rim glasses up his nose. He squinted as he scanned the page. "It's from Heinrich." He put a finger over his mouth as he read.

"Well, what does he say?" Katarina held her breath and rubbed her hands together. "How bad is it?" Although she wanted to know, she dreaded hearing the awful truth. Was the disaster an accident or something more sinister?

The color fell from Regier's face and the paper shook in his trembling hands. "Thirty-three dead. At least five more critically injured. Many more suffering. Men lined up and shot. Women ... children ..." he collapsed into a chair. The note fluttered to the floor.[1]

Katarina's eyes widened as she bent down and picked up the page. The last sentence read 'most horrific.' Her stomach knotted as she scanned the rest. "Everyone at the Thiessen estate is dead. He slaughtered an entire family? Servants, too?" She gasped and looked up at Regier for verification. He sat with a dazed expression on his face, a hand over his mouth. She reread the note, trying to comprehend the extent of the disaster. She shook her head and read it a third time. It couldn't be true, and yet it was.

Makhno. The room blurred as the images of the black stallion and the dead dog flashed. A wave of nausea washed over her, and she ran to the sink and vomited. When she rinsed away the nastiness and wiped her mouth, a fresh realization flooded through her mind — the world had dismissed her fears, but now her prophecies had come true. The very words she had held in her gut for the past two years could now be spoken and this time the universe would listen.

Her jaw clenched and her eyes narrowed as she braced against the wall. She turned back to face Regier and uttered her truth. "So ... Makhno has finally decided to show his true colors. He's a brutal killer with no conscience. He'll stop at nothing to destroy our people. He's ... he's a ... psychopath." She spat the words and her legs trembled with the force of their impact.

Regier didn't respond. Katarina dropped into her chair and joined him in his moment of silence. After a few minutes, Regier rose and walked over to his desk. "Katarina, do you remember completing the genealogical registry for this village?"

"Yes ... I believe I did."

"Can you retrieve it quickly?"

"It's in the cellar with the others. Why?"

"We need to verify the names of the dead with the listings. And we need to add an entry in the journal for posterity with the details of this disaster."

"Yes, of course. I'll go down and find it."

"And one other thing. We should warn the colonies. Let's quickly put together a newsletter for distribution to all the churches. They can disseminate the information to their parishioners faster than we can. I'll write the outline. We'll flush it out together. Can you help me with typesetting and editing?"

"Yes, of course. I'll stay as late as you need me."

"We'll need our little couriers too. Please see if any are hanging around outside. Today, they'll earn their kopeks."

---

1. On January 25, 1918, five members of the Aaron Thiessen family were executed in the Schonfeld region by the Makhnovists. For the purposes of literary dramatization, the facts and dates of this gruesome catastrophe have been altered. Makhno's Black Army was credited with violent military-type activities including mass murders in southern Ukraine during the years 1918-1921. The term Makhnovist was not used until late 1918. See https://www.libcom.org/history/makhnovists-mennonites-war-peace-ukrainian-civil-war

16

BLACK FLAG ON THE STEPPES

NOVEMBER 1917?

AFTER A LENGTHY MEETING, THE BOARD OF DIRECTORS agreed to the co-operative education plan on a trial basis for one term. Katarina selected the brightest boys between the ages of eight and ten, coaching them on proper behavior and procedures in the printing press. Each child was to train at *The Post* for a half day a week. Under the supervision of the headmaster, Katarina would conduct a formal examination at the end of the term. Based on this, and on Regier's reports, the school board would decide whether to continue the program.

In the beginning, the added tutoring time in mentoring students, plus Heinrich's frequent and lengthy absences in his dedicated position of field journalist, frustrated production. Katarina capitalized on the growing pains, convincing Regier to task her with editing Heinrich's work.

"You can't change his voice," Regier protested. "Spelling and grammar only." When she pushed to write a few articles on her own, he balked. "We can't have a female columnist in this paper. It'll be scandalous."

"I'll put your name on it, then. Or Heinrich's. Or Jacob's. Just let me write something," Katarina implored.

"Fine. But the tone must be masculine. And it must sound like me." He waved a finger in her face. "And don't be telling anyone. And don't expect any literary credit."

"Everyone knows I work here. What do they think my job is?"

"You're here to classify the church rosters, clean the office, and make coffee and sandwiches. Supervise the students. And keep the public's nose out of my business." He sighed and added, "I expect they know that you help with typesetting. I've been asked. I couldn't exactly deny it. Your blackened fingernails are much too obvious."

"Oh," Katarina cringed on examining her hands. "I guess they are. I'll need to do a better job with the soap."

"I soak mine in linseed oil. If that doesn't work, try petrol," Regier added.

That explains the manicure. "Huh. Thanks." Fingernails aside, Katarina wondered if Regier feared tarnishing his reputation or if he was protecting hers. Other than Anna, no one had cautioned her about working at *The Post*. The fact that the church leaders' visits — or spot-checks as she called them — had lessened as of late boosted her confidence about the community's acceptance of her position. Anyway, as far as she was concerned, those gray-haired heads could take their old-fashioned opinions to the grave. She rather enjoyed altering tradition.

Katarina quickly discovered that copy editing was a refined art with an intense learning curve in concise writing and headline creation. In addition to polishing her German spelling and grammar, every spare minute between class and lunch breaks was devoted to practice. After a dozen attempts, she presented Regier with a completed article for review.

"I underestimated your skills," he muttered. "Maybe you can do this after all."

Katarina could barely contain her excitement. "Just think, Anna," she announced one morning over breakfast. "One day, a female columnist will write for *The Post*. Maybe it will be me."

Anna choked on her prips and coughed. "The church will never agree. Get your head out of the clouds, Katarina. That's not in your future."

"The church doesn't control who works at *The Post*. Regier can hire anyone he wants."

"No. But he is a deacon in the church. So, everything he does is scrutinized."

"True enough. But imagine if they agreed; why ... maybe I could even become a reporter, like Heinrich."

Anna set her cup down. "Katarina, this nonsense has got to stop. Women cannot hold such roles. If they did, who would raise the children? Reporters travel all over the countryside and go into crime-infested areas. That would be extremely dangerous for any woman. I can't believe you fantasize about such nonsense. Have you been seduced by Bolshevism?"

Katarina grimaced. "I suppose you have a point there."

"I suggest that you stick to writing children's stories. Something you can teach at school. You can repurpose them later at home — reading to your nieces and nephews and one day to your own children."

"I want more for my life."

"You always do."

A few weeks later, Regier became more accommodating. "Katarina, can you review today's news wires? And highlight the best ones."

"Can I study the political maps, too? It'll help me understand what I'm reading."

"Yes, yes. We need to keep abreast of the war activities. The public needs to know. And see if there's anything new on that Makhnovsky character. If he's causing more problems, we must alert the colonies."

"Can I read *everything*?"

He looked over the top of his glasses and waved his hands. "I won't be held responsible if you faint on me. Read what you must."

As Katarina's work world expanded, her heart sank at the grim and often shocking global news. Daily reports of death and destruction suggested there was no escape from the chaos. As she watched Regier chart the movement of the front lines, her stomach tightened with the frightening reality that the war was headed directly towards the colonies. It was only a matter of time until they would be caught in the fray. She prayed it would end before reaching them.

As the days shortened and the nights grew longer, her yearning for freedom grew. But when David's letters to Anna verified the heavy truth of war hammering through the Teletype, her hopes of traveling the world as a teacher or a newspaper woman dampened. She consoled herself with reading fantasy. When that no longer satisfied, she joined Anna at teatime, a ball of wool and knitting needles in her hands, resigned to her predicted future.

Anna smiled but said nothing, only refilling her cup with more tea.

A few weeks later, Regier slapped a second apocalyptic report on top of her notebook. "Makhno struck again, this time close to his hometown of Gulai-Poyle. He's raiding the large estates. Katarina, you must speak with your sister. Chances are, you're in harm's way. I suggest you consider moving before he sets an ambush for your place."

"Moving? To where? The entire world is in turmoil." Katarina frowned as she read the paper.

"Somewhere you can hide until this war ends." Regier peered over his glasses and tapped a pencil on his palm. "Go to the mountains or the sea. Doesn't David's family own a summer house in the south? Somewhere near the royal family's estate? I hear the Imperial government has control of Sevastopol."

"The palace is in Yalta, I believe. But if there's any royals in hiding there, you can be assured Lenin will send his rebels and the entire place will blow up in a firestorm. There's already a red line heading that way. And the German warships along the coastline are shooting cannonballs at our men. I'd be surprised if the palace is still standing when this war ends.

"Besides, how can a small house in the middle of nowhere be more secure than our big estate with all our servants? Olek's got the entire place guarded like a fortress." A shadow passed over the window and blocked the light. She looked up and groaned at the sight of gray snow-filled clouds. "And Anna's with child. We can't go anywhere until next year, at least."

Regier shook his head. "I fear for your family. And I pray things go well for Anna this time. It's a risky year to be having babies. I can't imagine fleeing in the middle of winter with little ones. Hopefully, the snows will slow the bandits down. God willing this entire war turns around in the next few months." Regier waved the pencil in her face. "But Katarina, if the threat continues, you should make plans to leave in the spring. For your own safety. Consider it a back-up plan, if — God forbid — something awful happens. Think of the Black Sea as an exquisite and romantic destination to wait out this rebellious nonsense. Warships aside, ships offer escape routes to safer destinations. I'm considering taking my family to Crimea. I may even send them to Constantinople."

Katarina sighed. "I hear your concern, cousin. But Anna and I talked about your worries. First, she won't go anywhere without the encouragement of her husband. David's not recommending any changes right now. He's telling us to stay put. Secondly, Anna has full confidence in the servants. Some have been with the family their entire lives. She says they'd never harm us. They might even die for us."

"Don't be blinded by their politeness, Katarina. The junior ones could turn on you in a heartbeat. Be very careful what you say around them. There's a reason we call them cornstalks. They pretend to see and hear nothing, but that's not true. They all have big ears and eyes, and they pass information to each other. Although most are uneducated by our standards, they're not stupid. With exceptions of course. Olek being one — educated — I mean. He's in a class by himself. I don't consider him a local. Besides, like the other seniors — he knows who butters his bread. But I fear for you ladies. What if something happens to him?"

Regier took a deep breath and blew it out in a long, slow stream. "I'm not discounting David's advice. It may be premature to move. But you're right about me being nervous. And with good reason. Makhno's following is burgeoning. He's encouraging rebellion against the status quo. The wealthy — like your families, are the old guard, a threat to the new social order. The peasants want change too, but few trust the politics in Petrograd. They want a local solution.

"Now read this latest news." Regier thrust a Russian newspaper in front of her and pointed to the headline. "November 7, 1917. The Bolsheviks overthrow the provisional government and infiltrate the winter palace. Kerensky is out and Lenin is in charge. The Imperial government is finished. This means the Bolsheviks now dictate our future. And Lenin is declaring drastic changes to private land ownership. 'Collectivization' he calls it — the elimination of the sole ownership of property. Katarina, the entire economy of our world is about to change." Regier's eyes darted around the room. "Listen carefully. Read between the lines. We were born in an era of privilege where land was money, but this is no longer that Russia."

The worry in Regier's voice was almost palpable. Katarina's stomach tightened. "But Ukraine will achieve independence. We won't be subject to the Soviet's policies if that happens."

"Don't believe it. Ukraine has been in flux for the past three years and is in constant arguments with Mother Russia. Nothing is certain. Independence is an expensive commodity. Look at the surrounding upheaval. We've not had a consistent, reliable, or trustworthy government in a very long time.

"Who makes and enforces our laws in this part of the country today? Think, Katarina. Right now, Makhno is intimidating the colonies and making up his own rules as he goes along. Trust this — he's intent on erasing the Mennonite colonies — starting with the wealthy. You watch. He'll use the Bolsheviks' policies to achieve his personal agenda. You, my dear cousin, are a target." Regier pointed a long bony finger in her direction.

Katarina shifted in her seat and looked down so he wouldn't see her roll her eyes. The conversation was becoming tiresome. "I get it, cousin. We're living in scary times. But we can't hide out just because some local trouble-maker wants to shoot up our property. Many things could change in the coming months. Anyway, it's not my decision to make. I still depend on my family. Besides, Anna says she's not going anywhere until David is home from the war — unless it's life and death. And I can't abandon my sister in her hour of need. Look, I know the country's in disarray, and everyone's on edge, but there's still seed in the granaries for the spring planting, and we have plenty to eat. There's still hope ... by the way, I heard the old men are planning a Selbstschutz in every village."

"Another ridiculous idea. A self-defence unit in every village? And who is going to run that? Old men and little boys? And where will the guns come from? The government confiscated our weapons when they accused us of our German sympathies. Will we be fashioning replicas? That will terrify the rebels." Regier looked up at the ceiling and threw his arms in the air in mock horror.

"And think further, Katarina. The church forbids 'an eye for an eye.' Do you think that old men who've been indoctrinated by the church to never pull a trigger on a human being would have the guts to do so now? They'd sooner shoot themselves. And can you imagine the emotional impact on the young ones if they do so? They'll be traumatized for life. No, Katarina. It's a façade. Even if they do acquire enough real guns, Makhno and his bandits won't buy it. A Selbstschutz only makes a mockery of justice and our religion." Regier tapped a pencil on the desk, then sat down and scribbled a note. "That reminds me. I must get Heinrich to attend a few political meetings in Tokmak. It's the only way we can be certain of the truth behind the latest rumors. But he'll need a disguise to keep himself safe."

"That sounds dangerous."

"It is risky. If they discover him, he may not make it out of there alive. And it's his option to go in or not. But it's our responsibility to give the community firsthand information so they can prepare themselves. Whether it's Makhno or the broader war, we don't want to end up as fish in the pond trying to escape the net. War is fluid and we don't know what tomorrow brings."

"My father says war is temporary. We can't give up hope for brighter days. If not Russia, then Germany. He says there's a chance Little Russia could become part of Germany if they win this war."

"Germany is still too far away to hear our cries."

"*Ja*. For now. That may change. As for me, I'll focus on giving the schoolchildren a sense of continuity and stability while the storm rages around us. I tell them the war is not here, it's out there. Of course, part of me feels like I'm lying to them. Letting them know all is well, when it isn't. I tell myself that I'm helping in my own unique way. Besides, there hasn't been any fighting here yet, who's to say God won't keep it away from us?"

"Oh, it's here all right. Makhno is making sure of it. Perhaps it's not Russia and Germany marching the streets ... yet. That might be almost better. At least we would know what to expect. The only predictable thing about Makhno is that he is trouble with a capital T. And the youth love him. The black flag of anarchy flies from rooftops in Tokmak. Rebels wander the streets with their guns in plain view ...

stealing from honest citizens .... robbing stores ... it's all for the cause, they say." Regier pushed back his chair and strode to the cast-iron stove, tossed a log in the fire, and lit the match. "There must be a storm coming," he muttered as he pulled his wool sweater tighter and rubbed his arms.

"Olek says the rebels give to the less fortunate after they steal from the rich. If that's true, it's no wonder the locals admire him. I wonder if they really believe Makhno is doing good or that he will actually free them from their hardships?" Katarina made quotation marks in the air around the word hardship. "He's a conundrum of contradictions. Why the necessity for violence? He lived and worked among us. It's baffling."

"You're right, Katarina. They're confusing people, and their actions are illogical. Why did they need to murder those families ... and the servants, too? Are we to anticipate more of this? And why haven't they been arrested? Is there no law and order anymore?" Regier scratched his head and adjusted his glasses. "My questions are redundant. There is no rationale. And there is no law and order anymore. There's only chaos. We must tighten our security and keep a watchful eye on our neighbors.

"I fear it's the beginning of a season of horror like nothing we've ever seen before. Watch your back because you may not see tomorrow." Regier shook a finger in the air emphasizing his point.

The lights flickered as the wind howled in the empty streets. Katarina stretched her neck and pulled the shawl tightly around her shoulders, then shuffled to the stove and held her hands over the hot grate. "I hope he doesn't target us."

"Me too, Katarina. Me too."

CONFUSED HISTORY

1951 POST-WAR GERMANY

"This isn't right." Peter stopped reading and looked up.

"What do you mean?" Reinhart set the spectacles aside and scratched his bald spot.

"Her dates ... they're off. If it's the same incident ... it didn't happen until January of '18."

The gray cat with the yellow eyes ogled Peter before jumping off the oaken desk and landing on the floor in front of him. Peter pulled his feet under his chair and waited for the cat's next move.

The cat ignored him, padded over to the bookcase beside him and sat on its haunches scrutinizing the empty spaces. After identifying a potential resting place on the third shelf, it leapt up, nestled between two books, and curled up.

Peter waited for the cat to settle before continuing. "My notes indicate there were only five gruesome deaths. And that family *was* decapitated. That is, if we are indeed talking about the same Thiessen family. However, there were other vicious attacks in October of '17 in that region. But none accredited to Makhno. And I'd expect corroboration of such crimes."

"Didn't Katarina pride herself on her research? Why would she make such a mistake? From what we've learned so far, she was detail oriented and a perfectionist."

"Yes, that's what's throwing me off. I can't believe she'd do it deliberately. There must be something else going on here."

"Was there another Thiessen family murdered in such a gruesome way?" Reinhart linked his hands behind his head and stretched. His gaze drifted to the ceiling and flicked over the bookshelves before returning to rest on Peter.

Peter shrugged. "Your guess is as good as mine. Keep in mind, there was a general state of lawlessness in the region. Some disappeared and were never heard from again, others buried before identities were known. To be honest, I'm speculating. Most records are inaccessible, buried behind Stalin's iron curtain, and there are few documented survival stories. The diaspora is now all over the world. The challenge is to compile a complete picture before they die, but it's hard to do when the information is hidden — and God only knows where. If and when communism falls — and we hope it does — then we'll retrieve more concrete data, as long as it hasn't been destroyed and the graves are intact. If not, then we've got an even bigger mountain in front of us. We need the truth. This history's important."

"Relax, Peter. We'll figure this out. This is cultural anthropology — for lack of a better word — and Katarina's narrative is only one slice of the cake. When you explore other accounts, you'll get a more accurate picture. I understand the personal relevance to your life, but don't let the minutiae throw you off course. Chart it and set it aside until you can substantiate."

Peter exhaled in a long stream. Was Reinhart correct? Was he getting caught up in trivia or was Katarina trying to show him something? She seemed so sure until this point, and he wanted to believe her. But at the same time, he didn't.

The surreal stories seemed a bit exaggerated. He hadn't heard these tales told like this while growing up. Jacob Regier seemed like such an important person in Katarina's life and yet, he couldn't recall her ever talking about him. More to the point, the youthful Katarina didn't much resemble the mother he remembered. Had she changed that much since the war? If so, had he also been transformed by his own trauma? Was the development of his own problem-solving skills affected by how she — as his parent — coped with her dark shadows?

If he hadn't lived through Germany's recent and revolting history, or come face-to-face with the astonishing capacity of evil, he would never have believed Katarina's writings. But he had seen horror with his own eyes. Senseless murders, the cadavers in the streets, waking to ghosts in the dark night — Katarina and him, and even Reinhart shared these scars of war. Experience was truth to the survivor. It couldn't be discounted.

Still, his soul wanted proof. And he wanted to know the person she was then. He wanted to connect with her happy, innocent past and touch the pain that changed her. He wanted to hold her hands while she cried, hug her, and help her heal. Maybe then, his own nightmares would leave.

If he could go behind Russia's iron curtain and see the graves, read the ledgers, find the original documentation in her handwriting ... then, he could accept her diaries verbatim. When would those doors open? Or was there a way to cross into the forbidden zone without detection?

"Peter," Reinhart's voice jarred Peter from his musing. "Did Makhno personally take credit for his violence? If there were no survivors, how did they know who was responsible? Did he show up at every murder scene or leave a sign? I'm thinking of tokens ... the kind serial killers leave behind."

"Good question. I'm not aware of any souvenir finds. As for the legacy, well, you know how rumours spread. Undoubtedly, some tales were aggrandized. And his own followers bragged. And with the chaotic and fuzzy history in Ukraine, many crimes can't be attributed to any one party. However, as far as these murders, Makhno was present in October of '17, so it could have happened then. But I'm quite sure this crime happened in January."

"Are you positive your particulars are correct? Historians have been known to be wrong before. You're reading directly from her diary ... correct?"

"Yes, but ..." Peter flicked the pages, studied two, then rifled back to the original entry. He chewed his bottom lip.

"You look puzzled, Peter. Is this the first time you've seen this entry?" Reinhart leaned forward, placing both elbows on the desk.

"No, I've read this before, but I just noticed something new. She goes back and forth between German and Russian in her writing. I'm not fluent in Russian. It takes me awhile to translate." Peter tapped on the page. "Reinhart, do you remember asking me about the accuracy of this diary?"

"Yes. That was a huge concern of mine in the beginning."

"Maybe it's nothing ... I never paid attention to this

before. In the beginning of the diary, she switches between pencil and ink. There are pages of just pencilled notes — which look like they've been written in a hurry, then very neat sections in ink — which tells me that she was sitting down and carefully considering her words. I always assumed this meant some entries were written during breaks at work, while the neater ones were completed during her off hours at Anna's house. But that may not necessarily be the case."

"You've lost me. What does this have to do with the veracity of her notations?"

"This entry isn't dated like the others. She only gives the date of the incident, followed by a question mark. That tells me she wasn't exactly sure of when this happened. Plus, the rest of this diary is all scribed in the same ink and is in German only — as if written at the same time. And the style changes here. The angle of her lettering is different, the flowery romantic style of a young girl's penmanship is gone. This is a more mature script. It's as if she's no longer telling herself a story. Instead, she's writing to remember, either so she doesn't forget or to inform the reader."

"Can I see that?" Reinhart put on his eyeglasses, leaned forward and held out his hand.

"Sure." Peter shuffled around the desk to avoid the cat, handed the open book to Reinhart, and pointed. "Look at the earlier and later entries."

Reinhart leafed through the book. "I see what you mean. This is curious. When did she write this? Is she retracing her steps, or only fixing the legibility? Did she rewrite a missing piece of history later because she realized its importance? Or was the chronology relevant? Redundant questions, I suppose. I notice this book ends at the beginning of '18. Is there another?"

"Ja, there are three. I haven't yet studied the others extensively."

"I suggest comparing this handwriting against the others." Reinhart handed the text back to Peter.

Peter closed the book — ignoring the sleeping cat — he returned to the chair and plopped down in his seat. For the past week, he'd wondered if there was nothing more to this book than a young girl's fanciful imaginations. Now, he saw intention behind the scribbles. But why?

He poked at the hole. "I suppose it's not unusual for a young diarist to want to fill in the blank spaces weeks or months later, especially if they realize the significance of a particular incident. I've done that myself ... reviewed my notes only to realize I'd forgotten to mention something important. So then, I quickly add what I do remember at that time, even though I'm aware that my memory might be hazy."

"In my experience, Peter, it's easy to dismiss details when life gets hectic. And we know Katarina was a busy young woman. If she only wrote a few times a month, other things must have come up. She likely remembered other aspects of the murders later but was perhaps unclear on when. Especially, if multiple atrocities were going on at the same time." Reinhart removed his glasses and set them aside.

"That makes sense. She'd have recognized the historical importance during the Red Rage in '18 and Makhno's reign of terror in '19."

"Yes, especially after working on the genealogical data for *The Post*."

Peter agreed, but something was still off. He frowned and scratched his chin. "Except those graves were marked.

And the deaths recorded in the ledgers. What are we missing?"

"Good question, Peter. Did she have physical access to both the church records and *The Post's* ledgers when she wrote this?"

"Huh. Maybe not. Something must have happened. I'll need to review the next diary to find out." Peter drummed his fingers on the book. If only the trail could be more obvious. It would help if he knew exactly what he was looking for. But he didn't. Maybe the next journal would clarify this one.

"Texts get lost all the time. I know we're speculating here, but it could be that simple." Reinhart reached for a pad and jotted a note.

Peter nodded. "That's true. Except it doesn't fit with the person I knew. She had hiding spots for everything. And with her love of reading .... no. It was something else. And let's not forget this dramatic shift in her scrawl."

"All right. Let's say she was prevented from getting to the book for some reason. Time and maturity would have changed her handwriting."

"That drastically? How much time? Reinhart, in my experience a person's autograph changes in one of two ways — either slowly over many years — or by a significant event that alters their personality. This is one chapter with a dramatic switch. And she doesn't revert."

"Despair and worry can alter one's personality. Perhaps it's as simple as that. She fell into hard times and lost her joy."

Peter nodded. "I suppose it's possible."

The clock struck four. The gray cat with the yellow eyes awoke, yawned and jumped down from its perch. It brushed against Peter's pant leg, startling him and then circled the chair. Peter glared at the animal. "He better not jump on me. I'm going out for dinner. I don't want cat hair on me."

Reinhart whistled and opened his drawer and removed a *Nurnberger rostbratwurst*. He broke off a piece, held it out to the cat who ran over and nibbled from his hand; then popped the rest of the small sausage in his mouth. Reinhart cocked his head as the cat chewed, the corners of his mouth twitching with a slight grin. "Where's your spunk, boy? Have you always been so serious?"

Peter shook his head and toyed with the hem of his tweed jacket. "Cats make me think of the war. Please don't make me explain."

"Ghosts that keep you up at night? You're not alone. We all have them. But we can't hide under the blankets forever." Reinhart's blue eyes crinkled at the corners.

"I'm not hiding from mine. But I don't want to pull on the wrong thread in her story."

"Why? Will something unravel if you do?"

"Reinhart, when I had my accident ... do you remember me telling you about the day I was mugged in the park — after Mom and I had that fight?"

"Yes, I remember. You connected the impact of your trauma to Katarina's accident in the barn." Reinhart leaned back and folded his arms over his chest.

"Right. Well, I remember something else now. When the police questioned me about the details, I was confused. I couldn't answer questions about the hobos — what they looked like or what they were wearing. I walked back to the park weeks later, and I couldn't even remember where I was sitting at the time. I couldn't find the bench. Even now, almost fifteen years later, I walk the park and get a creepy feeling that I'm standing right where it happened, yet I don't recognize the exact spot. It's like there's a dead space in my memory. Yet, I can give you details about everything else that day — even what I had for breakfast."

"Memory is a funny thing, Peter. I've had my own experiences, too. Trauma and time impact our recall. Some events fade, others sharpen. How old were you then?"

"Nineteen. It was 1937. I wanted to join the Luftwaffe. Mom wouldn't hear of it. I searched her dresser for my records. Then I found them. And she caught me. Then we fought and I ran out."

"That's a different story than what you told me last time." Reinhart uncrossed his arms, leaned forward and picked up a pen.

"Is it? Maybe I'm getting the timelines mixed up." Peter ran his fingers through his hair.

"And there's your answer!" Reinhart tapped the side of the pen on the notepad.

"Huh? I'm not following." Peter frowned.

"You just admitted your own mix up. Do you see how easily that happens?"

"So ... when there's more than one version, how do we know which one is right?"

Reinhart smiled and nodded. "Peter, have you ever noticed the variances in the accounts of two individuals who were in the same place at the same time? Each remembers something the other missed. Then, when they remind each other of the omitted details, they correct their version. The story changes both in how it's told and in their recall. They don't remember what they forgot the first time. Here's my take on your memory. Let's see if we can flush this out and apply this process to Katarina's confusion."

"Go ahead." Peter cocked his head and gazed sideways at his friend.

"First. Humans have this incredible capacity to deny reality even when it's happening to them. In the middle of a life-threatening event, there's no awareness of fear. Instincts take over. We react. Later, when we comprehend our near-death experience, we collapse. When we tell the story later, we relate the most impactful moments.

"Katarina's accident shook her security and made her aware of the unpredictable nature of life. Then there was Margaretha's death. This triggered her awareness of her own mortality. She could have died but didn't. Instead, her infant niece who should have lived, died.

"Now, look at this through a young girl's lens. She's coming of age and wants adventure and excitement, but at the same time she needs safety and certainty. Just when she wants to step out on her own, the world slaps her with the ugly reality that nothing is as it should be. It shakes her to the core. Maybe, it hits her so hard that she can't write it down. Does her narrative change accordingly? Or does it shift her future perspective? That remains to be seen." Reinhart sat back and tapped the pen against his palm. He stared across the room.

"Peter, you were exposed to a life-threatening event, but your mind blocked that moment and silenced the fear. Why? Because we're built to survive. Whether it's adrenaline or a built-in God-inspired zeal to live, we don't willingly choose to die.

"Point number two: when fear overwhelms, we shut down. We must replace the fear with something in order to keep going. The denial of imminent death helps our soul to push back against the trauma and keep us alive.

"Peter, what kept the holocaust survivors alive in the camps without enough nourishment to sustain life? Hope. The belief that things would get better, and help would come. Believing that they were not forgotten. That someone cared. That, and with the sibling support of their fellow sufferers and sheer willpower, they felt they still had some ownership of their destiny.

"Why did the Mennonites fare better during the Holodomor than the average Ukrainian? Same reason."

"Reinhart, I agree with your theory, although I doubt the relevance to Katarina's confusion in dates. Are you speculating that the grotesque nature of the crime kept her from recording it properly?"

"When we don't know the truth, Peter, we need to keep asking until we find answers. There is no such thing as a stupid question. If you want to be a historical researcher, you need to accept vagueness. Don't bury the paperwork because you don't like how it's presented. Work with what you have."

"In that case, I'll carry on. There may be more answers later." Peter stood up and buttoned his jacket. "Reinhart, do you think traumatic events trigger decision points in our lives?"

Reinhart drew his eyebrows together. "I'm not sure I follow."

"I keep thinking about her accident and mine. They're different, of course. But then I remember something she said. She felt like the event had thrown her into an invisible intersection and she'd made a wrong turn. She wanted to run back and correct her course, but she couldn't."

Reinhart nodded. "Yes, that makes sense. Fear amplifies trauma and makes us insecure about our future. We're suddenly aware we can't control everything. The *what if's* grip our mind. Everything is now colored by the event. Didn't you feel that way after being mugged?"

"*Ja.* But in my case, the rush to grow up was only

delayed, the route wasn't altered. However, if I had joined the Luftwaffe when I wanted to, I might not be alive today. I shudder to think of the war crimes investigations. If I'd been in a different place and time, I could be in the middle of interrogations right now."

Reinhart raised his eyebrows. "You were spared."

"I was."

"Peter, if there is a God with a master plan, then he has a reason for everything and a purpose for everyone. If there isn't, then there are a lot of strange coincidences in the world. I understand why people turn to the Divine for answers. It gives them a sense of mastery over their life. As for me, after going through the war, I sense there's something bigger out there managing the bigger picture, but I can't believe that IT or HE cares about my daily life. I guess you could say I'm an agnostic."

"I suppose we all wrestle with faith at some point."

"Peter, did your religion sustain you through the war?"

"I don't know. Maybe." Peter pointed to the diary. "When I read the stories from those who survived such horrible tragedies, I see where faith was the essence of their hope. Despite their failings, they believed in a personal God who cared about them."

"Peter, inside every church, you'll find both true believers and pretenders. The Mennonites were no different. Katarina only desired truth. She clawed at the veneer of hypocrisy hoping to find it or tear it down."

"Yes. You are so right. In her younger years, Mom was both curious and idealistic. For a time, the truth was hidden under chocolate-covered plums and surrounded by Christmas trees. But everyone knows such seasons don't last." Peter lifted the crystal glass and sipped the last drop.

"Ah, but even those with the thickest skins have

romantic hearts," Reinhart chuckled as he raised his glass in a toast.

"And during the war, romance kept hope alive, too. Even when faith is tainted, everyone believes in love. At the age of fifteen, Mom swore she didn't want marriage, but the seed of her future had already been planted."

"Are you saying faith and love balance each other?"

"I don't know, Reinhart. But it seems to me that those are the two determinants of life that keep hope alive."

"And every trauma survivor needs hope to keep living. Perhaps that's what colors our memories."

"What do you mean?"

"The fight to live requires a belief in a brighter future. The seed of optimism exists inside our souls."

"Like Christmas."

"Yes, Peter, just like Christmas and chocolate-covered plums."

18

MENNONITE GAMES

NOVEMBER 1917, PENNER ESTATE, MOLOTSCHNA COLONY

THE END OF THE HARVEST ANNOUNCED THE BEGINNING of the pre-Christmas social season, commencing before the disruptions of the heavy winter snows. Traffic to the estate swelled as Anna's ladies' committees organized for church dinners and charity functions, while other visitors dropped in without warning — sometimes with the obvious motivation to garner invitations to more exclusive functions. Katarina considered the shoulder-rubbing pretentious and tried to avoid being dragged into what she considered tiresome gossip and snobbery.

When a second carriage rattled up the long driveway during Anna's self-proclaimed Saturday tea-time, Katarina pulled the curtains on the gabled windows and closed the door to the study. Just as she settled herself at the rolltop desk, a rapid triple-knock interrupted her thoughts and Anna breezed in. Katarina buried her face in her hands and groaned.

"Change your clothes, we have company. Tante Susz is here." Anna yanked open the floral drapes, roping them to the brass tie-backs with braided golden cords. "How can you sit in the dark when there's such brilliant sunshine today? See how the sun dances on the snow. And look at the colors through the stained glass. You should be enjoying this beauty, Katarina. Christmas is coming, and the snow is fresh. Winter will be dull and boring soon enough. You can hide then." She put her hands on her hips and stared at Katarina, a look of disdain on her face. "What's wrong with you. Are you feeling all right?"

"I'm fine. I have work to do. I didn't want to be interrupted."

"Well, too bad for you. Tante Susz is here. It must be important. Now go change your clothes before she criticizes them."

"What's she doing here? She hasn't been here since ..." *since Margaretha's funeral.* Katarina slammed her book shut and rolled down the wooden panel on the desk. "She's probably attending the funeral in town. She won't stay long. God forbid she misses the latest gossip."

"Alyona's pouring tea and preparing lunch. She'll expect it." Anna gave a critical eye to the stack of books beside the desk.

"She won't leave if you feed her." Katarina tossed a lace doily on top of the pile.

"Don't be so crass, Kat. Hurry. Go put on a darker dress. I don't want her berating us about our bright colors."

"Oh, *ja.* Blue is so shocking," Katarina said sarcastically and rolled her eyes. "Should I wear white?"

"Go. We'll be in the parlor." Anna fluffed her skirt and trotted out of the room, then did a dramatic U-turn and came back. "Oh, I almost forgot to tell you."

"What?"

Anna's face glowed. "I received David's letter today. He says there's a possibility he might be home for Christmas. There's buzz the war is ending soon. Isn't that exciting news?

There's always rumors. "I'm happy you're happy. What does that have to do with Tante Susz?" Katarina yawned as she walked to the window and pulled the drapes closed.

Anna gawked and put her hands on her hips. "Nothing. I'm just telling you. Good grief, Katarina. I just opened those. Don't you want to let the sunshine in?"

"It gets too warm and then I get sleepy and can't get anything done." *And I don't need the entire world seeing my work pile.*

"Fine," Anna chirped. "Well, hurry up and change. She's waiting." She fluffed her skirt again and scampered out of the room.

Katarina rubbed her face and grumbled before padding down the long hallway and up the stairs to her bedroom. After staring at the choices in her closet, she chose a simple black wool with an embroidered white collar, praying the dour aunt would ignore the fancy design. She tied her calf-skin shoes with a double knot, checked her appearance in the mirror, tightened her bun and covered it in black lace with simple rosettes and checked for stray blond threads; then patted her pale cheeks until the color rose before heading down to the parlor.

Their mother's elder sister sat in the floral wing chair with her stockinged feet resting on the stitched footstool, her Victorian lace-ups on the floor beside her. She raised the cup of mint tea to her lips and gave a curt nod as Katarina waltzed into the room.

"Tante Susz, how delightful to see you. What brings

you by in this frigid weather? We haven't seen you in months." Katarina bent down and kissed her aunt's cheeks.

The beady blue eyes followed Katarina to the loveseat. "I'm attending the funeral of the late elder Epp. I thought I might encourage you ladies to keep me company. They're expecting quite a crowd today." A smiled played with the corners of her mouth, emphasizing the bouncing jowls under her square chin, her curly silver hair adding exclamation marks as it poked out in feathery tufts beneath the black lace head covering. A trio of black silk roses pinned to the top of her head jutted out like a crow's tail feathers.

Katarina bit her lip to keep from laughing at the woman's comical costume. She wondered how many layers one could wear before they drowned in a sea of black. "Thanks for the invitation, but I think I'll pass. I'm not much in the funeral mood these days and I barely knew the man." She hoped an abrupt closure to the topic would deter the woman from pushing.

"Yes, me too. And I'm a bit under the weather." Anna patted her belly.

"It's nice to see you in the family way again, Anna. I pray all goes well this time." Susz set her cup down on the stand beside the chair and adjusted her knitted shawl. "I stopped by because I thought Katarina may wish to survey the crowd there. One never knows what eligible bachelors will attend."

"Thanks, but I'm not shopping for a husband," Katarina said with a chuckle. The pale wrinkled face peeking out from the dark clothing seemed to levitate in mid-air. It was hard to take her aunt seriously.

"Humpft!" Susz sighed. "Well, I hate to go alone. After my George passed last year, I don't pass up an event to assess potential new companions. Men don't want to live alone, you know. They need a strong woman to look after them. And I will not say no to a good offer."

Katarina clamped her lips between her teeth and poured a cup of tea. She looked over at Anna who sat poker straight, her mouth drawn in a tight smile, her eyes wide, but otherwise a blank look on her face while she stared at the elderly aunt. It was obvious Anna was restraining herself from bursting out laughing. After swallowing her own giggle bubble, Katarina turned back to her aunt. "I'm very sorry, but I'm quite busy. Isn't there anyone else who can keep you company today?"

The beady eyes flashed, and the wrinkled mouth formed into a perfect circle. The jowls bounced as the head nodded. "Dear Katarina, this isn't just about me. I stopped in because I'm concerned about you. The entire community is disturbed that you're not more involved with your peers. You spend all your time working and conversing with mature men. Now, if this is the type of man that meets your interest, then you need to attend events where they congregate. I can help you identify some eligible possibilities."

Katarina felt the color rise in her cheeks. "Tante Susz, I know you mean well, but I don't fit in with most of my peers. My interests differ. I prefer more solitary pursuits, and I doubt such men who share my interests will be attending elder Epps funeral."

"I disagree. I know of one young gentleman — escorting a friend of mine — who I believe you'd find quite endearing. With your permission, I'd like to make an introduction."

"An introduction?" Anna made eye contact with Katarina and wiggled her eyebrows. "Do tell, Tante Susz. Who do you have in mind?"

"My great nephew on my late husband's side."

Katarina's hand skimmed her mouth to stop another

giggle from surfacing. The elderly women in the community — whom she nicknamed the gossip crowd — saw it as
their personal mission to match up young couples for
wedlock. It was obvious that Tante Susz felt Katarina's
future was hers.

"Oh, which one are you referring to?" Curiosity
bubbled in Anna's voice as she refilled the teacups.

Katarina groaned. Surely her sister wasn't buying into
this nonsense. She didn't have time or energy to put into a
relationship with a man. They had discussed this more than
once. Only last week, Anna had agreed to leave the subject
alone.

"Young George Klassen. He's a hard worker and is very
committed to the church," the elder woman said in a matter-
of-fact way. The wrinkled hand quivered when she picked
up the teacup. Her eyes drifted to the oak leaf carvings on
the arched doorway.

There was something odd about the way Susz spoke the
man's name that triggered Katarina to scrutinize the
woman's demeanor. "Oh? what kind of work does he do?"

Susz transferred the teacup to her left hand and pulled
out a handkerchief from behind her waistband. "He's
training to become a blacksmith. I'm told he has an excellent aptitude."

"Aptitude? Is that his father's business?" Anna leaned
forward.

Katarina shook her head and looked down at her tea.
She wondered if Anna was playing mind games with their
aunt or truly misunderstood the comment.

"No, no, he's choosing the occupation." Susz took a sip
of her tea and looked at the wall. Her gaze drifted around
the room.

Choosing? Katarina and Anna made eye contact and

frowned in unison. Anna raised her eyebrows. The Kroeger clock struck eleven. Katarina turned and glared at Tante Susz while the chimes played. The woman had something up her sleeve. She could feel it.

"Who are his parents?" Katarina narrowed her eyes and tilted her head, evaluating her aunt with a suspicious gaze.

"George and Martha."

"Which George and Martha?" Anna asked.

"I told you, the boy's father is my late husband's family."

"And the mother?" Katarina probed.

"The mother? Let me think. Oh, yes ... I believe her parents were Peter P. Peters and Elisabeth Unger."

"Were?" Katarina frowned. *She's using the past tense, which means they've died. Did I record their history? Which church were they from? From what colony? Which village?* Katarina furrowed her brows as she mentally scanned through her lineage. "I don't think there's any Ungers in our family tree."

"The name doesn't ring a bell with me, either. I don't know of any estates with such owners. Do you, Katarina?" Anna drew her eyebrows together. Katarina shook her head.

"I'm sure he's your third cousin, once removed. On your mother's side." Tante Susz set the teacup down and removed her feet from the footstool. "Now, before you say anything, I want to confirm that this intelligent young man is loyal and decent and will make an excellent husband. He enjoys learning and reading, just like you do, Katarina."

"How old is he? Why isn't he serving in the forestry like the others? Or providing medical support on the trains?" What Katarina really wanted to ask was, *What's wrong with him?*

Susz closed her eyes and coughed in her handkerchief. "He's twenty-five and he has a limp."

"A limp? He has a handicap?" Anna sat back in her chair, aghast.

Tante Susz waved her handkerchief in the air. "It's not like that. He had an injury as a young child. The plow cut his foot. It's not serious, but it does prevent him from military service. Surely you can understand, Katarina. With your crippled arm and all. The two of you can appreciate each other's deficits."

Katarina gaped. "My deficits? My arm isn't crippled. It just doesn't work as good as the other one. I broke it. It didn't heal right. It's not that obvious." She looked at Anna. "It's not so obvious, is it Anna?" Katarina slumped back as a wave of embarrassment washed over her.

Anna's mouth twitched and her cornflower blue eyes bulged. "Well, I don't think you can scrub floors or wash windows, but we'd never ask you to, either."

"It won't get better with age. She's already walking crooked with that shoulder drooping. She looks like a bird with a broken wing. She needs to get a good man now, before they stop looking at her pretty face. When she loses her looks, her choices will be gone. Then what will she do?" The trio of black roses bobbed over the black covered silver head.

"I ... I don't care if I ever get married. I can work and support myself." A chill went down Katarina's back. How dare this woman just show up and dictate her future. She had no right. Her gaze drifted to the door. She wanted to leave the room, run away. But that would only cause a scene and make matters worse. She blinked away the tears forming and swallowed the lump in her throat.

"Katarina, we've talked about this. Women don't make

enough money to be self-sufficient. And one needs a man for other things, too." Anna gave a sympathetic smile.

"Your sister's right. We're the voices of experience and reason trying to look after your welfare. We know how the world works. If you follow our lead, you won't regret it. Now tell me, Katarina, have you been to the bone doctor?" Tante Susz's beady eyes flickered over the top of her teacup.

"Yes, and he can't fix me." Katarina clamped her teeth between her lips and narrowed her eyes while she glared at the aunt. She crossed her arms and caressed the old bump.

"Well, that's important to know. Then we show off what you have and minimize what you don't. You need a strong man who doesn't mind helping around the house, or one with enough money to hire a maid. With the government and the world in such disarray, we don't know what tomorrow may bring, so it's best to stick with the most practical. In my opinion, George is a wise choice and a good match."

"Tante Susz, Katarina appreciates your concern. And surely, we don't want to cast aside any decent prospect. Her physical weakness aside, Katarina is quite capable of being a good wife to any proper young man." Anna crossed her legs and leaned forward. "But she's young, so there's still time. Let's remember that with the war going on, her options are reduced right now. But when it ends, the men will return. She'll have her hands full of choices then."

Katarina clenched her jaw and squeezed her fists as she gave Anna a dirty look.

"Anna, men are dying out there. Few come home in the same shape as when they left. No woman wants to take care of a broken man. Katarina should grab one with a sound mind and strong body before they're all off the market. Now

George may have a bad foot, but the rest of him is quite healthy."

"Well, you have a point there, Tante Susz. I'd like to know more about this young man." Anna refilled her aunt's cup and her own from the teapot on the serving trolley, replaced the pot and then sat down on the edge of the lady chair, with her ankles crossed beneath her.

Katarina slammed her empty cup on the side table. She was being ignored. Again. Her feelings were about as important to these women as the lamp in the corner of the room. "Don't I get a say about my own life?"

Both women looked at her, surprised shock registering on their faces. "Why, of course, Katarina. You have the final say. We're only searching for eligible possibilities for you," Tante Susz exclaimed.

"Goodness me, Katarina. Don't be so sensitive. We only want to steer you in the right direction. That's all," Anna said. She waved a white handkerchief in Katarina's direction. "Just sit and listen. We can talk about this later."

Katarina sunk back in her seat and rubbed her face. This matchmaking was nothing more than a game to these two, a complete waste of time. She could be working right now, being productive. Instead, she was stuck here. She hated this nonsense. If there was a sink in the room, she'd vomit.

Anna took a deep breath and looked back at the aunt. "Now, before Katarina tosses this man out the window, she needs to know what she's throwing away. Tell us more about this George with the floppy foot. A blacksmith job is heavy work. How does he manage?"

"I told you, he's a hard worker. He'll do well."

"He's a little old to be starting a new career. Why isn't

he working in his family's business? They have a business, don't they?" Anna prodded.

Katarina's eyes narrowed as Tante Susz fidgeted in her seat. She could see the aunt thinking about her words before answering. The woman was either hiding something or there was another problem with this George.

"His father worked in the sunflower oil plant until his death a few years ago and his mother isn't well. He takes excellent care of her, and the married siblings have been quite supportive. He's the youngest, so taking care of his mother has been his obligation," Tante Susz said.

"He's doing women's work? That's very strange. Doesn't he have sisters?" Anna eyes widened. "Are you sure he's ... normal? I wouldn't want Katarina to be saddled with a man with odd predilections."

Tante Susz threw her head back and laughed, "Oh yes, Anna. He's completely fine."

Katarina rolled her eyes. "A man that takes cares of his mother ... now that's a first." *He sounds weird. Much too feminine for my liking.*

"Yes, it certainly is." Anna tipped her head at Katarina with a cock-eyed glare, "He's obviously very caring," she directed her gaze back to the aunt, "but what do you mean the father worked? You mean owned, don't you? Which plant is theirs? I don't know any Klassens who own a sunflower oil plant."

The aunt coughed into her handkerchief again, then stretched her neck.

A peculiar feeling scratched at Katarina's brain. The hair on the back of her arms bristled. This was it. She'd zeroed in on the target zone. It would only take one more question to verify her suspicions. She narrowed her eyes and leaned forward. "Tante Susz, where do they live?"

The woman coughed in her hanky again and cleared her throat before spitting out the word. "Baratov."

Anna and Katarina gasped in unison and turned to make eye contact with each other. Anna blinked several times, a look of disbelief on her face. "The Hebrew area? Do they live in the village? Is the father an overseer?" Anna groped for an explanation. "Please explain, Tante Susz. And please do not tell me he's related to Agatha's nurse-maid, Ruth Schmidt, or any of *those* Mennonites."

Katarina sat back and relaxed her pose. The game was clear. The aunt's priority was to find a wife for her poor great-nephew, and she was searching in the pool of eligible contenders from a higher social standing first in order to upgrade the family name. Tante Susz was hoping for a mutual attraction between the pair so that this tidbit of status would be overlooked. Katarina was familiar with this sport. It was the reason her parents had allowed her to live with Anna. They wanted Katarina to marry up, not down. Katarina smiled at her own clever uncovering of the deceit and swallowed a chuckle. She'd play along, but she would not capitulate.

She tapped her fingers on her forearm and furrowed her brow, trying to recall the names from the church ledgers in the area. "Wait a minute. Are they related to our father's second cousin, the veterinarian in Vitebsk?"

"Yes," Tante Susz beamed. "Their mothers are first cousins. How brilliant for you to figure that out, Katarina."

"Oh. I know who he is," Katarina said, as she recalled the guest list from Anna's wedding. "He was sitting beside Peter at the wedding party."

"Who?" Anna looked at Katarina in surprise.

"Oh, nothing. I had a minor accident at your wedding. A bit of a mishap. I tripped on a hole in the grass right beside those men. It was Peter that helped me up, though. Not George. I think they're friends."

"The veterinarian's son?" A smile toyed at the corners of Anna's mouth as she made eye contact with Katarina. "Very interesting."

Katarina felt her cheeks warm as the sapphire eyes and the lanky frame danced through her mind. She gulped and her stomach tightened. She prayed Anna wouldn't stray down this rabbit trail.

"So, you've met George?" The smile on the aunt's face widened.

Katarina was thankful the aunt hadn't noticed the verbal slip. "No. Not really. But I know who you're referring to. I was rather too busy to notice anyone else." Katarina put her hands over her hot cheeks and looked down at the floor.

"Yes, of course. There's nothing more embarrassing than falling in front of a room full of men. On that day, it was the entire back yard. I heard those horrible men laughing at you as you ran away. I don't blame you for not noticing the bachelors, Kat. What an awful experience."

"It's a pity she didn't meet him. But at least, now she knows who he is." Tante Susz put her teacup on the side table.

"Oh, you can't put anything past Katarina, Tante Susz. She's very observant. And she knows who's who. She's been recording the genealogies for the colonies." Seeing Katarina's pink cheeks, Anna winked, and a large grin spread across her face.

Katarina grimaced and looked away.

"Oh, Katarina. That's marvelous. God honors such diligence. You'll encourage your future husband's success with such attention to detail."

Katarina stretched a fake smile across her face. *I'll make myself successful, thank you very much.*

Anna clapped her hands. "Wonderful. Now that we've discovered the ancestral line, let's proceed. You were about to tell us about the man's position and family status."

The aunt hesitated, pursed her lips and looked down at her hands. "Please don't dismiss the boy because of his family's situation. He's a good catch."

The smile dropped from Anna's face and her eyes narrowed. "Tante Susz, how much land does his family own?"

The woman dabbed her mouth with the handkerchief.

"Tante Susz, how many *desiatina*? A hundred, sixty? Tell us," Anna said.

"They own a house."

"A house? No land? Nothing? Do they at least own a garden plot and a cow?"

"Oh yes, they have a garden and a cow. They live in the village."

"Are you saying the family is landless?" Katarina asked the question that she suspected was hovering in Anna's mind.

"Well ... there's no farmland." Tante Susz avoided eye contact as she defended herself. "But he's a good worker. Besides, the new government's proposing land redistribution. In a few years, such wealth won't matter. Katarina should get to know the man for his personal qualities, not for his property."

Anna slammed her cup down on the tray. "Tante Susz, I'm shocked at your boldness. You know that land ownership is how we distinguish between hard workers and lazy ones. I, for one, will not even consider my sister being courted by anyone from a lower class. I can't for the life of me understand how you could even contemplate such a suggestion."

The old woman shrank in her seat. "Anna, your husband and his family own most of the town and the surrounding farmland. If Katarina were to marry down — as you suggest — surely there's enough land at your disposal that you could share with the extended family."

"Give land to an outsider? Do you have any idea how hard David and his family have worked to keep the property in the family? I was fortunate that he chose me. I wouldn't think of asking him to gift land to a total stranger."

"Anna, the man is not a foreigner. His family didn't enjoy the luxury of being in the right place at the right time, as David's family did. There was an era when many were landless. The government wasn't generous in their allotments of crown land in the early years. Not everyone gets the same start in life. It's hardly his fault."

Anna stood up and dusted the crumbs from her apron. "I'm leaving you two to talk more. I'm going to check on lunch. Please excuse me."

Katarina didn't know whether to hug her sister or thumb her nose at her aunt. Instead, she decided to deliver her decision in a polite, adult manner. "Tante Susz, I don't really care whether someone owns land or not. You're right that common interests are more important than inherited property. But my family feels it's important, and at this time in my life, I must defer to their wisdom. Please understand, I appreciate your good intentions."

"Katarina, thank you for your kindness and for considering this offer. George is a wonderful young man, and I don't think he'll be single much longer. I believe you're foolish for at least not meeting with him to see how the two of you get along. Why don't you think about it some more?

At least, come to the funeral to meet him. Please do a favor for this old lady. Make me happy."

Katarina stood in the middle of the room and contemplated the request. Accompanying the old aunt wasn't unusual — but it might open the door to speculation and gossip. At her age, the older crowd would assume she was husband shopping, and next, gentlemen callers would start coming to the house. She didn't want to risk it. "Tante Susz, I'm not ready to marry. And if I show up there, people will talk. I have my school children to think about. I must be always above discretion. My reputation depends on it." The excuse was flimsy, but it was all she could come up with.

The aunt sighed. "I understand. I can arrange for him to visit your parents the next time you're out that way. Won't you at least consider it?"

"Tante Susz, I haven't been home since last Christmas, so honestly I can't say when I'll be back, as our parents enjoy visiting us here. And now with Anna in the family way, and David gone, I doubt I'll be going back to Chortitza until after the birth. So, I'll pass on George. If God wills it otherwise, then the man will still be here when I'm ... ready." *Or desperate.* Katarina smiled politely and set her teacup on the serving tray. "Allow me to remove your cup. I'm sure lunch is almost ready."

The older woman's shoulders slumped as she handed Katarina her cup and pushed herself up from the wing chair. "I'm only trying to help, Katarina."

"I know, Tante Susz. I completely understand. But it's wartime. The rebels are gaining ground. The future is unpredictable. Anything could happen. I can't risk loving someone only to lose them."

"I disagree, Katarina. That's exactly the reason you should marry. For you never know when you'll get another chance. Isn't it better to have loved and lost than never to have loved at all?" Susz tapped her on the arm. "That's a quote from Tennyson. I read too, you know. The Bible isn't the only source of good literature. But don't tell anyone I said that."

Katarina smiled. "I can't put anything past you, Tante Susz. You are a wise woman. And educated, too. As for your Mr. Klassen, I'll sleep on it." *In your dreams.*

"That's all I ask, my dear. That's all I ask."

19

SHIFTING SNOWS

CHRISTMAS, 1917 MOLOTSCHNA

"ARE YOU COMFORTABLE, ANNA? YOU'LL NOTICE I don't care much about the other two, just you," Olek joked as he positioned the horsehair blanket around the women and tucked in the ends.

Anna giggled and Katarina rolled her eyes as Olek climbed up to the driver's seat and snapped the reins. The women held onto Anna's arms as the sleigh jerked sideways on the icy patch, then slid forward. The sharp movement dislodged the covering from Katarina's end, slipped off her knees and shifted into Agatha's direction.

Katarina yanked it back only to hear a protest from Agatha. She gritted her teeth and gripped the edge between tight fists to keep it from floating to the other end of the bench. "Agatha, if you sit on it, I get nothing," she complained.

"I'm not. I'm barely covered." Agatha argued.

Katarina leaned to look beyond Anna's growing belly to Agatha's plump frame and saw her snuggled in with the blanket stretched around her girth. She narrowed her eyes and snorted. *Barely covered, indeed.* Agatha had enough fat to keep her warm. She didn't need extra layers. The woman was being selfish. If they could squeeze together any tighter on the narrow bench with their sheepskin coats, the horse-hair covering might stretch a bit further, but Katarina doubted that was possible as her elbows were already digging into Anna's side.

She flexed her feet. "It's brutally cold. My knees are practically bare. My feet are blocks of ice. I'll freeze to death before we get home."

"Katarina, that's enough. We'll be home soon," Anna scolded.

Katarina clenched her jaw and white-knuckled the thin end piece and fumed. Next time she'd bring her own blanket and refuse to share it with them. She wiggled her toes again. "I need new boots. I think the lining's worn out."

Anna groaned, "Well then, go to the shoemaker next week and order some new ones."

"I will. I'll have them lined with sheep's wool, too."

"Fine." Anna's firm tone told Katarina to bite her tongue from complaining further.

The horses' bells jingled in the still night air, soft snowflakes fluttered from the dark starlit sky, and the full moon shimmered through the patchy clouds. The romantic ambience might be dreamy for some, but Katarina considered it too cold for sentiment. She yanked at her coat to cover the gap at her knees, then snatched the blanket before it slipped away again, only to arouse another round of protests from the bench.

"I give up," she exclaimed loudly, throwing her hands in the air. She slouched back, crossed her arms over her chest, bit the inside of her cheek and swallowed her frustration. If she got frostbite, it would be their fault.

"Lovely church service as always." Agatha broke the awkward silence.

"Yes, it's wonderful to have this one day a year when we don't have to talk about the war. Just enjoy the birth of Christ as it was meant to be," Anna chirped.

"Amen." Katarina forced a tight smile, trying to squash her annoyance; although she believed politeness wouldn't change her feelings toward Agatha. She tried another angle to impress her point about the cold. "I hope Alyona has the hot milk ready. I need it."

"Me, too. With some sugar and cinnamon," Anna said, her eyes fluttering and raised to the starry sky, "in front of a roaring fire."

Good grief. Everything's romantic with her these days. It must be a baby thing. Time to drop it, Katarina. Think of something else. Except that her negative thinking refused to switch off. "Say, what did you think of the Weih-nachtsstollen tonight? Personally, I thought it tasted a bit off, not enough honey or fruit? What did Alyona miss? And I noticed the gravy at dinner was watery."

"She's trying to economize," Anna replied.

"It's Christmas. It's hardly the time to be cutting corners." Katarina frowned.

"You're sleeping too much. You've missed the family bulletin," Agatha said in a condescending tone.

Oh, here she goes again. She's trying to pick another fight. Katarina resisted the urge to punch back. "Bulletin? What news?"

"Rationing. Flour and sugar," Agatha said in a loud, firm tone. "Like you didn't know."

"What?" Katarina scrunched her eyebrows. "I know

about the sugar. But not about the flour. Why?" Why did everyone assume she knew everything? "Is there a problem at the mill?"

"Yes," Agatha snapped.

"What happened?" Katarina pushed for more information.

"There are shortages at the mills because of the fields being razed in the summer. Blame the rebels and the militants," Anna explained.

"Since when do we depend on community resources? We have our own granaries. Our own mills," Katarina said, puzzled.

"The government's confiscating everything for the army — even we must sacrifice for the good of the country."

"*Ja*, I know that." Katarina scanned the inky horizon. "But we've enough to feed ourselves first ... no?" She looked for a reaction, but both women were staring straight ahead.

"We had." Anna's soft voice could barely be heard over the sleigh bells. "The mill storehouse was broken into last week. The stockpile was stolen."

"The grain?"

"No, silly. The flour."

"*Oba.*" An icy finger trickled down her spine and the hair on the back of her neck rose. *How did I miss this news?* Her stomach tightened, and she shivered and bit her lip. *It must be that Makhnovsky.* Saying his name or sharing her feelings about the anarchist would cause more distress. The evening was tense enough.

The back of her neck prickled as she reflected on the conversation with Regier. "I thought the elders were organizing a Selbstschutz to protect the villages."

"Ha. Fat chance of that working," Agatha interrupted as she tugged on the blanket. "They're not very organized.

And they don't have much weaponry. It's a *schmozzle* — one big confusing mess. We've never needed self-protection before. It's all new to everyone."

Anna nodded. "After the government confiscated our guns, the elders worried when the German shipments arrived —"

"— And wait until the bandits see our men parading around with rifles. They'll think we're hiding our valuables. We'll suffer more break-ins than ever. With guns in our faces, too. This won't end well," Agatha said.

Katarina reflected. Mennonites and war were not compatible terms to be used in the same sentence. The possibility of this clash was terrifying. "*Ja.* It's scary. And they know we don't bear arms ... against people, that is."

"That's right. The bullies know our beliefs." A frosty bubble formed in front of Agatha's mouth. "And the elders are teaching the boys to shoot at the sky, so no one gets hurt. As if the bad guys will run away at the sight of a scared little Mennonite boy holding a gun."

"Baa, baa," Anna mimicked the bleating of sheep and sneered, "they'll laugh at us. We are like defenseless sheep without a shepherd, they say."

"Then how do we shield ourselves?" Katarina asked, "Violence is increasing, and some have been murdered. This can't go on."

Anna snorted, "Good question. I doubt our forefathers imagined this. Non-resistance seems highly impractical right now. Self-protection is a serious concern. Surely the church can't expect us to sacrifice everything under these conditions. I understand the importance of loving our neighbors and all, but good grief."

"We are taught to love completely, even if it costs us everything," Agatha interrupted.

"But surely not at the cost of our lives?" Anna asked. "There must be another solution."

The silence grew heavy as each contemplated the price of their faith under the threat of violence. Katarina thought about the latest senseless acts of cruelty. Did they fight back? What would she do if she was confronted by the villains? Would she go to hell if she did? *Could the church be wrong?* She reflected on their traditions. Fear percolated in her soul.

The principle of non-resistance required that interpersonal conflict be managed with words, not guns. Resolution was achieved through mediation and acts of forgiveness, justice through repentance and restitution. More severe cases inside the church membership were dealt with through shunning or excommunication. Non-violent solutions were also sought between members and outsiders. God's love and justice prevailed. For over three hundred years, this protocol of Menno Simons led the self-governing colonies.

On a global scale, the church taught that Christ's kingdom of peace and love was the answer to all of humanity's woes, and the world only needed to lay down the sword and embrace this solution. Total submission was the cost for God's will to be accomplished.

Katarina knew the teachings by heart, but she wasn't aware of any manifestos providing instructions or strategies to implement during warfare. If there ever was a time that they needed Biblical clarification, it was now.

"Is there no other answer?" Her voice quivered as she pushed the words past the fear rising in her throat.

"Yes, there is," Agatha replied.

Katarina and Anna turned to stare at Agatha. "What?" they asked simultaneously.

"We do what our forefathers did when they were threatened."

"Which was what?"

"We leave."

"And go where?"

"Anywhere we can find religious freedom. A country that respects our religion and doesn't threaten our way of life."

Katarina snorted. "And where — with all this war going on — will we find such a country?"

"The Americas," Agatha said in such a way that made Katarina think she should have known the answer all along but was stupid because she didn't.

"The Americas? You mean, like Canada and the United States?"

"Yes. Exactly. We need to move."

"Move? But when? Now?" Anna gaped and stared at Agatha. "Surely not yet. It hasn't come to that point, yet. Has it?"

"I think so. If our faith is important enough to us, then we must follow the example of our forefathers. Yes. Now is as good a time as ever."

"You don't mean forever, do you? Only for a while until things get better, right?" Katarina tried to grasp the implications behind what she considered Agatha's daft and impulsive suggestion.

"Let me put it this way. The Czar has lost control. Russia's collapsing. It's time to accept that it's not going to improve. We must move to a safe place ... start a new life. My Bergthal relatives left Russia in the '70s. They have productive farms over there. We can join them. They'll sponsor us."

"Emigrate? To Canada?" Katarina tried to picture the

process of such a move. "That's fine for you. But what about the rest of us? We must live with the war raging around us. How do we do that? Or are you suggesting we all run away ... together? What about our homes here? Our families? How does one do that?" She frowned, "Leave everything behind ... to never come back? I can see making a trip for a year or two, or even one person in a family moving away, but moving an entire family — lock, stock and barrel ... forever?" *Furniture, too?*

"Agatha," Anna's voice took on a serious tone, "Are you suggesting leaving everything behind ... giving up all our land, businesses and possessions and replant ourselves in another country? Everything we've worked for our whole lives? Just walk away and give it all up?"

"Yes, that's what I'm saying."

"Why not go to the colony in Crimea? I heard it's safer." Katarina reconsidered Regier's idea. Maybe it wasn't so bad after all. "Or even the mountains. Wait out the war."

"The politics are changing too fast. Eventually, even Crimea will be affected. Lenin's bloody fingers will leave no stone unturned. And that Makhnovsky, and others like him, are carving the path for more rebels."

"But Germany is coming. They could still win this thing." Katarina visualized the war map in her head.

"And if they don't? How long do we wait? And how do we protect ourselves in the meantime? I'm not putting my children's lives at risk anymore. There's only death and destruction here."

"*Oba.*" Katarina shivered, but rolled her eyes at the same time. When Anna elbowed her in the ribs, Katarina gritted her teeth to stop herself from arguing further.

Although Agatha's solution seemed a bit far-fetched, Katarina heard of others reaching the same conclusion. She simply hadn't connected the dots with her own life. Traveling for adventure, or teaching school in another country were compelling dreams, but abandoning her roots to relocate to a foreign land permanently felt daunting. Little Russia had always been her home and native land — a place of refuge to return to when life settled down — where her parents and siblings would wait for her. She couldn't envision not having such a safety net.

Agatha must be talking off the top of her head, Katarina thought. She couldn't be serious. Then again, Agatha was a strong-willed woman who insisted she was always right. She just might convince her hen-pecked husband to pack up and move out.

Katarina sank back on the wooden bench and flexed her numb fists, then rubbed her hands together. Her extremities ached from the freezing cold. She didn't want to argue with Agatha anymore. A roaring fire was waiting at home. She could keep her mouth shut for a few more minutes. Tomorrow — when everyone had calmed down — the future would look rosy again.

She shivered. Better answers to this crisis were bound to surface soon. The church elders and the old men were meeting weekly to discuss practical solutions. As an educated woman, she would rely on wiser sources before making such a critical decision. Katarina inhaled sharply and exhaled a slow stream, and watched her breath condense into white clouds in the frigid air. It was Christmas. It was time to think of something more joyful.

As she glanced down at Anna's growing middle, she remembered the words of Jesus in Matthew 24.

'And woe unto them that are with child, and to them that give suck in those days!

But pray ye that your flight be not in the winter,
neither on the sabbath day:
For then shall be great tribulation, such as was not
since the beginning of the world to this time, no, nor
ever shall be.[1]

"Dear God," she prayed silently, "Please protect us from this impending terror ... and may our flight not be in winter."

──────────────────

1. Matthew 24:19-21 KJV

20

AGATHA'S DEPARTURE

LATE JANUARY 1918, PENNER ESTATE

"WE'RE LEAVING," AGATHA ANNOUNCED AS SHE chomped on the strawberry jam covered rusk, then licked off the goop as it dripped onto her palm. She dropped the incongruent statement into the middle of the conversation as unemphatically as if she was announcing snow falling in January. Her input into the scheduled breakfast meeting about the family's dwindling winter food supply had been minimal. In fact, she was unusually quiet.

"Six barrels of cabbage in the main cellar ..." Katarina continued before realizing Agatha's comment didn't fit. "What?" She looked up from the notebook.

"We need to finish this today," Anna said. "We haven't even discussed your numbers yet. Where do you need to go so badly? Aren't you feeling well?"

Agatha's mouth twitched from side to side and her jaw tightened. Dewy clouds formed in her icy blue eyes. Her gaze drifted from one face to another, then down at her clasped hands, her thumbs toying with each other.

Anna and Katarina's eyes met across the kitchen table. Katarina raised her eyebrows and Anna shook her head from side to side in response and shrugged her shoulders.

Katarina put down the notebook, plunked her elbows on the table, picked up her glass of buttermilk and studied the woman. Whatever Agatha had to say, it had nothing to do with the food inventory.

"What's going on?" Anna pushed her plate aside. She had also picked up on her sister-in-law's preoccupation and lack of attention in the meeting. "Agatha, if something's bothering you, you know you can tell us anything. We're all sisters here. Spill your heart."

"We're going to Canada," Agatha blurted out. She tilted her head to the ceiling and blinked rapidly, then turned sideways, pulled a handkerchief from inside her buttoned sleeve and dabbed at her eyes.

"Well, good for you. I'd like to travel there one day, too. For a visit. But what does that have to do with the inventory?" Katarina frowned. She looked back and forth between the two women. Anna's head was cocked and her eyes wide. *She looks surprised but at the same, she doesn't.* "I'm confused. Am I missing something?"

"Our immigration papers arrived yesterday. We have tickets for Monday's train."

Katarina felt like her eyes were about to pop out of her head. "What? When did this get organized?" She set down her glass and stared across the breakfast table at the sister-in-law.

"Congratulations. I take it you got permission to leave?" Anna smiled as she picked up her coffee.

Katarina glared at Anna. "You knew?" *Why didn't you tell me?*

"Yes, everything's cleared with the government."

Agatha pushed her plate away and leaned back, a tight grin contradicting the tears brimming in her deep-set eyes.

"But that's so soon. What about the children? It's the middle of the school year. You can't just uproot four children ... besides, you just built a new house." Katarina scratched her head. The decision seemed hasty and irrational.

"*Ja*, tough luck for us. But Johann says the Soviets will confiscate it and give it to the locals. We can't fight this. Look how they're violating the other German colonies. They're even regulating how much machinery we can own. This new government is determined to collectivize everything," Agatha sighed and shook her head. "The writing's on the wall. They want to get rid of us. If we don't go voluntarily, they'll force us off our land and redistribute our wealth. Everything we've worked for .... it's all about to disappear." Her voice croaked as she waved her hands in the air to demonstrate her point. "Johann says there won't be anything left of the Mennonites when they're done with us. We're leaving before they destroy us."

Katarina noted that Agatha was calling her husband by his proper name. That meant the situation was serious and a firm decision had been reached. Objections from Agatha or anyone else would not be tolerated. Johann — also known as J.D. — would not back down easily.

"You're giving up ... quitting ... running away?" Katarina's pulse quickened. Could J.D. be right? "Is it really that bad, Agatha? Our men will protest such legislation. The legal committee will go to Petrograd and reason with the new government. It's just a misunderstanding. It's too soon to quit. All of this will get sorted out, eventually. It sounds to me like J.D. is being a bit impulsive."

"This does seem a bit rushed, Agatha." Anna brushed

aside a strand of blonde hair from her face and repositioned two pins around her plaited bun. "You should wait until the war is over. If Germany wins this, we'll enjoy full German citizenship. All property will be returned to the rightful owners. This chaos can't last forever."

Agatha's icy eyes flashed in reaction to the uncompassionate and unsupportive response. "Wars and rumors of wars, ladies. Don't you know the signs of the times? Russia's politically unstable. The world war has made things worse. With the communists in power, and their stupid ideas about equality ... imagine this lunacy — we are immoral because we have more than the locals. How did we get where we are? By working for it —"

"— This new leadership won't last. The Duma will sort itself out. These radical policies are just temporary — knee jerk reactions to the long war. We must hang on a bit longer," Anna protested. "Let's not dismiss that Ukraine has just declared independence and we now have a central Rada. It's only a matter of time until we have a functioning government. Lenin's promised to back it."

"It will take decades for this Ukraine to sort itself out. Johann says we can't trust the negotiations. The Rada is nothing more than a small committee of men. It can be dismantled with a snap of the fingers. And the Duma has plenty of infighting, too. Neither government can be trusted."

"True enough. A country can't be born in a day. All of this will take time. But the changes inspire hope, don't they?" Katarina asked.

"Sure ... in twenty or thirty years. What do we do in the meantime? I'm raising my children now. We worry about their future. I don't want them growing up in fear. To add to our angst, these rebels — Makhno and his bandit friends —

are pointing guns at people on the street, breaking into homes, stealing and killing. And no one's stopping them. He chopped off the heads of Thiessen's family. And no arrests."

Katarina shuddered at the re-telling of the gruesome story. Rumors of the details had spread quickly through the colonies. But only *The Post's* employees and the authorities had read the actual reports. She knew more than most, even though she had declined to read Heinrich's complete notes. The acid bile rose in her throat. She swallowed and squeezed her eyes shut to erase the mental images of the descriptions.

"The police won't even stop a crazy man," Agatha continued. "He's free to hold the colonies at ransom and do whatever he wants. There's no law and order. No protection for us. It's anarchy. I tell you, there's no hope for this country. Our children need a safe place to grow up. We want stability. We've got the opportunity now. My family in Canada is sponsoring us."

"*Ja.* We all feel the fear. I'd like to leave, too. No one is safe. But getting out of the country won't be easy with all the military zones. Besides, I heard we can't leave. How did you get papers?" Katarina scowled.

"We applied over a year ago. We just received the approval. If we wait too long, the papers will expire. We must go now."

"How will you get out? The German-Russian front is to the west ... there's civil conflict to the north and east ... you can't get to Moscow or Petrograd without going through a line of soldiers. The Crimea is blocked by ships — no one can get through the Black Sea — there's another line in the Mediterranean, and the western mountain passes are blocked. Everywhere there are either blockades, lockdowns, conflict, or curfews. We can't even get from one side of the

Dnieper to the other without a permit. And Makhno has the colonies surrounded with his men. How exactly are you planning to exit?" Katarina crossed her arms and wrinkled her brow. "This plan doesn't seem sound."

"Makhno aside, there's a cease-fire now between the Allies and the Central powers. It could be a sign of peace, but then again, who knows? Either way, there's still too much fearful activity in our neck of the woods for us to stay here. It's the best time to leave."

"But Germany's one step away from winning this war. If they take over Ukraine, everything will turn around. We'll become valid citizens of Germany. And if Ukraine independence is ratified, Germany will oversee the reorganization. Law and order will return. Life will go back to normal," Katarina protested.

"There's no guarantees of anything right now. The dominos are lining up, but they could fall in any direction," Agatha said. "We have to leave while it's safe to do so. If we can get through up north before they start shooting again ... if we wait, it could be too late."

"But how will you do it?" Katarina asked. "You will surely run into militarized zones ... soldiers with guns. They'll shoot before asking questions."

Agatha smirked. "We have a plan. I know you'll think it's silly. But we're taking the train to the front — or as far as we can — and we'll walk to the German lines and show them our travel papers. We'll be speaking in German, so we won't have a problem getting through. They'll escort us to safety."

"That's suicide. If it doesn't work, the government will revoke your passports and treat you as traitors ... or German spies." Katarina was shocked by the sheer lunacy of the plan. "They'll put you against the wall and shoot you ... and without a trial. I've seen the maps. I've read the daily war reports. I've listened to the reporters talk. The government has ordered everyone to stay home. We're not to leave our communities unless our lives are in jeopardy."

"Our lives *are* in danger, Katarina. How much worse does it have to get before you all realize this? As far as I'm concerned, we're like the proverbial frog in the boiling water. It's getting hot, and we're jumping out before we're cooked."

"I still can't believe you got permission to leave. No one's getting approval these days." Katarina pushed down the twinge of jealousy.

Concern resonated on Anna's face. "I agree with Katarina. It sounds risky. Personally, I'd wait until peace is formally declared. And I believe that day is close by. David's letters speak of great hope for the future. He should know. He's seeing the worst of the bloody horror, tending the injured from the frontlines. He expects to be coming home soon. But what does the rest of the family say? What about our dear mother-in-law? How can you abandon her so soon after Father Penner's death? She still needs you."

"Johann's discussed it with all, and they've agreed. Even mother said if father had survived and they had sponsors, they'd be leaving now, too," Agatha said. "She insists that it's silly for us to stay here when such an opportunity is being given to us practically on a silver platter. This is the other advantage, you know. We leave and get settled. Then we can send for the rest of the family to join us later."

"Agatha, what makes you think Canada is any safer? The entire world is at war," Katarina asked.

Agatha nodded. "Listen, Canada is fighting *in* the war, there is no actual war or conflict *there*. Canada is peaceful. And the Canadian government exempted our people from military service back in 1870. Our children will never have to take part in a war."

"Is that still valid? Our great-grandparents were promised the same when they moved here from Danzig. But governments change. Look what's happening here," Anna pointed out.

"*Ja.*" Agatha's square brown head bobbed up and down. "I know that. We're moving for the same reasons — freedom of religion and a better life. I can't bear the thought of raising our little ones under these conditions. Johann says that if things continue as they are, we'll lose the ability to live according to our beliefs. Instead, we'll be subject to spurious laws made by godless men."

"Now *that* I understand. I can vouch that our rights to self-determination within our school system are being eroded. They're overseeing our curriculum and language instruction —" Katarina flicked the pencil between her fingers.

"— See?" Agatha interrupted. "You worry about this too. The government is already telling you how to teach. Now, they forbid German instruction. Soon they'll discard the Bible and we'll be forced to learn things that are against the word of God."

"Oh, let's not get carried away, Agatha. They won't discard our Christian values. They'd have to fight every church in the country if they did that." Katarina leaned forward and put her elbows on the table. "What makes you think it will go that far?"

"Lenin wants complete control. He denies God and wants to abolish religion. For certain, he's the Antichrist. Soon, he'll demand we worship the state and their ideals. Next, he'll put statues of himself in every town and command people to bow down."

"Oh, Agatha, you've been listening to conspiracy theories again. Honestly ... statues of himself ... really," Anna scoffed. "Besides, a government can't dictate someone's heart. They can't change our beliefs."

"Not overnight; but they can indoctrinate children in the schools. When they change the beliefs of the next generation, they can change society. You've heard about that new nonsense called evolution, yes? A non-biblical theory of how the world was created and how life began?"

The women nodded. Katarina picked up her cup and traced her thumb around the blue and white patterns. She couldn't dispute Agatha's facts. Whether she'd gotten the information from her husband or read the newspapers and seen the Bolshevik manifestos, it was hard to tell. But the woman was definitely not ignorant.

She took a deep breath and exhaled slowly. "Agatha, I, for one, will never worship a statue or a political ideology. The Bible is clear that we must separate ourselves from such things. The first commandment says to worship only the one true God. The second warns about worshipping graven images. At the same time, Jesus told us to respect the leadership of our country. All leaders are given authority by God."

"Katarina, Russia is changing before our eyes. We don't trust this man, Lenin. He's a snake with a plan to kill and destroy. Mark my words. Not only will he eradicate religion from the schools, but he may also close the churches. They'll force you to teach that bizarre doctrine or lose your job ... or even your life. The colonies are about to be turned upside down. They already are. Look at how agriculture has changed over the last two years. We've lost our economic freedoms. They tell us what we can grow, how much we can keep for ourselves, and who we must sell to. They're putting our backs to the wall."

"The food shortage is temporary because of the war. Things will return to normal," Anna insisted.

"And you think sunshine grows on trees. What will you do when the cellars are empty, Anna? Will you kiss the clown when he holds a gun to your head and demands his taxes?"

Anna's eyes widened at the insult. Katarina cringed. "Lenin can't become a Czar. His control is limited and temporary."

"Ah, it won't take much for Lenin to put himself on the throne. He's probably eating the Czar's caviar right now. And washing it down with the palace's ice-cold vodka while his radical friends murder innocent citizens in the streets. Mark my words. This red rage will sweep the country. If it comes our way, we're all doomed."

"Agatha, we can't give in to threats and intimidation. We must wait this out and see what happens. As to education — even if Lenin has his way — if we stick together, we can teach our children in our homes. And Lenin won't live forever. God is watching over us. Evil cannot win." Katarina's surprised herself with her own optimism.

"Evil may not win. But it can reign triumphant while the chess pieces fall into place. Don't you know your Bible? Read how Israel became established. The Jews wandered in the desert for forty years. Generations died while borders shifted. Leaders came and went." Agatha slapped the table. "I am not interested in staying in a country waiting for God to reposition the world while my children are being indoctrinated with garbage. My fear is they'll forget about the God of our fathers and our way of life. I want them growing up without fear of tomorrow, in safety and learning Biblical truth — not some fairy-tales about evolution and being told God doesn't exist." Her voice quivered.

Katarina rose and stepped to the threshold of the kitchen alcove where Alyona was mixing and rolling the noodle dough. The cook winked. "We will always have vareniki and sausage. The government can't take our recipes away."

Katarina stretched her arms and leaned against the wall, "Maybe we can bribe them with the best food in the world." She hoped she could convert the table to a more palatable topic.

Agatha snorted. "Katarina, the Bolsheviks don't respect our food or our culture. Their idea of utopia is a cookie cutter world where everyone thinks and acts the same."

The speculative conversation was becoming tiresome. The simple announcement had turned into a political diatribe with Agatha defending her decision to move. However, Katarina also puzzled about the current societal shifts. If the Mennonite code was right, did that mean all others were wrong? "How are we any different ...? Our communities insist our members share the same basic Mennonites values. Granted, our churches have a few differences, but we have a common code of conduct to justice and right living. The bottom line is if you live here, you must obey our rules. We also believe the world would be a better place if everyone lived like us."

"Katarina, honestly, you have no understanding how the world works. We don't push our ideas on the unbelievers. We show our faith through our life and our good works. Our testimony spurs them to jealousy. Isn't that what God tells us to do? If we make the unbelievers jealous, they will want what we have. When we have their ear, we can testify that our blessings come from working hard and following God's laws of peace and justice. Sadly, these locals equate money with happiness. They don't realize that our true wealth isn't external. It's what inside that counts. These rebels can take our stuff, but they can't take our faith."

Anna nodded. "Amen to that, sister. Pastor Friesen preaches that success is an honest and quiet life and a close relationship with God."

"That's right. And we must seek that above all else. Now, I know we're making a costly move, and it'll be tough to start a new life in another country, but the result will be peace and prosperity. If not for us, then at least for our children."

"Agatha, what makes you think it'll be any different in the new world? Every society has expectations and laws," Katarina protested.

"Yes, but in a free society, anyone who doesn't believe the same is welcome to leave. Here, in our colonies, we don't force our beliefs on others. We respect the rights of outsiders to live as they wish. But fairness and justice are disappearing from Russia, Katarina. There's a movement afoot to take away our land, our homes, our property, our possessions and force us to share everything with those who never worked a day in their life. Vagrants already squat on our land and steal our food; soon they'll take our homes and barns too. It's unjust. They're spitting on our faith and everything we stand for."

"I understand. And I agree it's scary and wrong. But to give up all hope seems so pessimistic." Katarina sensed the circular argument was pointless. Agatha and her family were moving. Dozens of other families had made the same decision. She secretly wished she could join them.

Agatha refused to quit lecturing. "I don't trust any of it. Our people have been arguing with the government for years. Instead of getting better, persecution is escalating. Our rights to self-government are eroding. It's going downhill rapidly. We can get out now. And if you were smart, you would, too."

Anna snorted and pointed to her stomach. "We can't leave. Besides, I have a husband serving in the war. I'm not making any decisions until he gets back."

"When he does, you must beg him to take off his uniform and leave. Your lives and your children's futures are at stake," Agatha's voice strained with urgency.

"He can't abandon his post. He'll be shot," Anna scoffed.

"*Ja*, that's a risk. But if you stay here, you could starve to death. Isn't it better to die while running for freedom than dying alone in your bed because you were too afraid to? If there's one chance for peace, why not take it?" Agatha placed both hands on the table and leaned forward to press her point. "Let me emphasize something, ladies. Your life is worth more than stuff. One day all your possessions will dissolve into dust and disappear. Things are not important. Liberty is. If you have the opportunity to forge a new life in a country where you can worship and practice your faith without fear, grow your own vegetables, and raise your family in serenity and security, why wouldn't you grab it? Canada is where we're headed. We'd love it if the rest of the family could join us there. If not now, then later. We'll miss everyone terribly."

Katarina and Anna's eyes met across the table. Katarina guessed from her sister's cock-eyed reaction that she didn't think much about Agatha's under-handed invitation. Furthermore, she wasn't sure who Agatha was trying to convince — herself or them? Was it possible that she wasn't entirely convinced of the plan? However, there was strength and safety in numbers. If they could all leave together, it would be better on so many fronts. But they couldn't leave now. There were too many missing pieces.

Agatha's worry aside, Katarina agreed the world was a bit chaotic, but life in her corner still felt safe. In her opinion, Agatha's and J.D.'s decisions were both drastic and premature. She stared at the table and tapped her fingernails on the wood, then noted the awkward silence. She looked up in time to see a secret look pass between Anna and Agatha. Taking it as a cue to leave, she pushed her chair back and stood up. "I need to prepare next week's lessons. God give you safety on the move, Agatha."

"Wait, Katarina. Listen. You've always talked about leaving Russia to teach somewhere else. I neglected to tell you that when we applied last year, we added you to the paperwork in case you'd like to come with us. Surprise! You're approved, too!" Agatha announced. "God only knows when you'll get another opportunity like this."

Katarina startled and spun around. "You did ... what? I'm listed to leave the country? With you?" She looked back and forth at each of the women. Anna had a weird grin on her face. "Anna, did you know about this?"

"It was planned a year ago. I didn't think anything would come of it. Then, it seemed like the smartest thing to do. I'd sort of forgotten about it. We wanted it to be a surprise ... but if I'd known it would happen this fast, I would've prepared you. I'm sorry. I guess I should have ..." A sheepish look overshadowed Anna's face.

"Yes, you should have. Absolutely, you both should have. Tell me this. Why is everyone determined to plan my life for me? When will I be considered adult enough to make my own decisions?" Katarina looked with disgust at the women.

"I'm sorry, Kat." Anna grimaced and put a hand over her eyes.

Agatha looked shocked. "Katarina, honestly. I thought you'd be excited. Thrilled even. It's your dream to live in another country."

"On my own terms, Agatha. Not yours. I want to choose where I live and who to marry. It's my life, not yours."

"All right. You're right. We should have given you more time, included you in the planning. But the deed is done now. Are you coming with us or not? The door is still open."

"You expect me to leave ... just like that? On Monday ...? You think I can just pack a suitcase and run away that fast?" Her mind reeled with the complications of such an impromptu decision.

"Why not? You're almost eighteen. You've got your entire life ahead of you. You have nothing to lose by moving and everything to gain. You could meet a nice man in Canada, get married, have a wonderful life."

Katarina looked at Anna's expanding middle and recalled the last thing David said to her before he left for the war. "Katarina, please look after Anna while I'm gone. I couldn't bear it if anything happened to her or the baby."

If she left, she would never know Anna's baby. Then, what if war came to the colony and Anna was caught in the crossfire? She shuddered at the thought of Anna dying alone with an infant in her arms. David would never forgive her. The guilt would plague her forever.

She considered the precious school children. She would miss them. They would find another teacher. And she could teach foreign students all about Russia while she explored the new country. Her skin tingled with the excitement of that possibility.

Her mind drifted to Regier. They had become such

close friends, and he'd become dependent on her. *Katarina, you must find a safe place to hide if the war comes here. If anything happens to Olek, the rebels will swarm the estate. You won't survive.* If he was right, she could die if she stayed. And Anna could die. And the baby. Her gut tightened at the thought. *We only need to find a safe place to stay until the war is over. We could go to the Crimea ... But will we get out in time?*

The family. *Mom and Dad, Dietrich, Maria and George, Justina and Heinrich, my nieces and nephews, plus Anna and David. And the cousins. I'll never see them again. What if they die? I'll never get to say goodbye. If only we could all move to Canada together.*

Canada. *I won't know anyone there except Agatha. Do I really want to live with her and her family in a strange country? With strangers speaking that odd English tongue. I wonder what the homes are like.*

Katarina had learned that there were no servants in the American or Canadian homes, and the houses were small — like those in the village. Could she live with Agatha's family in such tight quarters? She could barely tolerate the woman now.

Before she moved to Halbstadt, her father said, 'Katarina, if I can only give you one bit of advice about your life, it's this. Never make big decisions until you have peace. Pray about everything. God's timing is always perfect.'

Her stomach churned. Staying meant waiting out the political crisis. If war arrived on their doorstep, she would have to live through it. There would be no escape then. Freedom beckoned with a crooked finger. But Anna wouldn't go with her now. Maybe after the war. She felt torn.

Leaving itself was a risk. Agatha was taking a big chance

walking into the front lines of a war zone. Anything could happen.

On the other hand, she wondered if the Russian crisis was truly so precarious? Perhaps it was exaggerated. Would the soldiers walk into the village and blow up the town? For what reason? The possibility seemed preposterous. *It won't happen. If Germany gets control of Ukraine, we'll be safe. Or we'll continue under Russian control. Or Ukraine will become an organized, independent government. With some changes. But we can live with change. Surely it won't be so bad.*

The required decision was too fast to make. There was barely time to pray about it. If God wanted her to go, she would feel confident. But she didn't.

Katarina looked at Agatha and then at Anna.

"It's all right, Kat," Anna said softly. "If you want to go, you have my blessing. I'll be fine." Except, she rubbed her stomach as she said the words.

"You have two days to decide, Katarina," Agatha said. "We'll make room for you. You'll be safe with us."

"I need to pray about this. I don't have peace today. Only questions." As she turned to leave the room, her crooked arm bumped against the door. A knife-like pain shot up her arm. She gripped the door handle and grimaced. *You can't scrub floors or wash windows. You'll depend on Agatha and her family forever. A lump formed in her throat and her heart dropped into her stomach.* She silently cursed the injury and spun around.

"I want to move to Canada, Agatha. I really do. I just think now is not the right time for me. This all feels too sudden ... too drastic. If the church is right, God will send us plenty of warning. The Bible says He won't abandon us. I must have faith. I'll travel ... after the war ... or when it's safer." Her eyes met Agatha's, "You can still sponsor us later, right? Once you're settled there?"

The sister-in-law nodded, her smile replaced by a somber expression. Anna gave a weak smile of understanding, then rose and walked over to her.

"You need to do what's right for you," Anna whispered in Katarina's ear as she gave her a big hug.

Tears burst through the dam of resistance as Katarina ran down the hallway to the study. *What if Agatha's right? What if we're wrong?*

21

REVISITING THE PAST

1951, POST-WAR GERMANY

THE ENORMOUS GRAY CAT WITH THE GLASSY YELLOW eyes yawned, arched its back in a lengthy stretch, then jumped over the short stacks of books and files on Reinhart's desk, and settled down in the few inches of uncluttered narrow space along the top outer edge. It turned to face Peter and examined him with a critical stare before yawning widely and displaying its large teeth.

Peter gulped, crossed his feet under the chair, straightened his posture, and placed the glass on the coaster beside the lamp.

"You don't like cats much, do you?" Reinhart chuckled.

"Not particularly. I told you, they remind me of the war. Cats and cadavers and all that. And I don't want to talk about it," Peter's voice croaked.

"*Ja*. The ghosts of war. Dark shadows that flicker on the ceilings at night. I have them, too. Do you speak about what you saw?"

Cats and cadavers. Stacks of bodies. Peter shook the

picture from his mind and downed the last of the amber liquid in his glass. "No."

"We can't drink it away, Peter. It's a chapter of our lives. We were part of the evil. The things we did ... somehow, we must forgive ourselves."

"She warned me not to go. I could have gone to Canada with my sister, Marta. I could've escaped it all. Mom sent her to live with Aunt Justina and Uncle Heinrich before the war began. She sensed what was about to happen here in Germany. I made the choice to be part of the killing machine."

"The memories of the first war were still fresh in her mind. How could she not guess at what was to come? Does Marta know about the diaries?"

Peter shook his head. "She's in Canada. We write occasionally. But she never came back, and I've never been there. Maybe one day, after I've transcribed everything, I'll bring them to her and explain it all. Hopefully, by then, I'll have some answers for her."

"She must struggle with her own guilt. The *what if* she hadn't gone across the ocean." Reinhart shook his head. "Daughters and mothers. They both want to fix everything. And now you, too. I'm sorry that things are so upside down in your family, Peter. And I'm puzzled why Katarina volunteered for the second war after having already lived through such horror once. Sacrificing time with the two of you ... for what? Chasing shadows?"

Peter blinked rapidly to hold back the welling tears. "I suppose so. It was the open door she'd been waiting for, to go back into Russia and find her son, Jacob. The second war made that search possible. She'd already seen death and destruction. She knew what to expect. She'd already been fighting ghosts almost every night. Like I do, now."

"You don't share the same ghosts, Peter. They may look similar, but they're not the same. Katarina was young, beautiful and naive. And we all know what happened to pretty, young girls in the war. And she was trained to be passive. Fighting back wouldn't come easily."

"She could have escaped it all if she'd left with Agatha and Johann."

"Are you blaming her for her own problems? She was a young woman. How could she fathom what was to come? Until 1918, she had only heard and read about the war. She had never actually seen it with her own eyes. You're being too judgmental of poor Katarina."

Peter shrugged. "Maybe I am."

"You know what I think, Peter? I suspect you're looking for a scapegoat to point a finger to the reason for your own problems. Instead of looking at yourself and accepting responsibility for your own part in whatever went wrong between the two of you."

"Ouch. That's harsh, Reinhart. I didn't realize you had a counseling degree."

"Here," Reinhart held up the bottle of dark amber liquid, "fill up your glass. We're not done, yet."

Peter welcomed the chance to stand and stretch his legs, if even for a minute. "Mind if I crack that window a bit more?"

"Be my guest. I realize that corner of the room tends to get a bit stuffy. I forget that sometimes. My apologies."

"Not a problem. I need to learn to speak up more." Peter angled the tilt on the window to direct the breeze towards his chair.

"Ah," Reinhart laughed. "Another trait you picked up from your mother."

"What do you mean?" Peter asked as he poured the shot, then repositioned his chair before sitting down.

"Passive, silent resistance. Denying your own needs. Expecting the world around you to mind-read your angst. Peter, are you trying to find Katarina? Or are you trying to find yourself?"

Peter swirled the drink in his glass. "Both, I suppose."

"Then you need to touch Katarina's pain. See what she saw, feel what she felt. If you can do that, and when you do, you'll reach a layer of understanding that you never knew existed."

"I'm trying," Peter insisted as he bit the inside of his cheek. Reinhart's digging at his core was darn uncomfortable. It was like sandpaper against his soul.

"Building walls around our vulnerabilities creates lonely and empty houses. Katarina wrote about her hurt, but you still don't understand."

Peter shook his head. "I guess not."

"My friend, sometimes I think you're just as bullheaded as your mother. Life is not a mathematical formula, Peter. There are many shades of gray between the black and white. If you can't grasp the nuances of her despair, then you need to reread her story."

"Maybe I am dull. I'm not finding any clues in these early years. And what does her personality have to do with anything?" Peter hugged his arms and scanned the leatherbound volumes filling the oak shelves lining the dark paneled walls. "She was just an ordinary, idealistic teenaged girl."

"A frightened one who felt very alone in the big, scary world that was falling apart. That's not how life is supposed to be. For anyone. Do I really need to spell it out to you, Peter? It's your story, but you're skipping important details."

Reinhart slipped the pencil behind his ear and rested an elbow on the desk.

Peter looked up and raised his hands to signify a question. "Please, explain it to me. What am I missing?"

"Peter, why didn't she want to get married?"

He shrugged. "I guess she wasn't ready."

"Come on, Peter. Really? Most people want to marry because they equate it with eternal love. Katarina didn't say she didn't believe in marriage. She screamed something else from the pages. But no one listened." Reinhart glared across the room at Peter, a smiling toying with the corner of his mouth.

"Oh." Peter blinked. "She didn't feel validated. No one cared about her opinions. She wanted a say in her life."

"My guess is she felt a bit like a china doll on a shelf. But she wanted to jump off and be a real person. Except, when she does (in the metaphorical sense), she discovers that the walls are made of glass, and no one can hear her."

"And then war hits, and the walls break, and she has trouble putting the pieces together." Peter nodded.

"That's a good start. She's first aware of those walls following her accident. The further she steps into the adult world, the more she struggles with both her identity and her faith. She has an interesting story. I'm interested to see how she develops."

"How would you summarize this drama thus far?" Peter picked up the tennis ball on the floor and threw it at Reinhart.

Reinhart chuckled as he caught it with one hand and lobbed it back. "Your synopsis is a wealthy German girl conflicted by her pacifist Mennonite faith while confronting the atrocities of war. Watching her insular and myopic world implode from external political winds didn't compute in young Katarina's head. Her fears and protests clashed with strong traditional walls that resisted change. Women didn't voice their viewpoints in that society. If they tried to, they were tempered, shut down or pushed aside. Undoubtedly, Katarina was an embarrassment to both her family and the community at large. I suspect she got away with things partly because of her social standing. Her life was anything but ordinary."

"Every teenager pushes limits to flex their independence." Peter tossed the ball in the air, caught it and threw it back.

"Yes, and most break away to do that. Katarina leaving her parents' home was a flagrant display of self-determination. It was convenient for her that Anna married up and created room for Katarina to respectfully rebel." Reinhart caught the ball and tossed it the air.

"Oh, I think my grandparents encouraged that opportunity. If for no other reason, so that she could find a suitable marriage partner."

"And as we said before, she didn't want to get married because —" Reinhart chucked the ball back.

"— marriage would chafe her independence. She wanted to travel, make her own way in the world." The cat perked up and watched the ball fly back and forth. Peter noticed the cat's attentiveness and fearing it might want to join in the game, he dropped the white orb on the floor beside the chair.

"Even so, she didn't make the big move to Canada when she had the chance." Reinhart leaned forward to pick up the cat and pulled it onto his lap, "Why do you think she stayed?"

"For several reasons. One. She'd seen the battle maps and knew war was hammering at every exit. Getting out of

Ukraine seemed impossible. Second, the advancement of the German army encouraged the ethnics to believe peace was at the doorstep. There was no justification to run when hope was high."

"But there was a deeper reason, wasn't there?"

Peter nodded. "Leaving home is a bit shocking for most new adults. There's an adjustment period with a push-pull between security and freedom. As an independent young woman and experiencing her first taste of the working world — making her own money and learning about a life outside the traditional domestic roles — the world was her oyster. The biggest thing holding her back was the war. She believed that when it ended, life would go back to normal.

"Eventually, she'd get to travel. But she didn't like Agatha's ultimatum. Going with Agatha was like trading one set of restrictions for another. It could be like moving home with her parents again. Then, she'd face pressure to marry someone she didn't love. Between that and the physical restriction of her bad arm—she'd feel trapped. I think the reality of leaving Ukraine felt like shaking the dust off her feet without saying a proper goodbye. It was too drastic and too fast."

"And her relationship with Anna?"

"Absolutely. Margaretha's death was a crushing blow, and now Anna was pregnant again. After the confrontation with her mother at the funeral, Katarina felt guilty for not being more supportive to Anna. With David away serving the frontlines, she couldn't abandon her sister in her greatest hour of need. She also didn't want to complicate Anna's precarious position with David's family."

"What do you mean, Peter?"

"Despite her sincere efforts, Anna never felt like she fit into David's family. Katarina's note of Anna's tea-drinking was a perfect example of that. Anna felt that the in-laws saw her as the lower-class member from the despised other side of the river. She would never be good enough for David, as far as the family was concerned, at least until she had children. She needed that legitimacy to be accepted. Katarina moved to the estate less than two years after Anna and David married and Anna had not yet given birth. Anna was still struggling with feelings of inferiority with her junior position in the new family. I suspect that Anna felt Katarina rescued her and was her ally against the Penner family's invisible thought and conduct police. If Katarina left for Canada, she worried that Anna would feel abandoned, like she'd cast her into a pack of wolves."

"You've portrayed the personality conflicts well, but weren't the three women aligned in a common front simply because they were in-laws?"

"Agatha had married into the family a decade earlier, and she'd learned to adjust. When it came to clan acceptance — Agatha had seniority rights over Anna. In-law or not — the women tolerated Agatha, but they didn't like her. Apparently, she was very judgemental. Katarina couldn't see herself spending the rest of her life under that woman's thumb. Besides, Agatha had been talking about emigrating for years. She'd always wanted to join her extended family in Canada. Our family was all in Ukraine. There was nothing to go to Canada for as far as Katarina was concerned — other than to travel and see the world. But living with Agatha stretched her imagination too far."

A loud roar with the gusto of a broken truck muffler rose from the bundle of fur in Reinhart's lap. He laughed, "We must sound bored, Peter. Old Willy wants input."

"You might want to get his pipes checked," Peter joked. "I've never heard one that loud before."

"He makes himself known. He's the king of his castle."

"He is that. Were you about to ask me something?"

"Yes." Reinhart nodded. "Why did Agatha and Johann go at such a risky time? Didn't it make more sense to wait until after the war?"

"Once their application for immigration was approved, they needed to take it or risk losing it. And it was a good thing they went when they did."

"What do you mean?"

"Yes. Canada closed the door to immigration of Russian Mennonites in 1919 for the next two years. They feared cultural disruption by the Mennonites' 'peculiar habits, modes of life and methods of holding property.'"[1]

"In other words, the importation of a strange religion and customs was too much for the Canadian public to tolerate."

"I suspect it was an excuse. They didn't fit into the WASPY ideas of normal. Bear in mind, German ethnics were treated as enemy aliens, placed in internment camps and kept there throughout the war. There were anti-German riots, German clubs were ransacked, stores vandalized, statues destroyed. Even the Canadian town of Berlin had a name change. Fear, hatred, and nationalism penetrated into the heart of the country."[2]

"Was it the same in America?"

"Similar. The anti-German sentiment was virtually global. Some changed their names to deny their German ethnic connection, cities and streets were renamed. Let's face it, Reinhart. We were ostracized by the world."

"Yes, Peter. Bigotry is an ugly thing. I'm not surprised Katarina decided to go to Germany after the war. There were few safe places for a German to live."

"Exactly. And as countries closed their doors in

response to the collective fear, massive numbers of displaced persons fled the war zones and a refugee crisis developed unlike anything the world had ever seen before."
3

"But at this point in the story, Katarina still believes that good will prevail, even though she worries there are more horrors to come."

"Correct. The German occupation empowers her confidence. She finds both positive support for her occupational roles and then experiences her first love. However, the war encroaches with such force and brutality, her life is forever altered. Ethnic discrimination and religious intolerance are not only ugly, they're deadly."

"And Makhno's Black Army?"

"As his popularity grew, so did his numbers ... it's estimated that his ranks swelled to more than a hundred thousand soldiers at one point. 4 And when opportunity presented, violence exploded. There were no laws or limits to his degraded savagery, and anyone with wealth or power was a target."

"Your family and their friends were on that list."

"Yes. And from this point on, the story becomes very dark."

"Then, we should prepare ourselves for the discomfort."

THIS IS THE END OF PART ONE.
Thank you for reading.

TO BE CONTINUED.
Sign up to the readers' group to get advance notice for the

release of book two. Click here for the Reader's group link (https://bit.ly/3gF2JMz).

Positive reviews encourage the author to write more books on this important historical period. If you enjoyed this book, kindly leave a review on Amazon. Click here (https://www.amazon.com/gp/product/B098LY2Z3N) for Amazon.

---

1. https://www.ccrweb.ca/en/hundred-years-immigration-canada-1900-1999
2. https://en.wikipedia.org/wiki/Anti-German_sentiment
3. https://encyclopedia.1914-1918-online.net/article/refugees
4. https://www.worldhistory.us/military-history/the-russian-civil-war-1917-1922/nestor-makhno-anarchist-general.php

BUY THE NEXT BOOK IN THIS SERIES

DISCOVER:

1918: The German occupation of Ukraine changes life for the Mennonite communities and new conflicts arise.

Learn how women coped and changed from the challenges of wartime.

Find answers to these questions and more:

- What are the horrors that Peter and Reinhart refer to?
- How does Makhno continue to be a threat?
- Does Katarina fall in love?
- How does war change Katarina and Anna?
- Who is Jacob and why is he pivotal in Katarina's future decisions?
- How does Peter's life change when he finds out the truth about his mother's secret past?

Follow the author on Amazon, check out the rest of her bookshelf and buy the next book in this continuing series: Click here for the Amazon author link.

RUSSIAN MENNONITE CHRONICLES

If you want to learn more about the Mennonite experience during the Russian revolution, check out the growing resource on this pivotal time in history. Google Mennonites in Russia and discover an intriguing world — guaranteed to keep you riveted through any pandemic.

Here are some references for you to review:
    mennoniteeducation.weebly.com
    gameo.org
    anabaptisthistorians.org
    encyclopediaofukraine.com
    mennonitegenealogy.com
    gerhardsjourney.wordpress.com

Turn the page to discover more.

JOIN MY READER'S GROUP

RUSSIAN MENNONITE CHRONICLES follows two wealthy Mennonite women from southern Ukraine during the Russian Revolution. While safe inside their patriarchal traditions, the World War seems a distant threat until Russia implodes, Ukraine pushes to separate and anarchy reigns. Then the jaws of war strike.

When conventional structures fail, and the religious prescriptions no longer fit, the women find themselves in a frightening and unfamiliar world. Raised under the banner of non-resistance, Katarina and Anna come face to face with life and death decisions. How will they survive the horrors to come? Can their faith endure?

As Peter tells the story based on the diary of his deceased mother, he struggles to understand the impact of trauma on Katarina's life and its effect on his childhood. At the same time, he struggles with his own emotional wounds.

This series tackles the eternal questions: Why do bad things happen to good people? Where is God in times of trouble?

Free stories, recipes and other fun giveaways. Get advance notice of upcoming releases. Sign up here: https://www.subscribepage.com/russianmennonitefiction

Email me for further information, let me know how this story impacted your life. I love to hear from my readers. Email here: themennogal@gmail.com

ACKNOWLEDGMENTS

Special thanks to the dedicated work of https://www. mennonitecentre.ca/Friends of the Mennonite Center in Ukraine Inc. and the Ukraine Headstone Project (through FOMCU) for your continued work in bringing awareness to the world of the importance of our Russian Mennonite heritage and being the hands and feet of Christ to the impoverished communities in Ukraine. Your dedication encouraged me.

Special thanks to R.E. Vance and the wonderful authors' community at Self-Publishing School who pushed me to complete this book. You're an amazing group. I couldn't have done this without you.

Extra special thanks to my editor Nicole Lamont.

To my accountability buddy: Author Violet Batejan, thanks for the virtual hugs and encouragement.

To my beta readers and proofreaders: Authors Nola Li Barr, Paul (P.C.) James, Louisa M Bauman, Ashley Peters.

To my historical research critics: Authors Evan Ostryzniuk and Gayle Goossen. Thank you for giving me the confidence to proceed in this venture.

To the vast community of Russian Mennonite cousins that I keep finding on the G.r.a.n.d.m.a. genealogical website and social media groups: you've inspired me to understand my roots from a whole new level. Thank you.

To my husband who cleans my house, takes care of the yard and tries to keep a low profile and never complains while I disappear for weeks on end. Your support means the world to me.

To those special friends who applauded my author journey and told me I could do it: thank you for your support.

To my granddaughter Artessa: you are my legacy and my inspiration. I hope one day you'll read these stories and desire to know your history. You are loved.

ABOUT THE AUTHOR

Author MJ Krause-Chivers is the fictional stream for award winning Christian Author Miranda J. Chivers.

A Canadian Christian author with Russian Mennonite heritage, MJ Krause-Chivers grew up in the German Mennonite culture surrounded by storytellers chronicling their intriguing and dangerous emigration treks to Canada following the Russian revolution. While listening to the mostly male narrators tell of their valiant exploits, she often wondered about the women's unspoken scars and darkest secrets experienced during the ethnic cleansing and refugee journeys.

In 2014, she learned more about her ancestral history when visiting Poland and Ukraine. Here, the path to portraying the incredible stories of survival became clear.

In developing the storyline of the *Russian Mennonite Chronicles*, the author draws on her own rich background, skillfully weaving the vivid imagery of her childhood, her religious understanding of that era, and both oral and documented history into a compelling and courageous tale of suffering and enduring faith.

Russian Mennonite Chronicles: Katarina's Dark Shadow is the first fictional novel in this continuing series about a young Mennonite woman growing up during the Russian Revolution in southern Ukraine.

Bonus: Buy the next book in this series on Amazon — Russian Mennonite Chronicles. *Join the mailing list* (https://bit.ly/3gF2JMz) *and get a FREE extra story.*

Follow on:
Amazon: https://amzn.to/3hPo6K3
FB: @mirandajchivers
FB: @russianmennonitechronicles
FB: @MJ-Krause-Chivers-Author
FB book launch group: https://www.facebook.com/groups/russianmennonitechronicles